She lowered the phone. "You're a cannibal."

Vom chuckled. "Cannibals eat their own kind. I am a singular entity. There is only one Vom the Hungering, and that is me. And you are?"

She ignored the question. "You're going to eat me?"

"Yeah, probably. Don't suppose it helps anything if I apologize in advance."

She put the phone to her ear. "Pay attention, Number Five. You are now Vom's warden. You will not age or grow sick and you cannot die by conventional means."

"Okay, this is sounding more and more like bullshit," she said.

"Don't interrupt. I have other responsibilities. If I don't bring Number Three an avocado in five minutes California will fall into the ocean."

"Yeah. Sure. Makes sense." She admitted defeat and just listened.

"One day, Number Five, you will release Vom. Maybe not today. Maybe not tomorrow. Maybe not a hundred years from now. But one day, when the crawl of eternity becomes too much for you, you will open that door. He will then devour you, go back into his prison, and wait for the next warden. That is just how this works. There's no point in complaining to me about it either. I don't have any control over any of it."

"But—"

"I'm not even obligated to give you this information, but you seem like a nice young woman. So best of luck."

He hung up, and she knew he wouldn't be calling back this time.

CHASING THE MOON

By A. Lee Martinez

CHASING

THE

MOON

A. LEE MARTINEZ

orbit

www.orbitbooks.net

This book is a work of fiction. Names, characters, places, and incidents are the product of the author's imagination or are used fictitiously. Any resemblance to actual events, locales, or persons, living or dead, is coincidental.

Orbit
Hachette Book Group
237 Park Avenue
New York, NY 10017
www.orbitbooks.net

Orbit is an imprint of Hachette Book Group. The Orbit name and logo are trademarks of Little, Brown Book Group Limited.

Printed in the United States of America

Originally published in hardcover: May 2011
First mass market edition: February 2012

10 9 8 7 6 5 4 3 2 1

ATTENTION CORPORATIONS AND ORGANIZATIONS:

Most HACHETTE BOOK GROUP books are available at quantity discounts with bulk purchase for educational, business, or sales promotional use. For information, please call or write:

Special Markets Department, Hachette Book Group
237 Park Avenue, New York, NY 10017
Telephone: 1-800-222-6747 Fax: 1-800-477-5925

For Mom and the DFW Writer's Workshop,
because you always have my back.

For my patient editor. Thanks for bearing with me on this work of
(nearly) overwhelming madness.

For every weird beast and every bizarre thing that has
ever existed in the imagination.

And for that guy in that movie. You know the one I'm talking
about. That one guy who you always see but can't ever remember
his name, but you recognize him immediately and then spend all
day racking your brain for where you've seen him before only to re-
alize that he is in EVERYTHING because movies and TV need
character actors and he's really good at it and you think it's a real
shame that he doesn't get acknowledged more often, because without
him the show would be just a little bit poorer for his absence.

We love you, guy. And if you're a woman,
we still love you. So thanks.

This one is for you.*

*I might have been thinking of Clint Howard, but then again, I might be mistaken. Although he does a hell of a job, and was excellent in *Ticks*. Kudos, Clint.

CHASING THE MOON

CHAPTER ONE

"You're doing it again," Sharon said.

"Am I?"

The moon called to Calvin. After all this time he should've become accustomed, but it was always a distraction. Especially during the new moon when the silver orb disappeared in darkness.

Fenris, the monstrous thing, trailed behind the moon. The moon god shone like a fireball on those nights.

Tonight was only a half moon, though, and in some ways that was worse. During the full moon the voice was barely a whisper, and the horrible thing chasing after it turned a mottled, dark green that almost made it disappear. During the new moon the voice was so strong he could almost hear what it was saying, finding some comfort in the alien voice. But at the half moon the balance between his own mind and the horrid thing above was just right to allow it to claw and rake at his soul. It wasn't intentional. Fenris was just as terrified and confused by the situation as he was, and it sought refuge in his mind, struggling against the endless, raging storm of madness.

Sharon turned Calvin gently away from the window and helped him with his tie. "I don't know why you can't ever make this straight."

"I don't know why it even matters," he replied. "Nobody cares about the tie."

"Oh, shush." She put a hand to his lips. "It's not going to kill you to dress up now and then."

Sharon was tall, about twenty-five pounds heavier than Hollywood permitted non–character actors to be, with a smile that always managed to bring him down to earth.

"I just don't see the point in—"

"You don't have to see the point, Calvin dear. Sometimes we just do things because we do them. It's tradition."

He chuckled. Traditions meant little to him. Probably because he'd seen a thousand come and go.

"How do I look?" she asked.

"Nice," he replied automatically, without taking the time to look at her.

She wasn't offended, having become accustomed to his moods. She put a hand on his cheek and turned his face away from the night sky. "Ready?"

He nodded absently. "I guess so. But couldn't you go without me just this once?"

Sharon frowned. "That's not how this works. You know better than that."

"Couldn't we put it off for a day or two?"

"We're on a very specific schedule," she replied. "Greg says that tonight is the night, that the arrangement of the heavens is exactly where—"

"Well, if Greg says so."

"Don't be like that." She fell just short of a scolding tone, the kind reserved for misbehaving three-year-olds.

"I really don't like that guy," said Calvin.

"Nobody does."

She always did know the right thing to say.

In point of fact, lots of people liked Greg. He was a likable person, almost pathologically so. Greg didn't just want you to like him. He needed it. Calvin found that need cloying.

"Does it really matter if we skip this one?" he asked.

"A lot of people are looking forward to tonight. You don't want to be responsible for ruining things, do you?"

"I guess not."

"Good. Now get your shoes on. The car service should be here any minute."

She gave him a light kiss on the cheek and left him to finish dressing. He owned more shoes than any straight, non-metrosexual man should. Sharon kept buying them. She said you could tell a lot about a man by his shoes. All he could tell was that he had too many shoes.

He reached for a pair of white sneakers.

"Oh, Calvin," called Sharon from the other room, "if you're going to insist on inappropriate shoes, could you at least wear the black ones?"

He grabbed the black sneakers and put the right one on. Something foreign wiggled between his toes. Annoyed, he removed the shoe and turned it upside down. A glop of yellow slime dropped onto the carpet.

"Ah, hell."

The slime sprouted thick brown hair. A single eye opened and blinked at him.

"Sharon, I did it again!"

He reached for the glop, only to have it skitter under the bed.

"Goddamn it." He dropped down onto the floor and probed in the darkness. "Sharon!"

"Oh, hell, Calvin," she said. "We don't have time for this."

"Don't tell me," he replied. "Tell it."

His hand closed on the moist, hairy thing, but it squirmed out of his fingers.

"Damn it," he said. "Come here, you little bastard."

The bed rocked as the thing growled and hissed. Spitting, it bit off Calvin's hand. He pulled back a bloody stump, except the blood was black and as thick as tar.

"Ah, damn."

The monster threw the bed to one side. The hairy lump turned to the window and howled at the moon. Then it hurled itself through the glass, plummeting to the ground far below with a long, startled gurgle that ended when it hit the pavement.

None of the lump beasts ever grasped the concept of gravity. More often than not, it was their undoing.

A new hand bubbled upward from his stump. The flesh was grayish, the veins a web of bright red. It would look more normal in a few minutes.

Sharon entered. She shook her head at the broken window.

"Honestly, Calvin. Sometimes I think you do this on purpose."

He shrugged. "Sorry."

"It's fine. Just get your shoes on."

The bed fell back into place. The window un-broke. An invisible hand tried to pluck Calvin from the fabric of reality. It failed, as it always did. He was a barb stuck beneath the skin of the universe, an unwanted invader that could not be removed. The invisible hand scratched at him like a dog scratching at a flea. It didn't hurt, but it was irritating.

The moon god wailed.

It was going to be one of those nights.

They went downstairs to a waiting black sedan. They sat in the back in silence. The driver didn't need to be told where to go, and there was nothing to discuss. The routine was set. Sharon read a *People* magazine while Calvin stared out the window, watching the city pass. They rode into the well-to-do suburbs, where the houses hid behind stone walls and iron gates. The car pulled onto an estate and traveled down the winding driveway. Sculpted topiaries and pavement fell away to gravel and untended bushes. The gravel turned to dirt, and the bushes became a forest. Calvin wasn't sure how large the estate was, but it took at least five minutes to drive from the gate to the house at its center. And the well-manicured lawns disappeared, consumed by a twisted wilderness.

The manor house was a foreign piece of civilization in an intentionally uncivilized place. Electric lights illuminated a few windows, but mostly fires in braziers or torches lit the way. Thirty-six cars were parked in the dirt clearing beside the front porch. Two more than last week, Calvin noted.

An older woman in a red dress and her young trophy

husband in a tuxedo followed the torches to the back of the house. He'd seen them before but had never bothered to learn their names.

When Calvin exited the car a bearded man in a turtleneck averted his eyes and bowed slightly before scrambling away in badly disguised panic. Calvin frowned.

"Why do they always do that?" he asked.

"Be nice," said Sharon.

"It's just goddamn annoying, that's all. I don't see you doing that kowtowing nonsense."

"And it's a good thing I don't. Someone has to make sure you keep your appointments."

They circled to the back porch, a sprawling alcove of stone columns with twisted, inhuman figures carved into them. Most of the figures were hidden under overgrown creeping moss. Just enough effort had been made to keep the invading wilderness at bay. A small gathering place was cleared, large enough for the guests to mill about a table of cheese, wine, and caviar.

They were a varied group. The Chosen made no distinction among age, race, or gender. Greg's need to be liked held no prejudice or preference.

The Chosen studiously avoided looking at Calvin. He thought about getting something to drink, but as soon as he stepped over there they'd bow and scrape and kiss his ass.

He was so sick of this.

Sharon read his mind. "I'll get you a glass. Why don't you have a seat?"

"Thanks. What would I do without you?"

He turned toward the marble throne at the top of the steps. It was hard and uncomfortable, but he'd gotten used to that. Greg, a smirking, sycophantic dullard decked out in that ridiculous lavender robe, stood beside the chair. Calvin glanced over his shoulder at Sharon for rescue, but she was already involved in a conversation with another guest.

"Might as well get this over with," mumbled Calvin to himself. He pushed forth a smile as he approached the throne.

"So good of you to join us, Lord of the Wilds," said Greg. "We are unworthy of your presence, much less your gifts."

"Yes. Don't suppose we could speed this up?" asked Calvin. "I'm not really feeling it tonight."

Greg smiled. His smile, either by design or incompetence, was a smarmy, counterproductive achievement. Maybe it was only Calvin who saw it as such. Greg never had a lack of friends.

It was always this kind of asshole that Calvin found himself associating with. He sometimes wondered what it said about him.

Greg looked into the night sky. The design of the alcove and the strange magic of the estate made every star closer and brighter. The half moon glittered like a polished nickel.

"The stars are almost right," he said. "Let them wipe away the corruption of civilization from these frail mortal shells."

"Mmm-hmm." Calvin sat on the throne. A charge tickled his elbows, and the moon and its pursuing god whispered its secrets. If only he could hear them clearly...

Sharon appeared with a plate of cheese and two glasses of wine. "Hello, Greg. Lovely night, isn't it?"

Greg nodded in that familiar, rehearsed, faraway manner. It was meant to be wise and thoughtful, but came across as ponderous and slow-witted. As if his brain were a rusty collection of gears that had to simultaneously process the question and crank his neck.

"I think the McKinneys were looking for you," she said. "Something about another donation to the temple, I believe."

With a hasty adieu, Greg scurried off in search of more of the material wealth he spent most of his life acquiring and condemning simultaneously.

"Thank you," said Calvin. "You're a lifesaver."

"I do what I can."

They tapped their glasses together and waited for the alignment. When it neared, the catering staff moved away the table, and the guests—everyone but Calvin on his throne and the staff hiding away behind locked doors—stood nude in the alcove. They formed a half circle, fell to their knees, and prostrated themselves before Calvin, their lord and master.

Greg, toned and tanned, his skin smoothed by lasers and obsessive waxing, a paradox of the natural world and humanity's obsession with grooming away his links to it, began to preach. Calvin didn't listen. He knew the gist of it. The new world was coming. Civilization would fall, replaced by something purer, more worthy. The strong would rule. The weak would perish. Glory, glory, something about beautiful chaos, blah, blah, blah, blah.

The crowd writhed and moved with the rhythm of Greg's words. There was always that moment near the end of the ceremony when Calvin considered just getting up and walking away. They'd just track him down again. They always did. Or someone like them.

A ray of silver moonlight shone down on the throne. Calvin felt the crackle of extranatural powers pass through him as if he were a prism. It filtered into the crowd, triggering the change.

Greg was the first. His body hunched over as patches of brown and black hair sprouted. A second pair of arms grew from his shoulders. The legs bent and twisted. And the head became a giant pair of jaws, filled with pristine white fangs. The beast clawed the marble, raised its head, and howled.

It turned and stalked toward Calvin as the other guests finished their transformations. Nostrils flaring, the creature studied Calvin with beady yellow eyes. Frowning, Calvin looked right back into its eyes until the monster cowered before him.

"Piss off, Greg."

The whimpering beast retreated. It joined the pack. Snapping, snarling, the wild creatures ran into the darkened forest. They wouldn't be back until morning, when the exhausted, naked humans would slink back to the manor with blood on their lips.

Somewhere in the darkness an inhuman monster bayed at the moon.

Calvin went to the small guesthouse. A beast waited for him, curled up on the couch. It raised its head at him and wagged its tail.

"Hi, Sharon."

He scratched her behind the ears, and she clawed the couch to shreds in her pleasure. She lowered her head.

He smiled. "It's all right. It's not my couch."

He sat beside her. She set her head on his lap. He turned on the television. *The Wolfman* was playing.

Sighing, he changed the channel and waited for the dawn.

CHAPTER TWO

"Third rule is don't pet the dog," said Mr. West.

A sad-eyed puppy sat in front of one of the three doors in the hallway. It was white with brown and black spots and big floppy ears, and it whined as they walked past.

"Does it bite?" Diana asked.

"No."

"Whose is it?"

"It belongs to Number Two," said West, "but he lost control of it about a year ago. Now he's lucky if it lets him out on the weekends to pick up groceries."

He wheeled and stared at her with tightly narrowed eyes. So much so she wasn't sure they were even open.

"Mark my words, Number Five. Bad things happen to those who don't follow the rules."

His long mustache twitched and he scratched his shaggy head, then turned back, walking up the six steps to Apartment Number Five. He fumbled with an overloaded key ring. As far as Diana could tell there were only seven apartments in this small building, but he must've had at least three dozen keys on that ring.

"This'll be yours," he said.

She wasn't so sure. The rent on this place was remarkably cheap, but if a creepy landlord came with the package, she'd have to think it over.

She didn't have to think it over for long.

The small apartment was fully furnished. It came with a brand-new sofa, a television, an old-fashioned jukebox like she'd always wanted. The jukebox even had all her favorite songs on it.

"Does this work?" she asked.

West shrugged and mumbled.

The kitchenette was bare except for some silverware in a drawer, but she didn't cook anyway. There were a few Mr. Fizz sodas in the fridge, though.

"I didn't know they still made this brand," she said. "They're my favorite."

"Help yourself."

"Really? Are you sure it's okay? What about the former tenant?"

"He's gone."

"But won't he be coming back for his stuff?"

"I doubt it."

She hesitated but decided that one soda wouldn't hurt anything. It tasted just as good as she remembered. Better.

He showed her the bedroom. Superman posters decorated the walls, along with art prints and a huge black-and-white photo of the Arc de Triomphe and another of the Eiffel Tower. It was bizarre. She knew she had eclectic tastes, and she had never expected anyone else to share them.

"There's no way anyone would leave this stuff behind," she said.

"It's not his stuff," he said. "It's yours. If you want it."

The rent on this place was half what she'd expected, and the décor meant she could just grab her three suitcases from the car and be unpacked within the hour. It was too good to be true.

"What's the catch?" she asked.

He smiled. "Ah, there's a smart girl."

She stiffened. Her first thought was that this guy was a fiend who lured innocent young women into a life of orgies and pornography, but it would take more than a jukebox and a sixpack of soda to get Diana to strip on a webcam. Maybe if a good cable package came with the deal . . .

"Rule number two," he said. "Never open this closet."

He pointed to a door tucked away beside the bathroom.

"Why?" she asked.

"A good question. People who ask too many questions don't usually last. Number Seven asked a lot of questions. Used to."

He fumbled with the key ring and managed, after some rattling and grumbling, to pull off the key to the apartment and offer it to her.

"It's all yours if you want it."

She didn't reach for the key just yet. A sixth sense warned her that she was striking a Faustian bargain. Odd, since she wasn't sure what a Faustian bargain was. But it was something not to be taken lightly. She knew that.

"If you don't want it," he said, "somebody else will."

"What's the first rule?" she asked. "You told me the third and second rules, but not the first."

He paused, chewed his lip.

"The first rule is turn the lights off when you leave a room. Just because I pay the utilities that doesn't mean I'm made of money."

Diana would've sold her soul for paid utilities, so she snatched the key. West was surprised enough to open his eyes to a softer squint.

"Where's the lease?" she asked.

"There's no lease. You stay as long as you're able, Number Five. Leave whenever you're willing."

She followed him out the door. Her three suitcases were already sitting in the hallway.

"Hmm," he said. "Apartment must like you. That's a good sign."

He waddled away without saying another word. The moment he was out of sight, even the jangle of his keys disappeared. Silence filled the hallway. No, that wasn't quite right. Music came from somewhere. So light it almost couldn't be heard. Like a chorus rehearsing. She couldn't figure out where it was coming from, though.

The puppy in front of Apartment Two glanced forlornly in her direction and whimpered.

She glanced around her shiny new apartment. So what if the landlord was a bit of a nut? This place was made for her, and with the run of bad luck she'd had in the last few weeks, this was a good omen. Things were turning around.

She fed the jukebox a nickel. The mechanical arm grabbed the gleaming vinyl disk and set it on the turntable. Frankie Avalon sang about the virtues of beach life, and she smiled.

Diana wasted no time getting unpacked. She needed to claim this apartment. She'd been living out of suitcases too long, bumming off of friends like a vagabond. She shoved her clothes into the dresser so eagerly that she didn't fold most of them. But once she closed the drawer she felt she'd made her mark. She lounged around for an hour, sitting on the sofa, drinking soda, watching TV, just relaxing. Chubby Checker, Aretha Franklin, and the Big Bopper kept her company. And when she was tired, she fell asleep on the nice comfortable bed and dreamed the strangest dreams.

She was herself, but she wasn't herself. She flew across other worlds, strange realms without form or substance, lost cities and ghosts of forgotten civilizations passing beneath her. Time rendered everyone and everything into dust. From the tiniest speck to the greatest of the ancients. In the center of it all the slumbering god lay still, wrapped in the dream that foolish mortals and inhuman deities alike called reality.

The god opened one of his countless eyes. An eye bigger than the sun. And though she was just a mote, the yellow-and-black orb focused on her. The weight of a vast, incomprehensible universe threatened to crush Diana. She tried screaming. Her throat filled with bile and her brain melted as every cell in her body convulsed in absolute horror before exploding.

She awoke covered in sweat. Her heart pounded. A chill in the air turned her breath frosty. And just for a moment she thought the walls were moving, and something else was swimming under the covers.

She turned on the lights. Everything snapped back to normal. Her terror vanished as quickly as it had come. The air warmed. She marveled at how alien and real the dream had been. Although it was all fading now, transforming into shadowy memory the way dreams did.

Diana got up, grabbed a glass of water, and headed back to bed.

"Bad dream?" someone asked.

She jumped and whirled around. Self-defense courses sprang to mind, and she was ready to shout and gouge and do what needed to be done.

Nobody was there.

"Settle down, girl," she told herself. "You're imagining things."

"No, you're not," said the voice.

She jumped again, but this time had the presence of mind to listen for the source.

It was coming from the closet.

"Hello?" she asked quietly. "Is there someone in there?"

There was no reply.

"Hello?"

No answer.

She went to the bathroom, splashed some cold water on her face, and dried herself with a towel. She was sticky with sweat, and a shower sounded appealing. But she'd seen enough slasher movies to know what happened next.

Part of her said it was time to leave. Don't pack anything. Don't change out of your pajamas. Just walk out of the apartment and never look back. But that was stupid.

She wasn't about to be spooked out of her new home by a crazy dream.

Another part of her suggested that this was still just a dream. She'd wake up in another moment and laugh at herself. But it was all so clear, so lucid. She'd never dreamed anything as weird as the flying segment at the beginning. Nor anything as ordinary as walking around her apartment, looking for a phantom voice.

"Bad feng shui," she remarked to herself, as if that explained everything.

"Oh, I agree," said the closet. "The couch really should be a few more feet to the right. And the coffee table counteracts the openness of the room."

The voice wasn't threatening. Diana was determined to stay calm, but she wasn't going to stick around or investigate. Most stupid victims in movies tended to die because they weren't smart enough to go away from the sound of the chain saw. She didn't want to run around in her underwear since that seemed like a cliché too, but stopping to get dressed in the name of vanity also got you killed in these situations.

The front door was gone. Only a wall. There weren't any windows, no other ways out.

She was trapped.

"Don't panic," said the closet. "Let's just keep our wits, and we'll work everything out."

Diana said, "This isn't funny."

"You don't think I find it funny, do you?" replied the closet. "I don't like this arrangement any more than you do."

She tried the phone.

"Don't open the closet," said West's familiar voice on the other end of the line.

She hung up, dialed 911.

"Don't open the closet," repeated West.

"Damn it. You can't do this. It's illegal. People will know I'm missing."

"You can leave any time you want, Number Five."

"How?"

"Open the closet."

"But you just said I'm not supposed to open the closet."

"Stay as long as you're able, Number Five," said West. "Leave whenever you're willing."

The line went dead.

"Looks like we're stuck with each other," said the closet.

Diana pounded on the walls and shouted for a few minutes. Nobody heard her. Or maybe somebody did. More prisoners ensnared in West's bizarre game. She used a tall standing lamp as a battering ram against the wall with negligible results. She stripped the paint and chipped away some of the wood. If this was her only option, it was going to be a lot of work. Even if he didn't have anything weird planned, even if he was just going to leave her locked in here with a guy trapped in a closet, she'd starve to death before doing any real damage.

Just the realization made her prematurely hungry. She'd have to settle for a soda, though she would've killed for a turkey sandwich. She found one waiting for her in the fridge. The Mr. Fizz five-pack had regenerated its sixth can as well.

Someone was in here with her. Someone other than the guy in the closet.

Lamp in hand, she searched the apartment. She came up empty.

"Where is it?" she asked.

"Where's what?" replied the closet.

"The secret door."

He chuckled. "There's only one way out, and you're talking to it."

"I'm not stupid. Somebody had to put that sandwich in the refrigerator."

"You did. By wishing for it."

"How gullible do you think I am?"

"What kind of sandwich is it?" asked the closet.

"What difference does that make?"

"What kind?"

She slumped against the wall and glared at the closet. "Turkey."

"And what kind of sandwich were you just thinking about?"

Diana dismissed the observation as irrelevant at first. But she hadn't verbalized her sandwich desires. Assuming that there was a secret door somewhere and that someone had sneaked into the small apartment and slipped in a sandwich before escaping, all without her noticing, they'd still have had to be telepathic to know what she wanted, and have some sort of super-speed sandwich-making ability.

The rational explanation had a lot of holes in it.

She returned to the fridge. The sandwich was still there. An inspection revealed that it was exactly how she liked it. With just a touch of mayo and mustard, a single leaf of lettuce and three tomato slices. She stuck it back in the fridge, closed the door, and stared at the appliance for ten seconds.

"Orange juice," she said, opening the door.

The sandwich was gone. In its place, a tall glass of juice.

She closed the door.

"Deep-fried Twinkie," she whispered, throwing open the door.

And there it was.

Diana had spent too much of her life in a logical world to be convinced just yet. Only after she had pulled the refrigerator away from the wall, checked for false walls and trapdoors, and come up with nothing did she see no other choice. The guy in the closet was strange but didn't require a supernatural explanation. A magic fridge wasn't so easy to dismiss.

"Damn." She circled the fridge twice before admitting defeat. "I'll take that sandwich now."

She ate the sandwich in the kitchen, not even sitting down, and tried to make sense of this, but it didn't click.

The phone rang. She went to the living room, stared at the phone, but didn't pick it up.

It kept ringing.

"Are you going to answer that?" asked the closet.

She put the receiver to her ear.

"West?"

"About time," West said. "I may be ageless, Number Five, but I don't have all day." He paused. "So did you open the closet yet?"

"No."

"Good. Don't."

"Will you shut up about the stupid closet already?"

"Suit yourself."

He hung up.

"Ah, damn it." Diana stared at the receiver, then the closet.

"Frustrating, isn't it?" said the closet. "Imagine how I feel. I was spawned at the dawn of time and now I find myself bound to a small clump of transient flesh."

"Bound by what?"

"Whatever decides these things. Primal forces that make even me piss myself. Or would if I pissed. It's a complicated universe. Sorry if I can't just summarize it in a pithy metaphor."

The phone rang again. She took a moment to steady herself. Losing her temper wasn't getting her anywhere.

"Hello."

"Hello," said West. "Ready to talk now?"

She sucked in a deep breath and replied in an even voice. "Yes."

"Good. Here's how it works. Inside that closet is an ancient entity known as Vom the Hungering. He's actually a pretty decent sort, as ancient spawns go. But if you let him out of that closet, he will eat you."

She lowered the phone. "You're a cannibal?"

Vom chuckled. "Cannibals eat their own kind. I am a singular entity. There is only one Vom the Hungering, and that is me. And you are?"

She ignored the question. "You're going to eat me?"

"Yeah, probably. Don't suppose it helps anything if I apologize in advance."

She put the phone to her ear. "Pay attention, Number Five. You are now Vom's warden. You will not age or grow sick and you cannot die by conventional means."

"Okay, this is sounding more and more like bullshit," she said.

"Don't interrupt. I have other responsibilities. If I don't bring Number Three an avocado in five minutes California will fall into the ocean."

"Yeah. Sure. Makes sense." She admitted defeat and just listened.

"One day, Number Five, you will release Vom. Maybe not today. Maybe not tomorrow. Maybe not a hundred years from now. But one day, when the crawl of eternity becomes too much for you, you will open that door. He will then devour you, go back into his prison, and wait for the next warden. That is just how this works. There's no point in complaining to me about it either. I don't have any control over any of it."

"But—"

"I'm not even obligated to give you this information, but you seem like a nice young woman. So best of luck."

He hung up, and she knew he wouldn't be calling back this time.

She checked the apartment again. Ran her fingers along every wall, probed every corner, moved every bit of furniture. If there was a way out she didn't find it, but just to be certain she checked one more time.

If West was to be believed (though she wasn't quite ready for that) she was a prisoner and her only way out was death. And if she was immortal there was only one form of death available, to be devoured by a monster living in her closet.

She found a butter knife in the cabinet and ran it across her palm. It wasn't easy getting the blade to draw blood, but she managed. The shallow cut closed immediately. There wasn't even a scar left behind.

It was as far as she was willing to go right now. Maybe

in a hundred years she'd be so bored that sawing her arms off with a dull butter knife would sound amusing.

Stay as long as she could. Leave whenever she was willing. She got it now.

She went back to bed. The clock radio on the nightstand counted the minutes. She turned the bright red numbers toward the wall and tried not to think about it. If she really was immortal she had all the time in the universe. It seemed pointless to obsess over every second. Diana turned the clock toward her and frowned. Twenty-two minutes had passed.

Twenty-two minutes.

She put the pillow over her face and reflected on infinity, breaking it up into twenty-two-minute chunks. Endless bits of twenty-two, one right after the other after the other.

The crawl of eternity indeed.

She got up and turned on the television. Nothing was on. Or maybe she just wasn't in the mood.

"Can't sleep either, huh?" asked the closet monster. "I hate that. Of course I only sleep seven minutes every other century. And believe me, that's annoying. I have a lot of time to kill and a nap now and then might help."

She turned up the volume.

"We're the only company we're going to have for a long, long while," Vom said. "We can at least try and be civil."

She stared at the TV, not really watching it, just thinking about the passage of time, listening to the tick-tick-tick of the clock on the wall. Where had that clock even come from, anyway? It hadn't been there before. She was certain of that. She'd been over every inch of this place.

Diana muted the television.

"This isn't fair," she said. "All I wanted was an apartment."

"You seem like a decent lady," said Vom. "I'm really sorry that I have to eat you."

She walked over to the closet. "You keep saying that, but if you were really sorry you wouldn't. Then I could open this closet, and we could both get out of here."

"Sounds like a good deal to me."

"So you agree then?"

"Sure. No eating. I promise."

She reached for the knob but stopped short of touching it.

"How do I know I can trust you?"

"You don't. And I'll admit I'm not trustworthy. I did promise not to eat all the others. And I really meant it when I said it. But it just sort of happens. Not always though. There was this Spanish guy who I didn't eat. Good guy, too. Lot of fun. I miss him."

"What made him different?"

"He had the stuff."

"The stuff?"

"You know what I'm talking about. The stuff. The goods. The mojo."

"What does that even mean?"

"It means what it means," said Vom. "When someone has the stuff, you just know it."

"That's not very helpful at all."

"There are mysteries beyond even my ken. Listen. I've done this plenty of times. I know how this game goes. Some people open the closet right away. Others hold out for a while. One guy made it a whole century. But you are going to open this door one day. So why don't we just cut the suspense and jump to the inevitable conclusion?"

Diana wanted to argue, but if what West and Vom had told her was true, then it really was unavoidable. The question wasn't *if* she would open the closet. The question was *when*.

It took her four days to get bored enough to think about finally opening the door. Four days of watching television, of staring at the ticks of the clock, of obsessively searching every nook and cranny of the apartment for some form of escape, of waiting for the phone to ring and for West to tell her that he'd changed his mind and she was free to go.

No one would be coming for her because no one knew she was here. If she was going to get out she'd have to do it herself. And four days of steady rumination on the subject always led back to that damn closet.

She went to the refrigerator and demanded another turkey sandwich. Then another. Then another. Then she stopped thinking small and demanded a turkey. Then she just started demanding "Food" and left it up to the refrigerator to supply whatever it felt like. She piled the sandwiches and turkeys and cakes and hamburgers and buckets of apples and haggis and everything else in the living room. When she ran out of room on the coffee table she started putting stuff on the floor. She threw everything in a huge messy heap. She didn't stop until the mound of food filled half the room and was nearly to the ceiling.

She didn't know if it would be enough to satisfy his appetite, but she was already tired of waiting. She wasn't going to spend the rest of her life in this cage, dreading the inevitable. Better to just get it over with.

She threw open the closet door.

Bright green fur covered Vom the Hungering. His flat, wide head had no eyes or ears or nose. Just one huge mouth. Another maw split his potbelly. He was simultaneously lanky and pudgy. Her first instinct was that he was an old puppet, rejected from *Sesame Street* and banished to a limbo alongside moldy raincoats and wingtip shoes. It was only when he lurched toward her, both of his mouths licking their lips, arms raised, that she realized he was alive.

She smacked him across the head with a rolled-up magazine.

"No!" She scolded him gently, but firmly.

Vom snarled and reached toward her again.

"No!" She hit him again. "Not for you!"

He frowned, rubbing his snout.

She pointed at the pile of food. "That's yours."

Vom pounced on the meal, gleefully shoving down everything. She was revolted and hypnotized by the sight and watched him gorge himself for several minutes. He wasn't slowing down, and she doubted he would be full once he finished—in another two or three minutes at most.

The front door was back. She tiptoed out into the hall and shut the door quietly behind her.

The puppy in front of Number Two wasn't a puppy anymore. It was something else. Something vaguely puppyshaped, but with a malformed skull, giant black eyes, and a sucker-like mouth.

The creature looked up at her with its three huge eyes, wagged the tentacle sticking out of its backside, and whimpered.

Diana waited until she had slunk past the hideous creature before she ran screaming into the streets.

CHAPTER THREE

She stopped shrieking after a minute.

It wasn't the crazy looks she drew from the other pedestrians that made her stop. And her damaged sanity hadn't managed to repair itself. She'd left something behind in that apartment. Something she'd always taken for granted. Faith in a rational world. It was like a tiny cog had been removed from her brain, and all the gears were still working, but a slight wobble was slowly and inevitably stripping the teeth until one day, without warning, the Rube Goldberg device that was her mind would fall apart with a loud *sproing*.

No, she eventually stopped screaming because she discovered that running and freaking out at the same time was exhausting. She doubted even an Olympic athlete could do it for very long. Also, she got stuck at a cross-walk, and it was hard to keep the momentum while standing there waiting for the light to change.

She sat on a bench and caught her breath. A glance back the way she'd come showed neither Vom nor West following her. She'd escaped. Too bad she'd lost her stuff, but there was no way she was going back for it. Her first thought was that it was just more crappy luck, but then she remembered that she'd avoided being trapped for eternity or being eaten by a gangly furry monster and decided it was the opposite. Things were starting to turn around. If she could escape unhurt from Vom the Hungering, everything else should be easy.

Leaning back on the bench, she exhaled a sigh of relief.

The early evening sky was torn in pieces.

Six slashes ran across it. They pulsed with a strange yellow glow. The weirdest thing was that the slashes didn't seem to be behind the stars, but on top of them. It was as if some gigantic monster had raked the fabric of the universe itself. And the universe had healed, but the scars remained.

The full moon appeared normal. But on the other side of the sky was another moon. The orb was sickly greenish. It writhed. It was covered in bright red eyes. The thing undulated, and she glimpsed a maw filled with rows of teeth.

She'd escaped the apartment, but she was still in the trap. The cage was just bigger. She'd seen enough *Twilight Zone* episodes to know a cosmic screw when she was in the middle of it.

She stood, carelessly bumping into a tall, angular man in a black trench coat. His face wasn't human, but insectile. Her first instinct was to cower or flee. But that was what *they* wanted her to do. And she wasn't about to give *them* the satisfaction. She pushed forth the most sincere smile she could manage while staring into the bug's six hundred eyes.

"Pardon me, sir."

The bug clicked its mandibles.

"No problem, miss."

It walked up to the curb, spread its coat, and soared away. Diana dug her claws into her fractured sanity and refused to let it go. Even as she noticed that one of the cars driving down the street was an SUV-sized crimson slug and that the hot dog vendor on the corner was a monster in an apron with a paper hat on his squid-like head, she convinced herself, through sheer force of will, that there was nothing to be concerned about. She didn't know if that meant she would be okay or if she'd just lost her mind. All she knew was that she wasn't gibbering, and she'd take whatever small victory she could manage.

A hairy hand grabbed her shoulder. "Hey, there you are."

Diana turned to the toothy jaws of Vom the Hungering.

"No!" she shouted forcefully as she punched him in the nose. Or at least the area of his mostly featureless face above his mouth.

"Ow." Vom rubbed his head. "Why'd you do that?"

"You were going to eat me."

"No, I wasn't."

His stomach rumbled, causing the earth beneath the concrete beneath their feet to tremble. He smiled sheepishly.

"Okay, maybe I was thinking about it."

"This is bullshit," she said. "I let you out of the closet. You were supposed to either eat me or let me go."

Vom shrugged. "Don't blame me. I don't make the rules. Oh, hot dog." He lumbered over to the cart on his stumpy legs. "One foot-long, please. Extra everything."

The squiddy vendor asked, "You got any money?"

"What? I'm good for it."

The vendor wiggled his tentacles and folded his floppy arms across his chest.

"Hey, could you loan me a couple of bucks?" Vom asked Diana.

She duplicated the vendor's stance.

"Oh, fine. I must've eaten someone with a wallet at some point." He opened his mouth and reached down his own throat. He spit out a variety of random objects: an old lipstick, a dog collar, a license plate, some buttons, and something small and squirmy that was apparently still alive.

Vom extracted a pair of wrinkled blue jeans from his bigger mouth. He rifled through the pockets and found a few dollars and some change. Enough to purchase two hot dogs. The sticky drool covering the cash didn't bother the slimy vendor beast, who started working on Vom's dogs. While waiting, Vom shoved the regurgitated items back into his mouths. Including the squirming thing.

"Don't skimp on the sauerkraut."

The vendor gave Vom the dogs. He offered one to Diana. She turned it down with a queasy twinge.

He swallowed the hot dogs in one gulp.

"You have something." She pointed to the mustard-stained pant leg snagged on one of his fangs. "Right there."

"Whoops."

He slurped down the denim like a stray noodle.

They walked through the park, and Vom tried to explain what was happening. Normally she wouldn't have been caught walking through a park alone after dark, but she figured that the ravenous creature beside her would discourage even the most determined mugger. Or not.

Nobody seemed to notice anything out of the ordinary. The giant bugs and slugs and misshapen things lurching on the city streets. Or the tears in the sky. Or the monstrous moon god. All these things remained unobserved by everyone else.

"Imagine the universe as a tesseract, a single multidimensional hypercube divided into thin, mostly self-contained slices. Now this model is, by its nature, flawed and incomplete. Mostly because each entity perceives its own slice to be the most important, simply from a lack of ability to perceive the other aspects of the complete universe which surrounds them. With me so far?"

"No."

He sighed. "This'd be easier if you had some experience with multidimensional geometric theory."

"Yeah, well, I don't. Didn't think it would be important. And I don't think they even offered it at the college I attended."

"Okay. We'll go with the dumbed-down version then." He spoke very slowly, using sweeping gestures to emphasize his points. "The universe is a very tall building with many floors but no elevators and great soundproofing. And every shred of matter in the universe exists on one of those floors."

He paused.

"Have I lost you again?"

"I'm not an idiot. I can follow a metaphor."

"Each floor is usually completely unaware of the other floors around it. Although sometimes, if one floor gets particularly noisy it might have an effect on nearby neighbors. And sometimes a floor will spring a leak or a window will open for a short while and things might get a little wonky for both floors until the anomaly corrects itself. And other times the floors get shuffled around and in the process something on Floor A ends up on Floor B, where it really doesn't belong. See, there are connections between floors. Like ventilation ducts or Jefferies tubes or crawl spaces or whatever. Invisible gaps in the fabric of the universe that probably serve some useful purpose, but that also some beings use, unintentionally in my case, to cross floors. And our apartment is one of those trap-doors.

"But you don't leave your old world behind. A part of it comes with you, no matter where you go. And so you and I are straddling floors. One foot in our own portion of reality and another in an alien perception we were never meant to have."

"But why?" she asked. "How does something like that happen?"

"Hell if I know," said Vom. "Until I came into contact with your world, I was just a merciless destructive force, a mindless devourer."

She flashed him a look.

"Hey, I'm working on it," he said. "I didn't eat you, did I?"

"You tried."

"If we're going to make this relationship work, you're going to have to get over that."

"What relationship?" she asked.

"Like it or not, we're bound together," said Vom.

"Oh no we're not."

He gnashed his teeth. Since he had a lot of teeth, several rows of them, it made a hell of a grating noise.

"Hey, consciousness isn't all it's cracked up to be. There are all these complicated thoughts running through my head now, and some of them are very confusing. They don't mesh together well. It's like you. Part of me wants to eat you. But another part of me feels like that would be a lousy thing to do since you freed me from that closet. But another part of me thinks that if I kill you, maybe it'll free me from this sliver of reality and I'll get to go home where all I had to worry about was digesting anything that found its way into any of my two thousand fourteen stomachs. But another part thinks that maybe I don't want to go back to that now that I've found a world where not everything is as simple as endless devouring hunger. But another—"

"I get it."

"The point is that once you gaze into the abyss—"

"The abyss gazes into you."

"Who told you that?"

"It's a cliché. Everybody knows that."

Vom frowned. "Damn. And I thought I'd made that up. Well, it doesn't matter. What matters is that we're stuck with each other, and we can't go back. Me, a timeless devouring force and you, a delicious chewy morsel wrapped around a crunchy calcium treat."

She moved a few steps farther from him.

"What?" he said. "It's a compliment."

She took stock of her situation. She was bound to a horror from beyond time and space, and she was probably going slowly mad because of it.

"Is the apartment still mine?"

"You bet," said Vom. "It's a package deal."

There was a bright side at least.

"So what do you say?" He extended his hand. "Roomies?"

Noticing snapping jaws buried in the fur in Vom's palms, she kept her hands in her pockets and nodded.

They walked back to West's apartment building of horrors. She wasn't crazy about living there, but she had no place else to go. She couldn't call on any of her friends. Not with Vom and his endless appetite following her.

The building didn't look right. She'd run away without glancing back upon her escape, but she saw it with new eyes this time. It was a jutting tower of strange angles, disappearing into a swirling green vortex in the sky. The brick walls shimmered and shifted as she walked closer, like one of those cheap 3-D card images that never quite worked the way the inventor had hoped.

The vortex growled, and the building shuddered, expanding and contracting. She climbed the short flight of stairs to the front doors. The creaky old doors opened without her touching the handles, and hot wind poured over her. She saw the portal as a huge mouth. One of thousands scattered across the cosmos, all part of a single impossibly huge creature dwelling across multiple realities. And all the people, animals, and even monsters like Vom were merely skittering atoms drifting between its toes. Although it probably didn't have toes. Or if it did, each of those toes could crush a universe. Except for the big toe. That could probably crush several at once.

Vom walked inside, and she expected the lesser devouring monster to be devoured by the larger one. But it didn't happen.

"Are you coming?" he asked her.

She pushed the inhuman thoughts away, gritted her teeth, and followed him. The otherness outside the apartment disappeared once she was across the threshold. The heat faded to a mildly uncomfortable warmth. The air was a bit humid, but nothing she couldn't handle.

One of the apartment doors opened, and West stuck his head out. He sported an extra pair of eyes above the normal set. And his bushy beard writhed a bit. Not the beard itself, but whatever was underneath it, whatever passed for West's chin. Not that she wanted to think about that.

"Still alive, Number Five?" he asked, though the answer should've been obvious.

She nodded.

"You wouldn't happen to have any Monopoly money on you, would you, Number Five?"

She shook her head.

"Damn. The mole lords are not going to be happy about that."

He withdrew into his room and shut the door without another word.

"He's a crazy old bird," said Vom, "but he's harmless."

Considering the source of the reassurance, Diana didn't find this very comforting.

She noticed for the first time that every door in the

building was different. Different size. Different color. Different style. Nothing in the building matched. The carpeting appeared to be assembled from a thousand discarded scraps. The walls were brick, then wood paneling, then stucco, then polka-dotted wallpaper. Nothing lined up in a conventional way. The hall seemed askew. The stairs curved downward, giving one the impression of walking down when going up. The doors tilted at odd angles, though never the same angle. And the numbers marking the apartments were all in different fonts. The entire building was like a hastily constructed model, put together from bits and pieces of other models by a maker who was only vaguely familiar with traditional design conventions.

She hadn't noticed any of this before. Or maybe it hadn't looked like this before. Maybe this was all a byproduct of her new perceptions. Either way, it weirded her out.

They passed the gruesome puppy beast in front of Apartment Two. The door opened a crack, and she glimpsed a shadowy figure.

"Hey," the figure whispered.

The puppy snarled, and the door slammed shut.

The apartment was exactly as she'd left it. She'd expected it to be as twisted and skewed as the rest of her new universe, but everything was in order. Except that the coffee table had had a big bite taken out of it.

"Sorry," said Vom. "Kind of hard to put on the brakes once I get going."

He helped her push the refrigerator back against the wall.

Someone knocked.

He answered the door before she could stop him.

A short blond woman in her forties and a hulking bat-like creature in a sweater vest stepped into the apartment.

"Congratulations." She gave Vom a polite hug. "We just heard about your early parole."

"Stacey, Peter. I thought you'd have moved out by now."

"We're working on it," she said.

The bat gurgled.

"Now, Peter," said the woman. "Be nice."

The creature lumbered over to Diana. She recoiled from the grinning monster and his saber-like fangs. He thrust a lump wrapped in tinfoil into her arms. "Yours," he said as drool dripped down his chin.

"Now, Peter," said Stacey. "Is that any way to treat our new neighbor?"

Diana held the lump in limp hands. It was warm. And was it squirming or was that just her imagination? How the hell could she even tell anymore?

"You'll have to excuse Peter. He always gets a little grumpy after a few hours of hosting."

"No problem," replied Diana.

Peter pounced on Stacey. He squeezed her in a tight embrace. They howled in one terrible harmony as his body collapsed into a frail mortal shell while she took on the bat-monster shape. The only difference was that now it wore a floral-print dress.

Peter smoothed the few strands of hair on his balding head. "That's better. You must be Vom's new warden."

"I must be," said Diana.

The Stacey-thing snatched the tinfoil lump and bit into it.

"We just got a new breadmaker," said Peter. "The missus has been dying for a chance to try it out."

"Pumpernickel," cooed Stacey-thing. "Goood."

"For Heaven's sake, honey, don't eat it all."

She offered the loaf to Diana with a sheepish smile. Bread crumbs and bits of tinfoil were stuck between Stacey's pointed teeth.

Diana politely turned the offering away. "No, thank you. Maybe later."

"I'll take that." Vom snatched the bread and shoved it into the mouth in his potbelly.

CHAPTER FOUR

Once a week Calvin and Sharon spent the night together, doing something. It was an informal arrangement, and since they lived together they already saw each other regularly. But there was only one night when it was expected, when they would leave the apartment together and see a movie, get some dinner, or maybe just hang out at a coffee shop and talk.

Sharon knew better than to think of it as date night, but sometimes she still did.

Dressing for almost-date night was tricky. She didn't want anything too formal or too casual. She wanted to be comfortable. She wanted to look nice. Although this was purely for her own satisfaction. Calvin didn't care what she looked like. She could've worn a clown suit and he wouldn't have noticed. Half the time he needed her help to dress himself.

He didn't need clothes, but having walked among humans for ages he had the basics down, though he did complain that fashion was always changing and was hard to keep up with. Shirt. Pants. Usually he remembered his shoes. She'd long ago accepted socks were hit-and-miss. Underwear was right out. Getting him to dress up was difficult because it was all just so many extra accessories as far as he was concerned. Ties escaped him. Cuff links he couldn't understand. Wrinkles were beneath his notice.

Given a choice he'd have walked around in a T-shirt, sweatpants, and sandals all day, every day. And that would've been just fine with her, but it wasn't up to her. Greg had established a rule that Calvin had to maintain a certain level of presentability at all times. It was necessary since most people would not worship a man who dressed slovenly. Not in this day and age. There were expectations, standards. If Jesus were walking the Earth today he'd have to get a shave and a haircut and invest in Armani. Probably no one would listen to him, but at least he'd have a fighting chance.

In addition to Calvin's underdeveloped appreciation of clothing, he also had no appreciation of the human form. To him all humans were merely walking bags of meat. If Calvin was a god (and who was to say he wasn't?), he was not the type of god to cavort with every piece of tempting mortal ass that came along. And while she wouldn't have minded some cavorting, Sharon had accepted it.

But when date night came along she still put on some makeup, still struggled to find the right pair of slacks that made her ass look good, still fretted about those few extra pounds, and still debated what level of cleavage was most flattering without drawing too much attention to itself.

She came out of her bedroom, wearing her carefully selected ensemble.

"How do I look?" she asked.

"Good," he replied automatically, like a trained dog. He didn't even look up at her, but at least he was trying.

They decided to go to the Mexican place just down the street. Although just where it popped up varied from week to week: it migrated from building to building, replacing the bookstore or the Italian restaurant or the church. And there were some days when it disappeared entirely.

The universe, while mostly stable, had its hiccups. The Mexican place was one of these. When it was there it was a vibrant restaurant full of life and energy with the best tacos in town. When it was gone...it was just gone. The sound of mariachi music remained, though, filling the block every hour of the day, the ghostly echoes of a phantom band.

She'd never seen the restaurant appear or disappear. It seemed to happen only when no one was looking. On occasion the restaurant would disappear with people still inside it. They would promptly be forgotten by everyone, never to return. Whether they ceased to exist, were devoured by some nameless thing, or were perhaps lured into a mysterious netherworld by the freshest handmade tortillas and most delectable enchiladas in the city, no one knew. All Sharon knew was that the food was delicious and reasonably priced, and they served a margarita that she was willing to die for. Or disappear. Or whatever.

The Mexican place was there, occupying the spot usually held by an electronics store. They grabbed a seat and munched chips. From the inside the world looked different. The city was gone, replaced by a vista of yellow grass and an emerald sun. Giant moths soared in the skies. Their colorful prismatic wings shimmered in great clouds. The view was part of what she liked about the place.

There was another reason she loved the Mexican place. She loved it because it was their place. Here she didn't have to share Calvin with anyone else. Here, and really only here, nothing else mattered.

The front door flew open and a mound of hairy blue thing with a face like a buffalo entered. A pair of giant black mantises hung on each of its arms.

"There goes the neighborhood," said Sharon.

The buffalo crept up to the employee in charge of seating, promptly devoured her in one bite, and lurched to a table. There was a couple already seated there, but they were all too happy to concede their table and meal to the creatures.

The buffalo slurped down the enchiladas while the bugs sniffed the beers. They chirped, chewing on the tablecloth and licking the wax from the candles.

"Should we go somewhere else?" she asked.

"You haven't even gotten your food yet," he replied.

"It's not that important."

The waiter tried to take the buffalo's order and was set upon by the bugs for his trouble.

"That's it." Calvin pushed away from the table.

"It's okay," she said. "You don't have to do that."

"Yes, I do."

"But—"

But he was already away.

"Excuse me."

The buffalo and bugs ignored him.

"I said, excuse me."

The bugs stopped tormenting the waiter and raised their heads. The buffalo snorted.

"People are trying to eat here," said Calvin.

The buffalo rose to its full height and howled at Calvin, spraying a healthy dose of phosphorescent drool across his face. The bugs chortled.

"I'm trying to be nice about this, but there is no call for this behavior. Everyone's just trying to have a pleasant evening, and you're ruining it for everyone."

The rude beast howled and shook its head, splattering copious amounts of drool throughout the room.

"Have it your way."

Calvin raised a hand and smacked the buffalo across the nose. The air cracked with thunder. The monster fell on one knee. Calvin grabbed it by the ear and yanked it to its feet. The buffalo squawked and roared, but Calvin pulled it helplessly toward the front door.

"And spit it out," he said.

The buffalo spit up the seating girl, whole and unharmed though covered in slime.

"Thank you," she said.

"Don't mention it."

Calvin tossed the beast out the front door. He helped the seating girl up, then turned on the bugs.

"You should probably leave now."

They scampered out the door. One tried to take the waiter to go, but a word from Calvin helped it change its mind.

"And don't come back unless you're willing to behave," shouted Calvin before returning to his table.

"Thanks," Sharon said.

"No problem." He reached across the table and used
his napkin to wipe away a smudge of glowing buffalo
drool from her chin. "I know how much you love this
place."

They shared a smile.

Their meal was on the house.

CHAPTER FIVE

Diana sold coats. Or, to be more honest, she stood around in the coat section of a department store and waited for people to come around and pick out coats. Buying coats was one of those shopping experiences in which a clerk served about the same purpose as a mannequin. Only instead of wearing the coat, she told people how good they looked in their potential new wardrobe additions.

She didn't lie. If someone looked genuinely bad in a coat, she usually told them this (in a gentle, soft-sell fashion). But it was hard to look bad in a coat, and it really wasn't hard to pick out one that you liked that looked fine on your body type. Although there was one dreadful red-and-orange eyesore that had been in the coat department since long before her and would probably still be there, waiting, long after she was gone.

As jobs went, it wasn't horrible. She'd had worse. She'd had better. She wasn't planning on making a career out of it, but it paid the bills for the time being. The only bad thing about it was that it could be dull and, when she was in the wrong frame of mind, a single shift could last thirty or forty hours.

Today felt like it would be one of those days.

After being trapped for four days and change in her apartment, she wasn't ready to be trapped in a bigger room. She also didn't feel like calling in sick because that would inevitably lead to questions. Where had she been? Why hadn't she called in? And so on.

It would almost be easier to go in to work and pretend she hadn't even missed. Except that even if she was willing to pretend, no one else would be. The same questions would still be waiting. *Why is there a hairy green monster following you?*

Oh, just something I picked up at the nexus of realities, she would reply. *Can I help you with a coat?*

She supposed she could have just skipped today and not called, but that wasn't the way she was hardwired. It was against her character to miss work four days in a row without letting someone know.

A glance at the clock confirmed she had two minutes before having to get up and get ready. She lay in bed and wished there were a way to miss and not call in and avoid the various hassles awaiting her on each and every path before her.

The phone rang in the other room. She was slow to answer it because she had to move the dresser blocking her door. The door didn't have a lock, and she didn't trust Vom to stay in control of his appetites while she slept. By the time she moved the dresser out of the way he had already answered the phone.

"Hello. Yes, yes. Oh really?" He listened, making generic *I'm listening* sounds to confirm this to both her and the person on the other end of the phone. "Okay. I'll tell her. No problem."

He hung up.

"There was a fire at the store," he said.

"Oh my . . . was anyone hurt?"

Vom shrugged. "Didn't say. Just said you don't have to bother coming in today."

She leaned against the wall and absorbed the news. On the bright side, her work problem was solved.

"Wait. I just moved in, and I haven't talked to anyone yet. How did they get this number? Even I don't know it yet."

Vom shrugged again, but she could tell he was holding out on her. Even though he didn't have any eyes, his mouths pursed suspiciously. She could feel he was lying to her. Probably part of that psychic bond they shared.

He withered beneath her glare.

"You'd probably call it magic. Or sorcery. Or wizardry. Or *majik* with a *j* and a *k*. Though I've always found that pretentious and unnecessary."

"Okay, so now you're telling me I have magical powers."

"It's just a side effect of straddling multiple floors of reality. Any intelligent being can do it, provided they have the will and desire. Also, you need a conduit to gather the appropriate metaphysical charge and—"

"Stop."

"What? Too technical again?"

"I'm sure you have a great metaphorical explanation you could give me, but it'll just be more mumbo jumbo that I really don't understand."

"You wished not to go to work. Magic took care of that for you."

"I didn't wish for a fire."

"You didn't *not* wish for a fire."

"What the hell does that mean?"

"Unguided reality manipulation will always take the path of least resistance. Since you didn't specify the details, you can hardly be upset by the results."

She hastily threw on some clothes, not bothering to shower.

"Where are you going?" asked Vom.

"To the store," she said.

"I thought you didn't want to go to the store."

"I didn't, but if I started a magic fire that killed somebody, I need to know."

"Why?"

"Why what?"

"Why do you need to know?" asked Vom.

"Because it's important."

"It's important to know if you killed someone?"

"Yes."

"And why is that?"

"Because I couldn't live with myself if I did."

Vom nodded. "Then why would you want to know?"

Diana said, "You don't understand."

"Oh, I understand. You may have killed someone by accident and now you think it'll make things better to torture yourself about it. Just because I don't agree with it doesn't mean I can't understand it."

"We can't all be amoral monsters with a complete indifference to human life."

"I'm not indifferent to human life as a whole," he said. "Just individual ones."

"My mistake. I'm going. You stay here."

Vom snarled. "I'm a cosmic entity. Not a puppy."

"Just do me a favor," she said. "Try not to chew on the furniture."

He grinned. "I promise nothing."

Diana rushed to the store, stopping only for a coffee and a bagel. When she was almost there she realized that seeing the fire wouldn't answer any questions. By then she was less concerned with the possible body count and just determined to see what the results of her careless wish might be. She envisioned the entire department store burned to the ground. Then, worrying that perhaps imagining something like that would make it happen, she did her best to wipe the image from her mind. But it was like asking herself not to think about a pink dinosaur. Once the idea was introduced it couldn't be removed.

She should've taken the time to listen to Vom's explanation. If she did have magical powers now, it was probably smart to understand them.

The department store had not been destroyed. CLOSED FOR REPAIRS read a sign on the door. She peered through the windows and, while the coat section wasn't visible from outside, she could see that most of the visible smoke damage was in that general area. The store was still standing, and it didn't look as if the fire department had had to soak the place down to stop the fire from spreading.

"Pretty bad, huh?" asked Wendall from behind her.

She turned toward him. He worked in housewares. Wendall was short, a little chubby, with curly hair and a perpetual smile. Always cheerful. Sometimes too much so. They hadn't talked much, but she liked him in a pleasant, casual-acquaintance way.

"Had to come and see for yourself, huh?" He joined her at the window. "Me too."

"Do they know how it happened?" she asked.

"They think it was an electrical short. You know how old the wiring is in this place. Thank God, nobody was hurt."

She breathed an inner sigh of relief.

"They say it'll probably take a week or two to fix the damage," he said. "Say, you want to go get a cup of coffee or something?"

"Actually, I just had some coffee," she replied.

"There's a great little bagel place just around the corner," he said.

"Uh, I just…"

"My treat."

Wendall grinned at her. He had a crush on her. Possibly. It wasn't easy to tell because he was always so friendly, but he was that special brand of nice guy who was so used to being overlooked that any woman who acknowledged his existence became attractive by default. Or maybe she was just flattering herself. Maybe he was just being friendly again.

"Yeah, sure."

She figured it couldn't hurt to spend some time with a regular, non-world-devouring person, and Wendall was as ordinary as reality could get.

The "great little bagel place just around the corner" was actually the "adequate little bagel place just around the corner where she ate lunch two or three times a week," but she found the familiarity comforting. Something like a half-cat, half-rabbit hopped around, unobserved by everyone else, under one of the tables, but she resolutely ignored it.

Wendall carried the bulk of most conversations. He wasn't a blabbermouth, but if you weren't feeling up to talking he didn't mind filling the silence himself. He talked about nothing important. She didn't hold it against him since most talk was about nothing important. She didn't have anything worthwhile to discuss either, aside from her recent induction into the world of the supernatural, and this was the last thing she wanted to talk about. But there were only so many variations of "Crazy weather we've been having lately," so much shop talk, before she found herself zoning out.

"Anyway," said Wendall, "how about it?"

"Hmmm."

"About the movie?" he asked.

It took her a moment to realize that he'd asked her out at some point in the conversation. She was having trouble focusing. The air crackled with a weird electricity.

She forced herself to look into his eyes. Bright, eager eyes above a hopeful smile.

"Uh, Wendall," she started, "I'm kind of in a bad place."

All the hope vanished from his face, though he was quick to recover.

"I'm not trying to blow you off," she said. "I'm not. It's . . . just . . . I'm going through something kind of . . . complicated right now."

She wanted to explain it to him, but it was too unbelievable.

A round purple monster waddled into view in the window. It stopped, pressed its face against the glass, and with its three eyes scanned the interior of the bagel place. In a world full of monsters, there was something different about this one. This one put her on edge. More on edge, anyway. And when its gaze settled on her, she was not surprised.

The creature jumped through the window, sending glass shattering in all directions. The other customers screamed. Some froze. Others jumped up in panic. But the monster lumbered with single-minded determination toward Diana. Lunging, the giant hedgehog-like beast prepared to pounce.

Suddenly Vom was there. He hoisted the purple creature into the air and threw it across the room.

"Are you okay?" asked Vom.

"I thought you said you weren't a puppy."

"Aren't you glad I lied?"

Roaring, the hedgehog threw itself into Vom.

Diana, along with half the customers, found herself trapped by the grappling horrors cutting off the exit. She didn't know what anyone else observed, but she saw a giant hedgehog with a thick, rubbery skin wrestling a fuzzy green puppet. The scene put Diana in mind of a *Scooby-Doo* episode. Except the villains were exactly what they appeared to be, and people were going to get hurt.

Vom took a bite out of his opponent, inflicting a gushing wound. A purple splotch jumped off the hedgehog's back and enlarged into a duplicate of the original. The new creature turned and charged at Diana.

Yelping, she threw her hands up to defend herself. A chill ran down her arms, and invisible forces catapulted the monster through the ceiling. She felt a little woozy after the effort. She definitely needed to get the hang of these new superpowers.

The hedgehog spawned two more duplicates. All three piled on Vom.

Wendall took her by the hand and pulled her out the door. Outside the restaurant she stopped him from dragging her any farther. The roars and shrieks coming from within were terrifying and bizarre. The struggle shook the street and cracked the building.

"We have to get out of here," said Wendall.

It was the smart thing to do, but it felt wrong. She'd left Vom to be mauled to death. Although she wasn't certain that he could die. He was ancient, and it was hard to imagine that a savage beating could destroy him. But the hedgehog was also some kind of monster, so maybe that was an exception.

She couldn't do anything about it. Her own magic powers were so new and unfamiliar that she didn't have the faintest idea how to help Vom, even if she had been sure it was the right thing to do.

A terrific howl rocked the earth. She was knocked off her feet. Dust obscured her vision as Wendall's shadowy figure offered her a hand. She took it, and a sharp pain ran down her spine.

It wasn't Wendall. It was the hedgehog. She pulled away, but his grip was unbreakable. He seized her by the throat.

Wendall came out of the dust and threw a sloppy punch that connected with the monster's shoulder. The

monster didn't move, but it was a noble effort. She'd
written off Wendall too soon. At least he'd tried when he
could've run away. Too bad she was going to die anyway.

Or not. She wasn't able to breathe but didn't seem to
need to. The monster wasn't hurting her. It didn't really
seem to want to, either. It threw her down to the ground,
and a quizzical expression crossed its face. It was confused, frightened.

Thunder cracked from the restaurant as a hedgehog
duplicate smashed through its façade, bounced off the
street, and nearly struck Diana and her attacker. Another
boom followed as a second hedgehog hurtled outward,
digging a trench in the pavement and coming to a stop a
few feet to their left.

Vom exited the building through its shattered front
door. He made a show of wiping his hands with big grins.

"Are you okay?"

"Yes. I think so." She rubbed her throat. The skin was
a little raw, but it wasn't a serious injury.

The hedgehog tilted its head at a curious angle and
stepped toward her.

"It's okay," she said in a soothing voice. "Everything
will be fine now."

The beast's face contorted into a snarl, and it lunged
at her. Instincts kicked in. Since flight had failed her, she
resorted to fight. Diana unleashed a haymaker under the
monster's chin. Its head exploded in a burst of green and
black. The body took several steps backward before collapsing.

"Holy crap," she said. "I didn't mean to…it was an
accident. I wasn't trying to—"

"He's not dead," said Vom.

Vom picked up the mushy purple body and started to eat it. It was a gruesome show as one unspeakable thing devoured another in the space of a half a minute.

He belched.

"Excuse me."

The pedestrians stood in shock at what they'd just witnessed. They weren't ready for a world gone mad filled with horrible monsters and exploding heads.

Several hedgehog beasts waddled beside Vom.

"You didn't have to hit me so hard," said one.

"Sorry about that," replied Diana. Only a moment later she was unsure of why she was apologizing.

"Diana, you know these things?" asked Wendall.

"I can explain," Diana lied. "It's not as crazy as it looks."

No, it was crazier. She couldn't explain because she didn't understand much of it herself.

He scrambled away as if she were every bit the horrible beasts beside her.

A whistling sound drew her attention skyward. The hedgehog she'd launched into the atmosphere plummeted downward. Before she could shout a warning it returned to Earth, landing right on Wendall, squashing him into a gooey mess. Or so she assumed. She turned away to avoid seeing all the gory details.

But she couldn't turn away from the carnage and destruction surrounding her. It was only in comic books that a whole city block could be destroyed without casualties. The ten-story building that housed the bagel shop looked as if it might collapse at any moment.

She was going to be sick.

"What's with her?" asked a hedgehog beast.

"She's new to this," replied Vom.

Vom and the hedgehogs faded away. Diana was still adjusting to this strange perspective on reality, so she wasn't able to see what happened. She sensed the ripples as the cosmos readjusted itself, but was aware of it only after it was over. She sat in the restored bagel shop. Everything was back to normal, returned to the state just before the monster attack.

"Wendall," she said. "You're alive."

He hesitated. She wondered if he remembered any of it. If anyone here did. There was an awkward quiet in the shop, and indeed the entire block, as the remnants of unacceptable memories faded.

Maybe it was all her imagination. Maybe Vom and the hedgehog were all just figments of her own deranged mind. It seemed more sensible to believe she was insane than that she was living in a universe filled with monsters that no one else saw.

Diana considered Wendall sitting before her. She never would've thought it, but he'd proven himself to be a good guy. And even if it was only in her imagination, she still thought he deserved a chance to prove it.

"Wendall, I'd love to go to the movies with you," she said.

"Yeah... about that," he stammered. "I'm pretty busy the next few weeks, but I'll check my schedule and get back to you."

She reached for his hand, but he recoiled.

"I have to get going," he said, "but I'll see you later, I'm sure."

He ran out the door without a backward glance. He was in such a hurry he steamrolled over an old lady.

He remembered, and he wasn't the only one. Nobody was looking at her. More than that. They were deliberately *not* looking at her. She had become something else to be ignored. Like the crumbs of rubble littering the floor or the spiderweb of cracks running through the shop window or the miniature hedgehog clone skittering across the floor. Bits and pieces of a not-quite-undone reality.

Diana's head hurt. The world was both too bright and not bright enough. Everything smelled funny. Her bagel tasted weird. The air blown by the ceiling fan scraped against her skin. She was aware of everything now, and everything seemed alien and unpleasant.

She threw away her bagel, dumped out her coffee, and walked out of the shop into a strange universe she could no longer call home.

CHAPTER SIX

The farther Diana walked, the more alien the universe around her became. She noticed more and more oddities. Like a ten-story building that floated a few feet above the ground. Or a dog with a human face being walked by a human with a dog face. Or the swelling and contraction of the pavement under her feet in a nearly imperceptible way, as if it were built on the back of a giant, slumbering monster.

That was what was so maddening. She couldn't rule out any possibilities now. She'd never been a contemplative soul. Like most people, she had usually been too busy living her day-to-day life to dwell on deeper mysteries that she was certain she'd never understand anyway. She had just taken most things on faith and trusted that someone would figure it out.

Now she'd discovered the human race was little more than a mass of microbes squirming on a thin slice of reality they foolishly labeled "the universe." The revelation that there was nothing special about humanity didn't shock her. Not specifically. She'd always been cynical about that sort of thing. The idea that reality was all too big to even quantify in any meaningful way didn't disturb her much either. Except, deep down, she'd assumed there was some inherent logic at work. Like ricocheting molecules congealing into planets and stars, dogs and cats. At least that made sense, even if it wasn't very comforting. At least it put things in neat little boxes with neat little labels that she didn't always understand but could rely on in terms of familiarity.

Too bad it had all turned out to be bullshit.

Instead she found herself in a world where everything was possible, without a mental filing cabinet into which she could collate her perceptions. Everything was one giant heap, too big to be swept under the rug, too noisy to shut the door on.

Too much imagination had never been a concern for Diana, but with her new perceptions a switch had been flipped. She envisioned the universe as being run by tremendous, godlike butterflies looking down on their creation and debating whether it was shiny enough to keep or whether they should just throw it away and start again. She pictured everything as a dream. Her dream. A never-ending fantasy that would start all over once she died. Over and over again. Or maybe it was the opposite. Maybe she was just a phantom in someone else's fantasy world. Hell, she might have been a robot for all she knew.

Every possibility, no matter how disturbing, inconceivable, or downright stupid seemed feasible now. She cursed every single *Twilight Zone* episode she'd seen for planting the seeds of schizophrenia in her brain. Although it wasn't technically mental illness if you were more aware, your sense of reality more expanded. Or maybe it was. Maybe all this was just her addled mind snapping, and she was just alert enough to realize it. She wondered whether you could be crazy and know it at the same time. Then she got pissed when she realized any answer she reached would be suspect by its very nature.

Diana mumbled to herself, targeting the first object for her annoyance that came to mind. "Screw you, Rod Serling."

She paused, stopping before her apartment building. She hadn't meant to come back here. She'd merely been walking without paying attention.

But here she was.

There was something comforting about the place. Something terrifying. Most terrifying was how comforting she found it. Like she belonged here now.

She entered the building, and everything suddenly felt better. The world outside was a strange, monstrous realm. The world inside was just as strange. So why did she find it less bizarre, less jarring?

The door to West's apartment opened, and he stuck his head out. "Hey, Number Five. Can you bring me that package on the stoop?"

Having just passed the stoop, she hadn't noticed a package. A glance over her shoulder showed a box wrapped in brown paper sitting behind her. She couldn't have entered without tripping over it.

"Hurry it up, Number Five," said West.

When Diana turned to pick up the package, it had disappeared. She walked back to the open apartment door and said, "It's gone."

"Better not be," replied West with a snort.

From her vantage point the package was back in its place. She walked toward it, each step taken with care and deliberation. With each step the package became lighter and lighter until it was transparent—then, just when she was within reach, it faded away. She walked back down the hallway, and when she reached West's door the package was back.

He swaggered over to her. "Well, where is it?"

"It keeps disappearing."

"Are you thinking about something else when you reach for it?"

"Something else?"

West's heavy eyebrows furrowed. "You can't think about picking up the package while you're picking up the package. It'll hear you coming that way."

She nodded, more to herself than to him. "Maybe it'd be easier if you just got it yourself."

He frowned. "That's no good. It knows me too well. Can smell me from a mile away."

So could she, but she refrained from suggesting a bath might be in order.

"If you don't get that package, every living thing in Barcelona is going to die," said West.

She believed him. Not just because she was in a state of mind to believe anything and everything, but because he said it so matter-of-factly, as if commenting on an annoying weather prediction. Oh, darn, the picnic is going to be ruined. Fiddle-dee-dee.

He vanished into his darkened apartment.

Diana decided that if she could save everyone in Barcelona, then at least she could say she'd done something worthwhile with her life. She moved toward the package.

It vanished.

Damn. It was onto her.

West's voice came from the darkness. "Three minutes."

"I'm working on it," she called back.

"Well, it's no problem. Not like anyone of any great importance is in Barcelona or anything. Not like the entire future of the human race hinges on the fate of one Spanish city."

She couldn't tell if he was joking or not. West's delivery was flat, and her gauge of reality was hardly reliable.

She stuck her hands in her pockets, whistled a jaunty tune, and sauntered toward the package. She attempted to occupy her mind with thoughts of turtles and jelly doughnuts. Why turtles and jelly doughnuts? She didn't have a clue. Just the first two things that popped into her head. Out of all the things in her expanding universe, she questioned what these two objects said about her. It wasn't that they were bad. It was just that they seemed an odd pairing, two things that didn't go together. And she wondered what it said about her perceptions and logic that these were the two things that sprang to her mind as if they were the most natural combination in the world.

"Aha!"

Diana pounced on the package. It vibrated in her hands as if trying to vanish, but she held tight. Her distracting thoughts had worked. Almost too well, as she must've wasted a good minute or two standing beside the package before grabbing it, but she had it now.

"Nineteen seconds," called West.

She ran in and handed him the paper-wrapped box. He took it and set it on a shelf beside several other identical boxes.

"Hummph," said West. "Didn't think you'd make it."

She said, "So what about Barcelona?"

"What about it?"

"Is it going to be okay?"

"Should hold for another day or two," replied West.

He shuffled over to an overstuffed couch and collapsed into it. "Something I can do for you, Number Five?"

She realized she was standing in West's apartment, a shadowy realm in perpetual twilight. The décor, what she could see of it, was straight out of the seventies. The brightest thing in the room was an unusually large lava lamp that cast a greenish glow. The wax inside swirled in strange patterns. If she squinted just right, she thought she saw an eye floating somewhere within, and it glared at her.

A black-light octopus poster squirmed on the wall. It twisted and distorted like one of those bad motion-imitation pictures won as Cracker Jack prizes. And West's couch swayed as if on board a boat, even though all the other furniture stayed put.

Yet the weirdness of this apartment was somehow less foreign and unsettling than the real world (whatever that meant) outside this building's front door.

"What's in the package?" she asked.

"There's nothing in the package, Number Five."

West jumped to his feet and marched forward.

"There's nothing in any of the packages if they know what's good for them."

Most of the boxes hopped deeper into the shelf recesses. One leaned forward, challenging West.

"Oh, someone's got an attitude, does he?" West's voice rose. Not much. But enough to be noticed, which in itself was surprising enough to unsettle Diana. "Someone thinks he's too good for the shelf, does he?"

The package growled.

"You'll stay formless, and you'll like it," said West. "Just remember that once you take on flesh, it means you'll have an ass for me to kick."

West stared down the package.

"Well, I can see you're busy," said Diana. "I'll just leave you to...uh...taunt the boxes."

She was a few steps out of the apartment and down the hall when West spoke up.

"It will get easier," said West.

His face, covered by hair, was as unreadable as his voice, but she thought she saw his thick mustache twitch with the traces of a smile.

"The period of adjustment varies from individual to individual," he said, "but it always gets better. One way or another."

"One way or another?"

"Oh, you know. Crossword puzzles. Pornography. Video games. Knitting. Madness. Death. We all find a way of coping, Number Five."

His dark eyes focused on a point on a distant horizon. He chuckled through a tight, closed mouth. Then an awkward silence, at least as far as Diana was concerned, passed between them. She suspected West didn't even notice.

"Uh... thanks," she said.

Something crashed inside his apartment. Grumbling, he went back to deal with the problem. She hoped Barcelona or Paris or whatever else would be okay, but it wasn't her problem anymore. Her problem was waiting in her apartment.

And he was not alone.

Vom the Hungering sat on the sofa. The green-furred monster had something stuck in his mouth. His cheek bulged. She wondered if it was a whole pig or a small child and decided she'd rather not know.

The giant rubber hedgehog hunched beside the coffee table.

"I know I saw it go under here," he said.

"I think it ran into the kitchen," said Vom. "Oh, hey, Diana." He grinned. Glimpses of red velvet showed between his sharp teeth. He spit out the sofa pillow he'd been sucking on like an industrial-sized Life Saver.

"Sorry. Helps to keep my mind off my eating disorder."

He returned the saliva-coated pillow to its spot on the couch.

"One day at a time and all that," said Vom.

She was annoyed, but only for a moment. Having Vom devour pillows was preferable to anything else that came to mind. She could've lived without his slimy drool soaking into the upholstery, but it wasn't her couch.

The hedgehog stood. He held a miniature version of himself in one hand.

"Oh, hello," said the monster to Diana.

"Diana, this is Unending Smorgaz," said Vom.

"Hi," she said.

"Do you want to take care of this for me, Vom?" Smorgaz threw his miniature to Vom, who snapped it down in a single bite. "Thanks."

"No problem."

Diana wanted to sit down but didn't want to sit next to Vom and his indiscriminate jaws. The air shimmered, and a recliner materialized beside her. She wasn't sure if she had caused it or if the apartment itself had created the chair, but it seemed a moot point. She plopped into the recliner.

"Smorgaz, could you excuse us a moment?" she asked. "I need to talk to Vom."

"Say no more. Think I'll go for a walk. Anyone want anything while I'm out?"

"Could you bring back a few dozen pizzas?" asked Vom.

Diana could've probably wished for pizzas, but eating magical pizzas conjured up from the nethersphere didn't sound very appetizing.

"Sure thing. Do you want the pizza delivery guy too?"

Vom's stomach growled. Literally, the mouth on his gut grumbled, licking its lips.

"No pizza delivery guys," said Diana. "Or gals. Or puppies or kittens or anything like that."

Vom frowned. "Can we at least get sausage on the pizzas?"

"Yes."

"Okay, a dozen sausage pizzas coming up." Smorgaz trundled out the door, but she stopped him.

"Do you have any money?"

"No."

"How do you intend to pay?"

"Pay?" Smorgaz tilted his head at an angle and a most curious expression crossed his face. "I'm sorry, but I don't understand the question."

"You have to pay for them somehow."

"I do?"

Unending Smorgaz glanced at Vom, who shrugged.

"She's unconventional."

Diana contemplated how Smorgaz planned on securing those pizzas, but, of course, he was a monster. Monsters didn't carry cash. They just took what they wanted without thought for the consequences. That wouldn't do. She couldn't unleash a beast into the streets to terrorize every pizza delivery vehicle he stumbled across.

She pulled some cash out of her wallet and handed it to Smorgaz. "Just seven blocks south, on the Corner of O'Brian and Swaim, there's a little shop that sells two medium cheese pizzas for a good price."

"Only two?" whined Vom. "And what about the sausage?"

"Fine." She gave Smorgaz another few dollars and some change to cover tax.

"What about garlic bread?"

She opened her wallet to let Vom see how empty it was. He slouched and stuffed the pillow back into his mouth with a pout.

Smorgaz left.

While she organized her thoughts, Vom noisily chewed like a petulant three-year-old.

"Pork is meat," he grumbled.

"Yes, it is."

"Puppies are meat," he said.

"You're not eating puppies. Not while I'm around."

"Have you ever eaten a puppy? They're delicious."

"Correct me if I'm wrong, but isn't everything delicious to you?"

"I don't care for broccoli," he replied.

She stared at him skeptically.

"Just because I'll eat it doesn't mean I like it." He leaned forward. "Anyway, when you get right down to it, everything in this universe is just a handful of atoms arranged in peculiar ways. Puppies aren't different than pigs, carbon and nitrogen. It seems unfair to just eat one because of your own arbitrary cultural standards of acceptability."

"Arbitrary, yes," she agreed. "But it doesn't change anything."

"What about dogs? Full-grown ones, I mean?"

"No dogs."

He opened his mouth, but she cut him off.

"Just assume that if I haven't okayed it, it's off-limits."

Annoyed, he swallowed the pillow.

"It's clear we need to lay some ground rules," she said. "If we're going to be stuck with each other, we have to figure a way to make this work."

"Agreed." Vom snorted. "I just don't see why I have to make all the sacrifices."

"My sense of reality has crumbled. I'm bound to a monster that wants to devour everything all the time, including me. And I'm pretty sure I'm going to lose my sanity eventually. So if I'm going to have to deal with all that, the least you can do is not eat puppies."

Vom shrugged. "Fair enough."

"What I need from you now is some explanations about how all this…weirdness functions. If this is the world I have to live in, I'm damn well going to understand it. For starters, I need to know why the hell that monster tried to kill me this morning and now he's hanging around, fetching us pizza."

"Do you want the complicated answer? Or the simple one?"

A three-inch Smorgaz climbed up the wall beside Vom. He nabbed it and stuffed it in one set of jaws while talking with another.

"The short answer is because of your connection with me, you aren't quite in tune with your native reality anymore. It's not a big deal, doesn't really have a big effect on the universe. But it makes you a beacon, a shining light that draws the attention of certain misplaced inter-dimensional entities, such as myself and Smorgaz, seeking to reorient themselves in a confusing, unfamiliar world."

"He was confused and frightened and that made him want to kill me."

"He wasn't trying to kill you. He was just attracted to the nearest thing that reminded him of home. It's like he's a lost rat that stumbled into someplace he doesn't belong and he scrambled toward the nearest…rat hole he came across."

She snarled.

"Maybe that came out wrong," he said. "These rules aren't universal. Plenty of alien things slip into your reality and either perish quickly or adjust without need of an anchoring force. But some are like me or Smorgaz, we don't die, but we also function at such different levels that without something to ground us, we'd eventually probably do some very bad stuff. Mind you, most of that stuff would be the unintentional damage of a bewildered animal thrashing around in an ill-fitting cage."

"So you must have known something like this was going to happen," she said. "Otherwise, why would you have followed me?"

"I expected it sooner or later, but I had figured later rather than sooner. Just the same, I tagged along because... well, it's not like I had anything better to do. And I like you. I like being around you. Being near you keeps me focused, relaxed, like a soothing melody." Vom snapped his fingers. "Hey, that sounds a lot better than the rat-hole metaphor I tried earlier, doesn't it?"

"Just a bit. Let me guess... now that I'm Smorgaz's reassuring tune I'm stuck with him just like I'm stuck with you."

"I'd avoid using the word *stuck* when Smorgaz is around. He's a little sensitive. And when he gets this insecure he starts spawning like mad. We'll be up to our eyeballs in clones before you know it."

"You don't have eyeballs."

"Figure of speech."

"That's his thing then?" she asked. "Spawning?"

"Yep. That's his *thing*. Nobody does it better."

The sound of tearing carpet drew her attention to another pint-sized Smorgaz.

"Yeah, you should probably get used to that," said Vom. "Even when he's trying to keep it under control, he usually spits out at least one Smorgaz Jr. every ten minutes. The unintentional ones tend to dissolve after about an hour, but they can be a handful."

The small creature raised its head and smiled at Diana as it shredded some carpet with its claws. Vom leaned forward as if to spring off the couch and pounce on the creature.

"Oh, I forgot the new policy. Is it okay for me to eat Smorgaz's half-formed spawns? Or are they on the puppy list?"

She mulled it over.

"Oh, come on," said Vom. "You can't seriously have a problem with that? They're destructive little bastards who were never meant to exist in this slice of reality and have a shelf life of an hour."

His argument was hard to counter aside from some squeamishness on her part. But of all the things he could request to eat, this seemed most reasonable.

"Okay, okay."

The small Smorgaz yipped and dashed behind the entertainment center.

"Just as well," said Vom. "They have a weird aftertaste."

There was a knock on the door.

Vom perked up. "Is that Smorgaz? Are those the pizzas?"

"Down, boy."

"I call dibs on the four biggest slices."

She suspected it wasn't Smorgaz. He wasn't a fast creature, and even if he had returned with the pizzas she wouldn't expect him to knock. He lived here. She didn't know what to expect, but it wouldn't have been surprising to discover yet another weird monster entering her life. Instead it was a tall, good-looking stranger.

It was weirder than a monster.

"Hi, I'm Chuck. Chuck from Apartment Number Two. Down the hall." He glanced to his left, then his right, then down, then up. Then, just to be perfectly sure, he looked behind himself and double-checked his right flank again. "Could I borrow a cup of sugar?"

"Number Two?" she said. "Oh, that's the apartment with the...dog in front of it, right?"

He nodded, put his finger to his lips. "Keep your voice down. It'll hear you."

She peeked out into the hallway. The scaly creature was curled up outside Apartment Two's door, and it appeared to be sleeping. But it didn't have eyelids, so its bulbous dark eyes were always wide open.

"Do you want to come in?" she asked.

"I don't think that's a good idea. I just need some sugar. I'm baking a cake, and I'm a little low."

"Cake?" said Vom. "What kind of cake?"

"Does it really matter?" asked Diana.

Vom scowled. "We get it. I'm a voracious omnivore. You don't have to keep pointing it out."

"Sorry. Didn't realize you were sensitive about it."

"Sugar?" repeated Chuck.

"One second. Let me go check." She jogged into the kitchen, opened all the cupboards and drawers, but came up empty. Reality-warping magical powers at her disposal, and she couldn't find a single sugar packet.

Vom poked his head in the kitchen. "Check your pockets."

She found handfuls of sugar in her pants. She emptied a small pile onto the counter.

"Did I do that or did you?" she asked.

"Does it matter?"

"Don't suppose you have a cup on you?"

Vom opened the freezer and pulled out an irregularly shaped mug.

"Thanks," she said.

"Don't mention it, but if lover boy happens to have an extra slice of cake lying around—"

"You got it."

Diana scooped the sugar into the mug and returned to Chuck.

"Here. Hope this is enough."

He took the cup. He glanced at the beast guarding his door, then silently mouthed a thank-you.

You're welcome, she mouthed back.

She smiled, and he returned it with a warm, if slightly nervous, grin. He tiptoed down the hall and disappeared back into his apartment. When the door clicked shut, the dog hopped up and unleashed a long, high-pitched shriek. It sniffed along the edge of the door before snorting, retching up a glob of snot that it immediately gobbled down.

Unending Smorgaz trundled up the stairs, past the dog, and pushed his way past Diana.

"One side," he said. "Hot pie, coming through."

"Finally!"

Vom seized one of the boxes and jammed it halfway into his mouth, but he paused under Diana's and Smorgaz's watchful stares. Vom removed the pizza, set it on the coffee table, and slouched in a sulk.

"Oh, okay," said Diana. "You can have one pizza all to yourself, but you might want to savor—"

Gleefully he snatched up the coffee table and swallowed the pizza box and a third of the table in one huge bite.

"This is a great pie. Love the touch of sawdust." His attention turned to the second pizza.

"Are you going to eat all that?"

CHAPTER SEVEN

"It'll only be a few hours," said Sharon. "Are you sure you don't want to come?"

Calvin didn't look up from his book. "Think I'll skip this one, if it's just the same to you."

"Everyone will be disappointed."

He dog-eared the page and set the book aside to help her put on her coat.

"I wish you wouldn't do that." She winced.

"I am the lord of beautiful anarchy, aren't I? So I don't use bookmarks, and I don't attend every annoying pep rally Greg feels like throwing just because he's bored."

"Now you're just being snarky."

He helped her on with her coat.

"You know how he adores you," she said. "How they all adore you."

"Have you ever been adored by four dozen people at once? Trust me. It's not as cool as it sounds. Anyway, if I showed up to all of these events, it'd stop being special."

"I guess you're right." She leaned in, gave him a polite hug. "Try to stay out of trouble now."

"I think I can manage on my own for an evening. Just going to hang out with the guys."

She paused. "So soon? Do you really think that's a good idea?"

"I'm not allowed to have friends now?"

"You have friends."

"Greg and his loonies are not my friends. At best, they're coworkers. Although really I do all the work."

"Yes, you do. It's just...you know how crazy things can get when you get together with the old gang. Just promise me you'll take it easy."

"You worry too much. Not like it's the end of the world."

She patted him on the chest. "Make sure that it isn't. Not yet anyway."

An elderly woman with wild gray hair, the nub of a green crayon clutched in withered, clawlike fingers, scrawled an endless string of numbers on the hallway just outside Benny's door.

She glanced up from her work and smiled. Her eyes glinted with madness.

"Hello," she croaked.

Calvin nodded at her. Benny's mere presence had this effect on people. He improved the efficiency of their squishy biological brains until they functioned like obsessive-compulsive supercomputers. This poor woman was working on an equation that disproved the universe. She had at least forty more years of scrawling to do, though.

He knocked on the apartment door, and a fat worm with translucent skin showing pulsing, multicolored veins answered. Limbs ringed his body in peculiar asymmetry. Most ended in hands, though two were just stumps and one served as his nose. He wore a baseball cap secured to his "head" with masking tape. The rules for greater eldritch horrors varied. Calvin had no trouble passing for human, but it had less to do with his appearance than with his separation from his more otherworldly self.

The worm, on the other hand, required a disguise to avoid driving mortals mad. It didn't take much: a T-shirt, a hat, sunglasses. Just something for the human mind to grab on to. Calvin wondered if the disguise itself created an illusion or if humans found the idea of a Benny, a giant, glistening maggot in a Raiders cap, so absurd that their peculiar brains decided to just accept it and move on. The end result was the same.

Benny said, "Cal, what kept ya?"

Calvin held up a grocery bag. "I stopped off for snacks."

He stepped inside, but before Benny closed the door Calvin told the woman, "You dropped a decimal point around the corner."

Frowning, she shuffled off to correct the mistake.

Calvin handed the snacks to Benny. "You should probably move before you cause irreversible damage to that poor woman."

"I'd like to, but where am I going to find another place this good? Plus, it's got rent control."

Benny slipped into the kitchen to put the beers in the fridge. Calvin had a seat next to Swoozie, who was playing video games.

Even among eldritch horrors, Swoozie was one of the most incomprehensible. Her body was little more than a random collection of colors and alien geometries. She'd molded a pair of mismatched hands to hold the game controller, but the twisted fingers had a hard time reaching all the buttons.

"Shit," she said as she guided her pixilated hero off a cliff.

Swoozie was lousy at video games. Hardly surprising since she was barely connected to this universe to begin with. She was like a puppeteer trying to control a marionette via a very, very long string and a telescope. And right now she was like a woman trying to use that marionette to control a second puppet composed of a few electrons dancing across a television screen. Sometimes Calvin envied Swoozie, who was almost free of the trap they were stuck in. And sometimes Calvin figured it had to be worse for Swoozie than for any of them. Like having to walk around with a bucket on your head for eternity.

"Press the A button to jump," said Calvin.

Swoozie's digital protagonist jumped the chasm. She hooted, and the sound caused the wallpaper to peel.

"Hey, watch it," said Benny.

"Sorry."

A virtual gargoyle swooped down and decapitated Swoozie's hero. The corpse collapsed in a heap.

"What the hell?" growled Swoozie. "Get up, you stupid bastard."

"Humans can't live without their heads," explained Calvin. It was easy to forget that.

"That's crap. I don't see why I have to be saddled with such a silly weakness just because humans don't have the imagination to realize that their limitations are not required for a video game character."

"These games are marketed with a human audience in mind," said Benny.

"It's discrimination." Swoozie reached around space and grabbed one of the beers from the fridge without getting up from her seat. The hole in space she pulled the beverage from didn't disappear right away. It just hovered there.

"Hey, hey, hey," said Benny. "What the hell did I tell you about respecting the space-time continuum in my home?"

"Oh, just sweep it under a rug or something," replied Swoozie.

Calvin reached into the hole and grabbed a beer of his own. Benny glared.

"What?" Calvin smiled. "It's there. Why not use it?"

The teeth in Benny's circular mouth twirled counterclockwise. His version of a frown.

"So what are we doing tonight?" asked Swoozie.

"I don't know," said Benny. "We could get something to eat, maybe see a movie."

"Oh no." Calvin waved his arms emphatically. "Not after the last time."

Individually, Calvin's, Swoozie's, and Benny's presences were corrosive tumors on thin-skinned reality.

When they were together, the effect was only increased. That was why they got together only once every few weeks, only for a few hours, and rarely in the same location. Predictability could go right out the window. Or the door. Or maybe up the chimney. Or screaming into the night while riding a chicken and dragging the mangled corpse of causality behind. Because even metaphors were fair game for their influence.

The last time the three had gone to the movies, a giant lizard had stepped off the screen and roasted the audience to cinders with its radioactive breath. Within hours the city had been reduced to a smoldering ruin. Reality's way of fixing itself eventually erased most the damage, but that sort of thing could put an undue strain on the already fragile sanity of most human minds. A concession-stand girl was still in a mental ward, haunted by nightmares of rampaging mutant dinosaurs.

Calvin had sent her a few apology cards. Unsigned, no return address, with an inspirational quote and SORRY ABOUT THE DREAMS written in the corner. Eventually he realized this probably wasn't helping her, so he stopped.

"We'll go see something safe," suggested Benny. "Maybe a chick flick."

"I don't think so." Swoozie formed a face. The eyes were misaligned, different colors, and the ears rotated like pinwheels. But the mouth grimaced just fine. "If it doesn't have ninjas in it, I'm not interested."

"And I promised Sharon no more movies," added Calvin.

Benny clicked his teeth.

"What?" asked Calvin. "Do you have a problem with that?"

"Not at all," said Benny. "If you're happy being kept on a short leash, it's none of my business."

"So says the insurance adjustor."

"Hey, a worm's gotta eat."

"Do you?" asked Swoozie.

"Actually, I'm not sure about that," said Benny. "Never tested it."

"Face it, guys," said Calvin. "We're neutered. Let's not fool ourselves."

Swoozie drifted off the couch and over to the window. "We don't have to be. Why don't we go out and show this world how insignificant it is?"

"And where would that get us?" asked Calvin.

"It'll make us feel better."

"For about ten minutes. Then everything will restore itself, and we'll be reminded that this world isn't the only thing that's insignificant."

The three ancient entities said nothing for a while. For a timeless being from beyond eternity, Calvin suddenly felt very old.

They carried on with the evening, tried to have a good time and forget their problems, but the damage was done. They were all trapped in circumstances beyond their control. Calvin figured that must be how humans felt, or would feel if they weren't saddled with their limited perceptions. They were a remarkably dim-witted species, and he envied that.

They called it a night early. Benny offered a half-hearted excuse, saying he had to get up early. Swoozie mumbled something about having to eat a dying star.

She faded to a sparkling point of light. "See you in a few weeks then?"

"I'll have to check my calendar," replied Benny. "Think I might be cocooning."

"And there's this thing I have to do." Calvin tried to downplay it, but there was guilt in his voice.

Swoozie rematerialized. "A thing? What kind of thing?"

"Just...a thing."

Benny's veins darkened. "Spit it out, Cal. What are you keeping from us?"

"I might be getting out," said Calvin softly.

"No kidding? For real this time?"

"I don't know. Maybe. There's this stellar alignment thingamajig, and it might allow full reintegration. That's what Greg says anyway."

"I thought you said he was a dumbass," said Benny.

"He is." Calvin half-smiled. "But he usually knows what he's talking about when it comes to this sort of thing."

"So what do you think?" asked Swoozie. "Do you think he's right?"

"He could be. I have been feeling a little different lately."

"Different how?"

"I don't know. Just different."

Calvin gazed out the window, at the moon rising. Fenris pursued. Calvin felt the boiling ache in his gut. He couldn't quantify it with inadequate human words built upon inadequate human concepts.

"Hell, buddy," said Benny. "Why didn't you tell us?"

"I guess I just didn't want you guys feeling bad about it."

"Are you kidding us? You're in deeper than either of

us." Swoozie slapped Calvin on the back with a twisted tentacle. "If you get out, then there's hope for everybody."

"We have to celebrate," said Benny.

"We don't have to make a big deal about this," said Calvin.

He'd been close to integration before. But in the end it was just chaos and madness and the collapse of a civilization or two, a lot of sound and fury signifying nothing. The real reason he had been reluctant to bring it up had nothing to do with Swoozie's or Benny's possible jealousy. They understood how important it was to him more than anyone. He just didn't want to get his hopes up.

"It's probably not going to pan out," he mumbled. "It never does."

"Can you believe this guy?" asked Benny. "He's about to get what we all want and he's moping."

"Have you told your better half yet?" asked Swoozie.

"No, I'd rather not bother—"

Swoozie vanished so swiftly that she tore a hole in the space-time continuum. A hideous many-eyed thing tried to slip through the portal and into this reality. Benny unleashed a warning shriek that made his upstairs neighbors' ears bleed. It was the cosmic horror equivalent of "Watch out. You're about to step into an alien universe, and it'll be hell to scrape off your shoe."

With a thankful screech, the thing withdrew.

Swoozie returned through the same warp in reality she had left, plugging it. She formed a pair of disembodied shoulders and shrugged. "He didn't seem excited to hear the news."

"I could've told you that," said Calvin.

Fenris was blessed with a single-minded stupidity. The moon, his eternal prey, occupied what little sentience he had. And that sentience wasn't even developed enough to catch a celestial body following a fixed orbit.

"This is great news," said Benny. "We should celebrate."

"I thought we were going to call it a night."

"This could be our last chance to hang out. You can't leave your friends behind without one last night. For old times' sake. Back me up here, Swoozie."

"Ah, what the hell?" Swoozie said. "I can always find another star to eat."

Benny changed out of his baseball cap. He draped a sports jacket over his back, taping it on his absent shoulders.

They found a T.G.I. Friday's just around the corner, where they spent the rest of the evening reminiscing about the many millennia they'd shared in this common cage. Then Swoozie had one too many beers and belched forth a yellow fog, and everyone in the restaurant began to shriek and claw at their own faces. It put a damper on the mood.

As they left the establishment, reality fixed itself. Like it almost always did. That was the real annoyance that the three eldritch faced. They didn't belong here, and the universe reminded them of that every day.

"Look at the time," said Swoozie. "There's a binary system in collapse, and if I don't make it, it'll just go to waste."

"And I've got a big meeting," added Benny.

They exchanged one last round of handshakes.

"Hope I won't be seeing you around, guys," said

Calvin with a smile. "At least not on this particular realm of existence."

"I hear you," said Benny.

Swoozie vanished. Benny slithered away.

Calvin studied the moon and Fenris. The horrible thing in the sky above stared back at him. It was hard to measure, but it seemed just a little closer to its prey tonight.

Fenris howled a long, mournful cry that resonated through the universe. Lost souls, madmen, and marooned horrors felt the merest twinges of yearning in the heart of the beast.

Calvin pushed away the malaise, and with cautious optimism walked into the night.

CHAPTER EIGHT

A howl shook Diana out of the first deep sleep she'd had in a week. A great despair seized her. It was an alien thing, a tidal wave of grave emotion sweeping across her. Because she was so slight, it picked her up and flowed beneath her as if she were a leaf caught in the swirl of a gale-force wind. Shaken and twirled, but set down safely and spared the bulk of the force.

Her head cleared as she pushed away the alien fear and confusion. It was only then that she noticed she wasn't alone. Something else was in her bedroom.

Her first thought was that it was Vom, who had finally come to eat her. The thing was the same size, and had the same general proportions in the darkness. But then she noticed that it had eyes, something Vom lacked, and that those eyes were bright green orbs.

They were hypnotic, and though she wanted to look away, she couldn't escape them. Her body went rigid. She couldn't move. She couldn't think. She should've been frightened to death, but those eyes even robbed her of fear. They left only a hollow chill in her gut.

"Who are you?" someone asked.

It was her. She did have some control over her body. She recognized her voice, even if she couldn't feel her lips move. But if she focused she could sense the air slipping out of her lungs and out of her throat.

The eyes narrowed. The thing growled.

It moved toward her. In the unnatural dark around her bed, the thing's mottled orange hands, shaped like seven-pointed stars, grasped her blanket and pulled. She tried to hold on to it. The monster was cheating. You weren't supposed to be in danger if you could hide under the covers.

If she could just reach the lamp, if she could just turn it on. The light would drive away this thing. Even if the covers couldn't protect her, the light would. But even as she thought this, she noticed in her peripheral vision that her arm was already reaching for the lamp. She wasn't paralyzed. Not technically. She was just so disconnected from herself that moving required absolute focus.

Concentrating on her arm, she managed to gather just enough sensation to realize that the lamp and the end table were missing. And now that she looked, she understood that everything in the room was gone except the bed, and that, as she willed her gaze upward, she saw a sky filled with dim stars that did nothing to light the darkness.

The thing ripped away her blanket with a shriek and wrapped one hand around her ankle. It was going to drag her into the shadows and kill her, and there wasn't a damn thing she could do about it.

A flare lit this inky void, just beside her bed, and its harsh glare drove the thing away. It disappeared, though its howls of discontent echoed for a while yet.

Suddenly she could move again.

West, his pockmarked face lit by a flare in his right hand, squinted at her. "Is that you, Number Five?"

She covered her eyes. The light was so bright.

"Yes, it's me. What the hell was that?"

"You shouldn't be awake," said West.

She wasn't about to let him dodge the question. "What the hell was that?"

"Dream eater. I wouldn't be too concerned about it."

"Not concerned? It was going to kill me."

"It was just feeding on your nightmares."

"But I wasn't having a nightmare."

"Well, of course you weren't. It was eating them. The dream eaters perform a valuable service, consuming negativity and other dangerous emotions while you sleep. Without dream eaters, the entire human race would've gone mad some time ago."

"Wait a minute. You're telling me those things keep us sane."

"You didn't think your fragile psyche was able to hold itself together all on its own, did you? Something has to clean out the baggage, remove the excess goop clogging the gears."

"*Labroides dimidiatus*," said Diana.

"Uh-hmm."

"Cleaner fish. It forms a symbiotic relationship with other fish by eating the particles that—"

"I know what *Labroides dimidiatus* is, Number Five." He took another flare out of his coat pocket and handed it to her. "We should get you out of here. Before they come back. They don't like being seen. Puts a fright into them, can make them dangerous."

"But you said they were symbiotic."

"Symbiotic and easily frightened. Not that it matters unless you wake up too suddenly, like you did."

The dream eater's cries were echoed by others of its kind. Lots of them.

"You should probably follow me now."

She was wearing her pajamas, and the ground under her feet felt warm and squishy. Like sand that wasn't quite mud. Every step made a wet, plopping noise. A few steps, and her bed disappeared into the emptiness. She could see some shapes in the dark. Maybe trees. Maybe rocks. But aside from that, all she could see was West's torch, which she followed closely.

"It was that howl. It's what woke me up."

She could still hear it. Low and mournful. Inhuman and pitiable.

"That'd do it," said West. "You must've heard Fenris's pain. You must be an empathic soul, Number Five."

Diana had always assumed empathy was a good thing, but if it meant waking up in an alien corner of the universe, she wasn't so sure. That's what she got for assuming anything.

"Who's Fenris?" she asked.

"The wolf that chases, the herald of Ragnarok, the ravenous godling. The big green thing that forever chases the moon."

"Shouldn't it be called Managarmr then? Because in Norse mythology—"

"I'm well aware of the mistake."

They walked a little farther. The cries of the dream eaters variously seemed to come from behind them or ahead of them. It was impossible to tell. Aside from the light of the flares and a dim shape glimpsed here and there, the world was nothing but black.

"Why is Fenris in pain?" She asked the question as much to keep her mind off what was happening as to satisfy any personal curiosity.

"It's trapped."

She chuckled to herself. "Aren't we all? Take a number, pal."

"True, Number Five. But for a being like Fenris imprisonment is unbearable. Most creatures were meant to occupy a single sphere of existence, but Fenris is one of the rarest of beings, made to swim the oceans of existence like you walk from room to room. Imagine being entangled in a net from which you cannot escape that only tightens itself the more you struggle."

It did sound pretty damn awful. "Isn't there some way to free it?"

West looked over his shoulder. His face was nothing but shadows, except for his four eyes that glinted in the torchlight. "The net is your universe. Or what you once thought of as your universe before your eyes were opened."

"Oh."

"If it makes you feel any better, this is merely an inconvenience for Fenris. His efforts to free himself are why there are tears in your reality in the first place. His thrashing snaps and strains the fabric of your world. While it might contain him for a while, he is greater than the forces that bind him. Inevitably, he will escape, even if he must obliterate your world in the process."

"But—"

"Oh, I wouldn't worry too much about that, Number Five. Now that you live in the building, your existence doesn't depend on anything as delicate as reality. So it's really not your problem anymore, is it?"

She didn't find that very comforting.

"Hasn't anyone figured out a way to help him escape without destroying the world?"

"If there are forces at work with the power to do so, they're largely indifferent to the well-being of this small universe."

"But—"

"It's a long ways off," he said. "At least a day or two."

She stopped. "What?"

He kept walking. "Or perhaps the day after that. Or the day after that. Eternity is measured one moment at a time."

She used one of those moments to focus on what was important, escaping from the dream eaters, and caught up with him.

"Where are we?"

"Do you know where you go when you sleep? When you close your eyes and no one is looking at you, not even you?"

"Here?"

"Sometimes here," said West. "Sometimes other places."

"You're telling me that when I go to sleep, my body is transported to a place like this?"

"More or less. Unless someone's watching you."

They passed another bed where an elderly couple dozed. A pair of those things were lurking beside them.

"Should we do something?" she asked.

"Do what? As long as they're asleep, they're fine. Trust me, waking them up would only cause problems."

"How often does this happen?"

"I already told you," he said. "Every time you aren't seen."

"I get that, although I won't ask the obvious question like how does that work with the blind because...well...because it's probably pointless. But how often do people wake up too soon? And what happens to them if those things get them?"

"It happens infrequently, and you don't really want to know what happens. Now we're almost there. Ah, here we are."

West reached out and flicked a switch, dispelling the dark. The dreamworld disappeared and her bedroom fell into place. Everything was normal. West and the dream eaters were gone. She might've convinced herself it had all been a vivid dream, if not for the flare still clutched in her right hand.

She threw on her slippers, pushed the dresser aside, and stalked out of the apartment and downstairs. She pounded on West's door. She didn't expect him to answer right away, but she resolved to stick with it until he did. She was midway through her second round of knocks when the door opened.

"How in the hell am I supposed to sleep now?" she asked.

West leaned against the door frame and sighed. "If you don't sleep, how can the dream eaters clean out your mind?"

"And knowing that dream eaters are out there or that my world is destined to be destroyed by a cosmic monster, how am I supposed to get to sleep then?"

"All you need to do is close your eyes," he said. "The eaters take care of the rest. Now that you've nearly seen them, they'll be drawn to you. You'll probably sleep better than you've ever imagined you could. All the tenants that survived the longest woke up too soon at least once or twice in their first few months in the building. It's a good sign."

"But when I'll close my eyes, all I'll see is—"

"You'll see nothing. The eaters will give you blessed oblivion, relieve you of the burden of jumbled thoughts and overheated memories. They'll allow you the sanctuary of a state of pure, untroubled unconsciousness, eight precious hours at a time. If I were you, I'd be thankful for every moment of peace you can get in this hectic universe."

He closed the door.

Diana trudged back to her room. He was insane if he thought she could get back to sleep, knowing what she did. She cracked open a book and read to stay awake. At some point, she fell asleep.

It was the best night's rest she'd ever had.

CHAPTER NINE

Diana awoke, slid the dresser away from her door, took a shower, and got dressed. Today was a new day. She was determined to make the most of it. And she was determined to do that by proving she could have an ordinary, run-of-the-mill experience from start to finish. She still had to ignore her monstrous roommates and all the weird things only she could see. But she could do that.

Unending Smorgaz lay flat on his stomach in a corner of the living room. He was a huge, purple lump. Unlike Vom, Smorgaz slept on a human schedule. His steady snore sounded very much like a buzz saw wrapped in cotton.

Vom reclined on the couch, reading a book. As he finished each page he tore it out and gulped it down.

Diana had time for a quick breakfast. Unable to find

anything to eat, she used her powers to will a carton of orange juice and some cereal into existence. The multidimensional qualities of the apartment made using her magical abilities easy, and she figured it was a good place to practice. Her box of Frosted Flakes came without a bowl, milk, or a spoon, though. It was annoying how the magic lacked common sense. She created these items as well. Everything molded itself out of the kitchen counters, rising up as if budded from the tile, and she wondered if she was creating reality or if the apartment, like some obedient living thing, was reshaping bits and pieces of itself to her desires. Was she eating cereal or some small piece of an otherworldly monster? Like a tick sucking blood from a dog?

When she bit a spoonful of cereal, she thought she felt the kitchen tremble. Whether the feeling was real or not she couldn't know, but that was just par for the course now. Better to not overthink it. She picked up her bowl and orange juice and went into the living room.

"Hey, did you hear that sound last night?" she asked Vom. "That long sort of howl?"

"Oh, that's just Fenris. The wolf that chases, the herald of Ragnarok, the ravenous godling..."

"I got that covered last night. Although shouldn't he be named Managarmr?"

"What?"

She took a swig of juice, right out of the carton because she didn't feel like wishing for a glass. "In Norse mythology, Fenris is the giant wolf that bites off Tyr's hand and kills Odin at the end of time. Managarmr is the wolf that pursues the moon and swallows it as one of the events leading to Ragnarok."

Vom lowered his book. "How the hell do you know that?"

She shrugged. "Internet."

"So you were just looking up obscure mythological references at some point in the past because you thought it might come in handy someday?"

"I don't know. Must have had some time to kill."

"I'm just shocked you remembered that name."

She smiled. It pleased her to shock a cosmic horror, even if only a little.

"Fenris is easier to say than Mana—Moona—Maga—"

"Managarmr," she said.

"Yes, that."

"Do you know him?" she asked.

"Fenris? Oh no. Can't say we've ever met. He's a greater eldritch while I'm only a lesser embodiment. We don't travel in the same circles. And if we did ever meet, he'd probably just eat me because he is as far above me as I am above…"

Vom trailed off, not finishing the sentence, and she ignored the potential insult.

"You guys have cliques?"

"In a way. It's like high school, except instead of jocks versus nerds, it's things who eat civilizations versus things who eat galaxies. I could devour the universe if you gave me a few billion years, but Fenris could do it in a few years, a decade at most if he put his mind to it." He crumpled another page into a ball, tossed it in the air, and caught it in his gut mouth. "I'm a big fan."

"So why is he wasting his time chasing one insignificant moon? I thought he wanted to escape our reality?"

"Maybe the moon has something to do with it. I don't know. You'd have to ask him that. It probably has to do with the same reason I like hanging around you. There's something about it that draws him, something he needs. All anyone knows is that he's been after the Earth's moon for...oh, about five billion years or so...give or take."

"Weird."

"Takes all kinds," said Vom.

She deposited her bowl into the sink. "Crap, I'm late for work."

"I thought the fire ruined your job."

"No, I fixed that."

"How?"

"The same way I started the fire in the first place," she said. "Magic."

Vom sat up. "Well, aren't you the fast learner?"

She smiled. "I don't know if it really worked yet. I just know that I concentrated really hard last night on undoing my first spell." She frowned. "That doesn't sound right. Do you call it a spell?"

"You can call it whatever you like."

"Spell just makes it seem too...ordinary," she said. "New Agey. Like something hippies do." She imagined herself dancing in darkened forests, wearing long, lacy sleeves, and honoring the mother goddess. She didn't have anything against it. Seemed like it might be more fun than church.

It didn't feel right because there was nothing mystical about her newfound powers. No rituals, no incantations or prayers, no sacred tomes. No commandments or law of threefold return to guide her. She was on her own here with what little help Vom could supply. And that wasn't much, since, in many ways, he was just as lost as she was.

All she knew was that she could make things happen by editing reality, and if she could start a fire by accidentally revising it into existence, she didn't see why she couldn't re-revise it out of existence. She'd willed away her original fire last night for fifteen minutes until a tingle along her spine suggested that the edit had taken place. She'd considered calling this morning to double-check, but couldn't think of a way to phrase that phone call.

"Hi. It's Diana. I was just checking if the department store was still burned to a crisp or if that thing I just mentioned no longer happened."

It'd be easier to just go and see for herself.

Vom swallowed his entire book and woke Smorgaz. "Get up. We're going to work."

"*I'm* going to work," she said. "You're staying here."

"Is that a good idea?" asked Vom. "What if you run into another lost entity seeking a focus? You'll want us around."

"I thought you said that didn't happen very often."

"It doesn't. Not usually. But it's not as if there's a cap on how many deranged other-dimensional monsters will be drawn to you in a week. You seem to have a knack for it."

She didn't want them to tag along. Two pet monsters, even well-meaning ones, could wreck the illusion of normality she was going for, but that was already a lost cause. Outside this apartment, on the streets, was a city filled with monsters and contradictions that a sane mind could only ignore.

"You can come," she said, "but try not to be conspicuous."

The fuzzy green beast and the giant rubber hedgehog saluted.

"You won't even notice we're around," said Vom.

Her magic wish had worked. The department store was restored. Diana noticed the remnants of the undone reality. Some black smudges, leftover smoke damage she assumed, clung to spots on the ceiling, and the whole place had a subtle, seared-wood-and-insulation scent throughout. But otherwise everything appeared in order, and once the managers had lectured the cleaning staff (something Diana felt bad about but couldn't prevent) everything went back to normal. She even succeeded in making everyone forget that she'd been absent for five days.

That was the thing that bothered her most about this experience. It was one thing to unmake her previous mistake. It was another to go around screwing with people's minds. It was a violation of their innermost selves. People weren't robots for her to reprogram at her whim, but she didn't see a choice. Undoing the fire and allowing everyone the memory of her absence would only leave questions she couldn't answer and very probably cost her job too.

Just this once, she decided. No more. The resolution would've held more weight if she'd even understood these new powers.

"Very nice work," said Vom. "Not many human minds can pick up the subtleties of reality manipulation. Usually it's all 'I am like unto a living god. Quake before me, mere mortals! I wish for a million dollars, a gold-plated robot butler, and adoration from all around me.'"

Diana said, "Jesus, is everyone that petty and dumb?"

"Not everybody," said Smorgaz. "But most."

"Of course, those kinds of eager beavers don't last long. They end up drawing too much attention to themselves, and the universe usually has to slap them down to keep things in order."

Smorgaz pulled a coat off a rack, checked it in the mirror. "Does this color work for me?"

"Yes, it goes great with your eyes," replied Diana reflexively. She snatched the garment away and put it back. "You guys promised you'd be unobtrusive."

"Sorry," said Vom. "We didn't realize it would be so dull."

"Didn't you just spend one hundred years locked in a closet?"

Unending Smorgaz hiccuped, and two spawns rolled off his back. They scampered away to wreak whatever havoc they could in their brief life span.

Smorgaz cringed. "Whoops. Sorry."

She handed them a few dollars. "Go to the food court and buy a soda or something. Just behave, please."

"We'll be nearby. Just whistle if you need us for anything."

"And remember," she called just before they turned the corner. "Don't eat anything that doesn't come on a menu!"

And then they were around the corner and gone.

She leaned against a display and gathered her wits. When the monsters were around they caused all manner of trouble, but she could keep an eye on them. When they were gone she didn't have to think about it, but it didn't mean they were behaving. Either situation was both a relief and frustrating.

She spotted Wendall walking by and waved to him. He lowered his head and picked up his pace away from her.

She wondered if she could alter his memory just enough that he wouldn't freak out when he saw her, but immediately ruled it out. This magic stuff wasn't a cure-all. It wasn't perfect, and even if it had been, she'd only been using it for two days. She was no expert.

Wendall's half-memories of yesterday were important. She was dangerous company, and he would be better off keeping his distance.

Diana hadn't thought much of Wendall in the time they'd worked together. Now he embodied that ultimate normality that had gone missing from her life. Something she'd taken for granted when it'd been around. Something that actively avoided her now.

She'd fix that by ignoring the weirdness and concentrating on the ordinary. So even though there was a shadowy blob-like entity browsing skis in sporting goods and a snaky thing swimming through the air, she ignored these things and thought about selling coats.

She was going to sell an assload of coats. To prove that she could, and to make up for burning down the store, even if that now technically had never happened. And also because she wanted to do something normal.

A mother with two children in tow stepped into her section. Diana, smiling perhaps a bit too widely, approached.

"Can I help you, miss?"

The woman acknowledged Diana in the vaguest manner, like a mosquito buzzing in her ear.

"I think it's time the children bought some new jackets."

The boys were noticeably annoyed by this.

"Mom," whined one, "we just went jacket shopping last week."

The woman ignored them and started looking through the racks. Diana, knowing the drill, stepped aside and waited to compliment the woman's choices. She bought two new coats for the kids and two new coats for herself. It was an auspicious beginning, and Diana took it as a good omen.

No sooner had the family left than another man appeared. This one sneaked up while she was working the register. He was tall with sallow skin and a big, waxed mustache.

"Excuse me, young miss, but I seem to have a great need of a new coat."

She smiled. "Right this way, sir."

He bought the first garment she showed him. He paid in cash, then wandered away in a bit of a daze.

Almost immediately two more customers appeared to take his place. They were just as eager to buy, and all Diana had to do was point them toward the racks. A woman with a distant stare set her purchase on the counter.

"Anything else for you, miss?" asked Diana.

The woman's gaze focused on Diana. "Oh…of course. Yes, something else."

She grabbed a random coat within reach and put it beside her original purchase.

Diana got the nagging suspicion that normality was about to slip out of her fingers again.

"Do you really want that?" she asked.

"Yes, I do," said the woman in staggering syllables, almost as if she didn't know where the words came from. "I want a coat."

"I want a coat too," said the elderly woman in line behind her.

"Coats are good," they said in unison. "We need coats."

Wendall walked up beside her.

"Hey," she said. "How's it going?"

"I want to buy a coat," he replied.

He reached for one of the garments beside the register. The customer grabbed him by the wrist.

"This is my coat." There was an edge to her voice.

"Have you bought this coat?" he asked.

"Not yet."

"Then it's not yours," he replied. "I will buy this coat since you haven't bought this coat yet."

"Hey, I'm next to buy a coat," said the old woman. "You can't buy a coat before me."

"No, I will buy all your coats too," said Wendall. "One can never have too many coats."

A new customer, carrying more jackets than he could reasonably hold and struggling to keep them all in his grasp, jumped in line. "These are my coats. You can't have them."

Diana sighed. Things were weird again. She tried to bring them under control. "Can everyone please stop saying the word *coat* so much?"

They all paused.

"But coats are important things," they intoned in one cultish voice.

With that point of commonality settled, they resumed squabbling over who was in greatest need of a coat and who deserved the lion's share of the sacred garments.

Diana lowered her head and muttered to herself and the universe.

"This isn't what I had in mind."

Only a moment later the coat department was brimming with customers, all of them fighting over purchases. A young man with crunchy, unkempt hair tried to grab a garment from a frail middle-aged woman. Shrieking, she pounced on him.

There was madness as coat-mania caused the crowd to turn on each other. A dozen melees broke out. A group of children wrestled with a leather-clad biker. A blind man beat a chunky nerd with his cane. And a slimy tentacle monster battled a duck-like Neanderthal over a blue hoodie. The combatants were hampered by their refusal to put down their prized clothing, which limited the damage they could do to each other, but things were getting out of hand.

Diana focused her willpower.

"Stop it!"

The mob hesitated. A few people carried on halfheartedly. The feathery Neanderthal yanked away the hoodie. The tentacle monster growled.

"I said stop." Diana sensed the shift in reality. "Everybody...just go home."

"Go home," they chanted in unison, turning and shuffling away.

"No, no. Stop."

They stopped.

"Give me a second here. I need to think this through."

She leaned against the counter and pondered. These magical powers were messed up, a monkey's paw she couldn't throw away.

"Okay, I have it," she said. "I want you all to put down your coats and just go about the rest of your lives as if everything that just happened never actually took place. Oh, and it's okay to like coats, just don't like them too much. I guess what I'm saying is that coats are nice, but they're nothing to kill someone over."

"Coats are nice," her cult agreed in unison, "but don't kill for them."

"Oh, and stop doing that, please. It's starting to creep me out. Now go on. Get out of here." She adopted the kind of gentle voice reserved for stray cats. "Shoo now."

The short-lived Church of the Hallowed Windbreaker quietly dispersed. Diana spent the next half hour putting coats back on the racks. Her department remained empty until lunch rolled around. She grabbed a piece of warmed-over pizza at the food court and sat at the table with Vom and Smorgaz.

"I just don't get it," she said. "There has to be a way to turn this off."

"Why would you want to turn it off?" asked Vom. "Most people are unwilling victims of reality."

"And now I'm the victimizer."

"You're just being melodramatic."

She slurped her soda, nibbled her pizza.

"It's not right. People weren't meant to have this kind of power."

"Says who?"

"Says everyone."

Vom shook his head. "Everyone is idiots."

"Everyone *are* idiots," corrected Smorgaz. He pursed his lips. "Everyone am idiots?"

"Regardless of whether you were meant to have this

kind of power, you have it," said Vom. "And there's no way to get rid of it. Are you going to finish that?"

She slid her paper plate across the table. Vom devoured it.

"I know how to get rid of it," said Smorgaz.

"You do not." Vom slurped Diana's soda without asking, then ate the cup.

"Sure, I do. It's not permanent, but it works." Smorgaz leaned forward and spoke in a quiet tone. "World peace."

He sat back with a knowing grin.

"How the hell does that work?" asked Vom.

Smorgaz winked. "It doesn't."

Diana used her patient voice. "Can you explain it to the rest of us in a little more detail?"

"It's simple really. Manipulating reality takes power. Your connection with Vom and myself gives you that power. But it has its limits. Screwing with a few minds here and there, rebuilding department stores, that's easy. You could do that all day without exhausting yourself. But world peace...that's a tall order. Trying to make it happen would be like trying to push a mountain with a bulldozer. You'll run out of gas, but you won't get results. Unless running out of gas is the result you wanted in the first place."

"That actually makes sense," said Vom.

"Why shouldn't it? I'm not just a mindless spawning machine, y'know."

A trio of clones budded off his back. Vom caught one and promptly ate it, but the other two bolted across the food court, eliciting surprised yelps from the lunch crowd, who assumed they were rats or puppies or some similar nuisance.

Diana excused herself from the minor chaos and went to the bathroom in order to concentrate. She found an empty stall, sat on the toilet, and cleared her head.

She pictured all the people in all the world getting along, accepting each other's differences with tolerance and grace. She went the extra mile and pictured everyone holding hands in a grassy field, singing songs, drinking Coca-Cola together. Just living together in a great big harmonious sing-along.

Her gut tightened. A knot formed in her shoulders. She felt queasy, but the power was leaving her, spreading outward, trying to manipulate reality to her desires.

She hit a wall. The nebulous forces she was attempting to unleash flowed back into her.

"Damn it."

She gritted her teeth. This wasn't going to be as easy as she'd hoped. Maybe her magical powers were aware of themselves and didn't want to be wasted. Or possibly reality itself was pushing back, trying to avoid holding the hot potato. She didn't understand the metaphysics. She just closed her eyes and pushed back.

"Come on..." Her heart beat faster. She could smell burning bacon and hoped it wasn't coming from her. "...Get happy, damn it."

The magic stream slowed to a trickle, then stopped altogether. It sloshed between Diana and the universe in a delicate balance. Humming "Imagine," she exerted every ounce of willpower she had. It was easier now that her body had gone completely numb, and there was nothing to distract her.

"Happy happy, joy joy, you bastards," she groaned.

The resistance crumbled, and all the magic rushed out

of her like a flood. She could actually see it, a rainbow of colors and shapes that twisted and altered reality on a primordial level, deeper than molecules. Deeper than atoms. Even deeper than quarks, gluons, other mysterious science-tastic words Diana had picked up from watching Discovery Channel. It was like reaching underneath all that to get to the core programming at the heart of the video game that was the universe, and using a cheat code to alter an inalterable law. Infinite lives. Endless ammunition. Level skip. World peace.

An invisible force snapped back at Diana and knocked her off the toilet. She wasn't hurt, but her hand did end up in the bowl. She was drained, exhausted, but it was gone. All the strange power within her was used up.

She was out of gas.

She pulled her hand out of the water. Bad day for long sleeves, but all things considered, *It could've been worse*, she thought.

Right before she threw up.

CHAPTER TEN

The problem with using up all her magic was that Diana didn't have anything left to undo the prominent vomit stain running down her blouse.

The nice thing was that, even if she hadn't brought about world peace, she'd brought a warm humanity to the mall. Every single person was smiling, exceedingly polite, and full of good cheer.

Ginger in women's wear helped Diana pick out a new blouse.

"Maybe you should go home. You don't look very good."

"I'm fine," Diana lied. She'd felt better after vomiting, but her legs were shaky. Her hands trembled. Along with all her supernatural powers, she'd exhausted something else. It was like a piece of her life force had been torn away. She told herself she was exaggerating, but she was only guessing. But she was immortal now. Or at least she could die only in very specific ways.

"I'm just a little woozy." She checked a new blouse in a three-way mirror. She didn't like the color, and it didn't go with her slacks. But it was the cheapest in the store.

"Here, take this one." Ginger gave her a much better match.

Diana checked the tag. "I'd rather not. Even with my employee discount, it's a bit much."

"So don't pay. Take it. You're obviously having a rough day, and you do your damnedest in coats every day. Don't think of it as a gift. Think of it as appreciation for all the terrific work you do here."

Beaming, Ginger gave Diana a warm hug, heedless of the moist stain between them.

"You're super, Diana," said Ginger, "and I want only the best for you."

Diana nodded very slowly. "Ooooookaaaay. I appreciate the offer. I do. But I can't ask you to pay for this."

"Oh, I'm not going to pay for it. Why pay for it? It's just a blouse. Not nearly as important as you are. If you ask me, we place too much value on these things when what really matters is all of us, together, making the most of every moment—"

"I can't steal it," she whispered, so as not to get Ginger in trouble.

"Steal it?" Ginger laughed. "It's not stealing. Not if you really need it."

She shouted at a manager, "Hey, Shaun! Is it cool if I let Diana have this blouse?"

"Absolutely!" Shaun gave the thumbs-up. "You're doing a super job, Diana!"

"Thanks," said Diana.

"What was that?" shouted Shaun.

"She said thanks!" yelled back Ginger.

"Cool. Thanks for passing that along, Ginger! Great job!"

"Thanks, Shaun! You too!"

Diana didn't want to take the new blouse, but she soon realized there wasn't any point in arguing. Everyone in her immediate vicinity was in a state of absolute good-will. If she kicked them in the face they'd probably compliment her on her high kicking ability, even as they spat out their teeth.

It wasn't genuine, just an illusion she'd forced on the universe. She had no idea how long it would last or how far it had spread past the mall. But she wasn't going to try changing it back, no matter how unnatural all this joy to the world was at heart. She'd learned the hard way that magic wasn't controllable. Not for her, at least. If she tried to get everyone to act normal, it'd probably end up in a chain saw battle royal that she'd have to undo.

Not that she had the power to change anything. Smorgaz's plan had worked. She was empty, unable to alter reality in any supernatural way. Although she wouldn't have minded feeling a little less mortal at the moment.

"So a bunch of us are going out for drinks after work," said Ginger. "You should come."

"Thanks, but I have other plans."

"Well, I guess you can't help that. Too bad though. Been ages since we've just sat around, catching up."

Diana nodded. It had been a while since she'd just hung out with friends. Most of her coworkers weren't much more than acquaintances, but it was a nice, normal thing to do. She would've gladly taken Ginger up on the offer except for the two monsters in her care. She didn't see a way around that.

"Did you know that Vicki's son is almost two?" asked Ginger.

"Already? Damn, where does the time go?"

"I know, right. Sorry you can't make it. I'm sure everyone will be super disappointed."

Diana thanked Ginger for the new blouse, walked a few steps, and stopped. If she was going to maintain her sanity, she needed a normal life. Or at least as many bits and pieces of a normal life as she could scrape together. Spending time with ordinary people who had ordinary-people concerns might just keep her grounded. Even if it didn't have any long-term effect, it would be good for a distraction for the evening.

"Ginger, count me in."

Ginger smiled, and even though Diana knew that smile was partly due to her own cosmic powers, she still found it reassuring.

She managed to finish her shift, even if her strength never quite returned. She stopped trembling, but she couldn't shake the hollow sensation. By the end of the day the mall was already restored. Everyone was cheerful, but they stopped going out of their way to compliment each other. Maybe in an hour or two they'd be back to normal. Kind of a shame that it couldn't last, but it wasn't right. When world peace happened, she mused on the drive to the bar to meet her coworkers, *if* it ever happened, it shouldn't be as absurd as someone making a wish that did it.

"That's ridiculous," said Vom.

She glanced over at the passenger seat. He was in her mind again.

"Sorry," he said.

She turned the radio up in an attempt to drown out the unreliable and unrequested telepathic communication. It came and went, and while she occasionally picked up a thought from Vom, he was more often the receiver in the relationship. She preferred that, because those foreign thoughts that came to her were strange, inhuman desires. Usually involving eating something. Or everything.

She also caught one or two thoughts from Unending Smorgaz, but these were less bizarre. His most pressing need was to be fruitful and multiply, but this seemed easier to repress. Just like it was easier to be celibate than to be hungry, she guessed.

"If humanity has to wait for everyone to get on board with world peace," said Vom, "then it'll never happen."

"Maybe, but just making it happen is cheating."

He smirked. "Why?"

"Because I can't just force my desires on the world."

"Why not? Everyone else does."

"I don't believe that."

"No, and just believing something is enough to make it a fact," said Vom. "Oh, wait. I'm talking to a human where this is literally true. So never mind."

She was content to let it drop, but Vom wasn't.

"Every interaction you have with this universe is exerting unwanted influence on it. Even before you joined up with me and Smorgaz."

"Mmmm." She hoped the vagueness of her reply would convince him that his point was made.

"When you eat something, you're deciding that your continued survival is more important than something else that would probably rather exist if given the choice."

"What about vegetarians?" Smorgaz countered.

"Potatoes and carrots are still alive. They might not possess will, but they exist. And they only cease to exist when something else decides they shouldn't. Even if that something is just bacteria."

"It's always about eating with you," said Diana.

"That's because consuming is the purest form of existence, the most primal of all desires throughout all realities."

"Actually the most primal force throughout the universe is spawning," said Smorgaz.

Vom chuckled. "Don't be ridiculous. Spawning is only a tool to ensure that you will produce more mouths to consume more than the other guy."

"No," said Smorgaz. "Consuming is only a tool to ensure that you will spawn more effectively than the other guy."

"Most things die if they don't consume. They don't die if they fail to spawn."

"No, even with consuming, most things die. Eventually. Spawning is the only reliable method of ensuring the continuation of existence. In fact, not spawning is the only way to die."

"What about adoption?" asked Vom. "Or cultural contribution?"

Smorgaz chuckled. "Those are all just derivatives of spawning."

"Oh, I see. Anything important is spawning-related by default."

"Makes more sense than everything important being consumption-related."

Diana zoned out while the monsters continued their debate. They were still going strong when she parked the car.

"Let's go over the ground rules, guys," she said.

"Again?" asked Vom. "How many times do we have to do this?"

"As many times as it takes for me to convince myself that this isn't a terrible mistake that is going to go horribly awry. So give it to me."

"When in doubt, don't eat it," said Vom with mechanical indifference.

"If you absolutely have to spawn," said Smorgaz, "excuse yourself to go to the bathroom."

Diana nodded. "Good. And..."

"Try not to talk but be polite," intoned Vom and Smorgaz in unison. "If anyone asks, we're old college friends in town for the week, and we have to go back to Stockholm to complete a research paper on soil samples."

"No, not Stockholm," she said.

Vom sighed. "But you said—"

"I know what I said, but Stockholm is too exotic. It invites questions. We need someplace less interesting. Sacramento. Or maybe Denver."

"I've been to Denver," said Smorgaz. "It's a surprisingly interesting place."

"Okay. We'll go with Kansas. Kansas is boring."

"Really?" asked Smorgaz. "So I take it you've been there."

"No, I haven't, but it's not important if Kansas really is boring. It's just important that it seems boring."

"So you're willing to impugn a whole state for an elaborate charade?"

"Yes, I am. I'm sure the state of Kansas will forgive me just this once."

"Can I say we used to date?" asked Smorgaz.

"No."

"Can I say I used to be worshipped as a god?" asked Vom.

"What?" She shook her head. "No."

"Not even if someone asks? Like maybe it just comes up randomly in the table conversation?"

"When is something like that going to come up?"

"You never know. A lively conversation can be unpredictable."

"You're a guy who studies dirt," she said. "That's it."

"Can I be gay?" asked Smorgaz.

She covered her face and ground her teeth.

"Okay. You can be gay."

"That's no fair. Why does he get to be gay?" said Vom.

"You can be gay too," she replied.

"Wait," said Smorgaz. "We can't both be gay. Then it won't be special."

She said, "Maybe we should just forget the whole thing."

"No. It's fine. We can both be gay. But since I thought of it, I'll be flamboyantly gay and you will just have to be ordinary gay."

"I can live with that," said Vom.

"Just don't be a stereotype," added Diana.

Smorgaz snapped his fingers. "You got it, girlfriend."

They climbed out of the car and walked toward the bar. Diana was already getting a bad feeling about this. She thought about turning around, forgetting the whole thing. But she'd come this far.

Her sanity hung in the balance. If she was going to avoid death and madness, she needed to find a way to ground herself. This might not be the solution, but it was worth a shot.

"How are they going to see you?" she asked. "What do you look like to normal people?"

They shrugged.

"You don't wear any clothes," she said. "Even if you appear like human beings, wouldn't you be naked? I mean, why do they even perceive you as male or female to begin with? You aren't really either, right?"

They shrugged again.

"Sometimes I wish you two were more helpful."

"If you want everything to make sense," said Vom, "you're only going to be continually disappointed."

They entered the bar, and she spotted her coworkers occupying a group of tables. They waved her over.

"So glad you could make it," said Ginger. "And these must be your friends."

"Yes, this is..." Only then did she realize that she'd overlooked coming up with normal human names for her monsters. In the few seconds it took for her to come up with John and James, they stepped forward and introduced themselves.

"I'm Vom."

"Smorgaz."

Ginger said, "Those are interesting names."

"Albanian," said Smorgaz.

"I thought you looked Albanian."

Diana understood. Vom and Smorgaz were blanks, seen however the viewer wanted or expected to see them. Just as long as it was a conceivable alternative to seeing what they actually were.

"I'm gay," said Vom.

"I'm gay, too," added Smorgaz. "Flamboyantly."

Smiling, Ginger nodded. "I see."

Diana sat. Vom and Smorgaz sat to her left.

This wasn't going to work. She couldn't relax with the monsters here. It wasn't their fault. They were behaving themselves. But she couldn't shake the image of Vom, in a moment of weakness, setting upon everyone, eagerly devouring them within moments. Or someone, in a moment of unusual clarity, might glimpse a clone rolling off of Smorgaz's back. It wasn't implausible. People were not uniformly oblivious. She could see that.

Wendall watched her from a distance. When she sat down he moved to the far end of the table. And he kept nervously glancing at Vom and Smorgaz. He might not have been able to see them for what they were, but he could certainly sense something was off about them.

She wanted to straighten things out somehow for the poor guy. He'd seen something mortal minds weren't meant to see, and it was obvious he was having trouble reconciling himself to it. She couldn't blame him for that. She wasted a few minutes trying to come up with a simple way to ease his troubled mind, but aside from telling him he wasn't crazy and that the universe was filled with terrifying cosmic horrors, she was coming up short. That news hardly seemed reassuring.

Just brushing up against this horrible secret had jostled loose his sanity. Confirming it could very well destroy it.

Yet here she was, neck-deep in this madness, and she wasn't doing nearly as badly. But maybe it was easier when you were all the way in. Perhaps a full immersion allowed her to adjust. Rather than seeing only bits and pieces of a half-remembered madness, she saw the whole thing. And that allowed her to accept it more easily, to bounce back.

More likely, she'd already gone mad and just didn't realize it. She found some comfort in that. Hitting bottom meant the worst was over.

Diana didn't believe it. Not for a moment. Not even enough to lie to herself about it.

Her coworkers engaged in small talk. They made jokes. Vicki showed pictures of her kid. Ginger talked about a funny thing that had happened during her morning commute. That guy from the shoe department (Steve or Bob or Fred, she could never remember his name) recommended a movie he'd seen. It was a lively, perfectly harmless conversation.

And it bored the ever-living hell out of Diana.

Although perhaps boredom was the wrong word. Small talk like this was always boring, but everyone played along, pretending to be fully invested in the mundane trials and tribulations of human existence. The unspoken social contract went like this: you listened sympathetically to other people's problems, and they listened sympathetically to yours. While she had enough faith in humanity to believe this wasn't always an act, it didn't really matter if you genuinely empathized just as long as you could fake it.

She couldn't fake it. Not the way she used to.

It was, she knew, selfish of her. These were good people with real problems that mattered to them. Only a few days ago she'd shared those problems. Little things like paying bills, relationship difficulties, and traffic annoyances. She just couldn't relate.

It all just seemed so insignificant, so petty and trivial. It always had been, but now she couldn't even pretend it wasn't.

She envied all the ordinary people in this bar. She despised them. The internal conflict, along with her effort to hide it, made her queasy. Diana didn't know why she bothered. People were obviously clueless. If they couldn't see the monsters among them, then why would they notice her disinterest?

Meanwhile, Vom and Smorgaz were getting along just fine. Better than her. She had no idea how that was possible. They weren't even human. Maybe that worked in their favor. That distance gave them a more objective viewpoint. Rather than judging humanity for the clueless race of cosmic microbes it was, Vom and Smorgaz could just enjoy it without reservation.

Regardless of the reason, within the hour Diana found herself the odd woman out of the conversation. It wasn't intentional. She had so little to contribute that the natural give-and-take of an ordinary conversation just slipped away from her. She sat at her end of the table, not even pretending to listen.

Wendall sat at the other end. Only he seemed even remotely aware of the weirdness of the monsters. He'd turn his head and study Vom and Smorgaz from different angles. He'd squint and stare, and just when he managed to see them for what they truly were, he'd chicken out and look away.

He couldn't even look at her, much less meet her eyes. He left early. Then all her coworkers left, one by one, until she was left sitting at a table with only a pair of monsters to keep her company.

CHAPTER ELEVEN

Diana didn't feel like going home, so she found a pool hall and rented a table. She bought three beers and handed one to Vom, another to Smorgaz.

"Drink it slow now," she cautioned. "I'm not made of—"

Vom had already eaten his, bottle and all. He hadn't even bothered to open it.

"I'll rack," said Smorgaz.

Diana wasn't very good at the game, but she handily beat the two monsters. Neither could sink a ball, even when everything lined up perfectly. They didn't seem to care.

Halfway through their third game she went back to the bar to get another beer for herself and one for Vom and

Smorgaz to split. A tall, blond woman in jeans waited for her own order. The woman nodded at Diana. Diana nodded back.

"They're cute," said the woman. "Your friends."

Diana glanced over at her monsters. She had no idea what the woman saw, but Diana saw a furry green eating machine and a giant rubber hedgehog. They were kind of cute. In a strange, not-of-this-Earth way.

"You're lucky," said the woman. "I know a guy who is stuck with a slime-covered spider-thing."

Diana nodded. If that was her other option, she was lucky.

The woman took her drink and started to walk away, but Diana stopped her.

"Hey, can you see my friends for what they are?"

The woman smiled. "Of course."

"And you're not freaked out by that?"

"Why should I be? Believe me, the stuff I've seen…it makes those guys look like a couple of teddy bears."

The woman went to a table where she was playing by herself. Diana followed her.

"I don't mean to bother you, but—"

"But you're new to this and had a few questions." The woman leaned over the table and sank three balls in one shot.

"I'm sorry," said Diana.

"No. Don't worry. I understand where you're coming from."

She lined up another shot. The cue ball zipped across the felt and knocked two more balls into pockets. Diana noticed that the balls all moved in odd zigzagging patterns. At one point the cue ball circled the eight ball twice before completely reversing direction and smacking another target hard enough to send it arcing through the air to land in a pocket on the far side of the table.

"How did you do that?" asked Diana.

"It's all angles," the woman replied. "I just like to use the ones most people ignore. I'm Sharon by the way."

"Diana."

She took Sharon's hand. A zap passed between them. It startled Diana but didn't hurt.

"Sorry," said Sharon. "That happens sometimes to people like us who have slipped just a bit into the beyond."

She made it sound so casual, so everyday. Diana found that comforting.

Diana scanned the hall. There was a dog-sized housefly crawling along one of the walls.

"Is that one yours?"

"That's just a phase fly. They're all over the place this time of year. No, my partner isn't here right now."

"Aren't you worried?" asked Diana. "What if something attacks you?"

"Why would anything attack me?"

"Because that's what they do, right? I think that's what they do. I don't know if I quite get it yet, but displaced monsters might attack you in confusion."

"I don't really shine like you do. If anything, my bond has the opposite effect. I make most displaced entities uncomfortable. They tend to avoid me."

"That's a neat trick. Don't suppose you could teach it to me?"

"I wish I could, but it doesn't work like that."

Sharon joined Diana at their table. They played a few

games while Sharon explained some things. Vom had tried to enlighten Diana, but there was a chasm of perception between them. Their situation was similar. Both were struggling to make sense of an alien universe, but it was the difference in the areas they defined as alien that made things difficult.

The game of billiards was the perfect example. The reason Vom and Smorgaz had trouble sinking shots was that simple geometry was a bit confusing. They understood walking around solid objects, accepted the inconvenience of gravity, and could work with a one-way time continuum, but multicolored balls bouncing around a few square yards of felt was simply too subtle.

It didn't help that Sharon's presence proved distracting. If Diana was a comforting melody that kept the monsters calm, then Sharon was a low-pitched hum, too soft to be heard but rattling them on a cellular level, making them queasy.

Smorgaz smacked the cue ball with far too much spin. The ball leaped off the table, shattering someone's beer bottle.

"Dang," he said. "Thought I had it that time."

Diana resisted the urge to smile and headed to the restroom. She was washing her hands when she heard a peculiar gurgle coming from the stall she had just used.

"Did you hear that?" asked the short, black-haired woman beside her.

"Must be problems with the plumbing," replied Diana.

The woman opened the stall door as the toilet began spilling water across the tile. "Gross."

Diana was getting a bad feeling about this. "Maybe we should get the manager."

A bolt of lightning erupted from the toilet. The woman was disintegrated in a flash. She didn't even have time to scream. The crisp smell of ozone filled the smoky bathroom, and a giant eyeball floated toward Diana. That was all it was. A huge eye rimmed by a dozen tentacles. Strange energies crackled in the orb's interior.

Diana's attempts to flee were hampered by the slick floor. She fell on her butt just as the eye creature unleashed a blast that blew a hole in the wall. She kept her head down and scrambled toward the exit. The eye monster looped a slippery tentacle around her ankle and pulled her back.

The creature studied her with its single eye. She remembered that this monster, just like Vom and Smorgaz, didn't mean her any specific harm. It was just lost, confused, and trying to figure things out, figure her out. If she remained calm she could provide it with the anchor it sought.

"It's okay," she said soothingly. "It's okay."

The eye narrowed, but it didn't blast her, so she felt confident.

Vom and Smorgaz flung open the bathroom door.

"Don't worry, Diana!" said Vom. "We're here!"

"No, it's cool," she said. "I have this under control."

But her defenders had already sprung into action, tackling the eyeball.

"Hey, no! Stop!" she shouted. "Damn it, listen to me!"

Sharon grabbed Diana.

"It's too late for that. You need to put some distance between them, let them work it out on their own."

"But—"

Sharon yanked Diana out the door. The people in the

pool hall stood in shocked confusion at the howls and shrieks coming from the restroom. Diana resolved to, first, always save at least a little bit of her magic, and, second, avoid public bathrooms in the future. She realized that the second resolution was nothing more than superstitious impulse, but it couldn't hurt to keep to it.

The foreboding crackle warned Diana to hit the deck just a moment before the bathroom exploded. She didn't know what had happened to Smorgaz or Vom, but the eyeball hovered toward her. She stood, focusing her calming influence over the bizarre thing.

Sharon leaped in front of Diana. Her claim to be disruptive to alien monsters must have been true because the eye retreated.

Diana said, "Thanks, but I think I can—"

Several Smorgaz clones jumped the eye from behind.

"Damn it!" shouted Diana. "Everybody needs to calm the hell down!"

The eye unleashed blasts at random. A sizzling beam cut a swath of destruction through the hall. Pool tables and people were scorched into piles of dust.

She waved her arms and screamed in a futile attempt to get things in order. Instead she found herself looking into the eyeball's destructive gaze. She didn't have time to ponder the limits of her immortality as the creature prepared to obliterate her.

A red beast leaped from somewhere. It swept Diana off her feet and tossed her over its shoulder. The eye beast unleashed its blast from point-blank range, but Diana's furry savior was a blur, sweeping her from the line of fire.

The red beast darted from one side to the other, dancing with unnatural speed and grace around the eye's pursuing beam. Everything the ray struck, including several people, dissolved. Quickly her furry rescuer was trapped in a corner. The beam swept toward Diana and the beast.

Several Smorgazes tackled the eye creature. They buried it under a rapidly growing pile. Flashes of light would lance out from deep within the mound of monsters, and one or two of Smorgaz's spawn would disintegrate, only to be replaced by three or four more.

All Diana could do was stare at the devastation the eye had unleashed. Everything was just gone. Erased like it'd never been there at all. As far as she could tell the creature's blasts just kept going forever. The trench that had been dug into the floor went down into the darkness, and she was willing to bet the blast had come out the other side of the Earth and was even now traveling through space, cutting an endless destructive scar across the universe.

The red beast shook Diana alert to more pressing concerns. She looked into its huge maw. Its head was almost wolflike, but not really. It had long ears like a rabbit's, and two low-set black eyes. Its fur was long and wild. It opened its mouth, and she wondered if it was going to bite her face off.

"Snap out of it, Diana."

The voice, buried under a savage growl, was almost unrecognizable.

"Sharon?"

Diana was almost too fixated on Sharon's slavering jaws to notice her nod.

"You're one of them?" asked Diana.

"No," replied Sharon. "I'm not like them. I'm like you."

A chill ran through Diana. Because whatever Sharon was, she wasn't quite human anymore. And Diana was just like her. Only the realization that this was exactly the wrong time for this insight kept Diana from going mad.

The monsters spun around, knocking over tables. The pile of Smorgazes atop the laser eye creature filled half the pool hall, and it continued to expand. This would just keep going on and on if she didn't stop it.

She dug deeper. She had some magic left. There was always more, she realized. She could never run out for long.

She stepped forward and unleashed a thunderclap to get everyone's attention. The Smorgazes and the eye monster stopped fighting.

"Knock it off, you idiots."

The Smorgaz spawn whined. The eye hovered toward her. She sensed its confusion. It threatened to overwhelm her, but only for a moment. She stayed calm, collected. The battle of wills was short because the eye wanted her to help it.

The world shifted. Everything went back to the quiet seconds before the pool hall had erupted into chaos. Because monsters didn't exist. Or at least they shouldn't exist in this reality, and this reality did a bang-up job of erasing their titanic battles. The damage was undone, the building repaired. But it was the people Diana found most confusing. It was one thing to erase their memories. It was another to reconstruct their flesh-and-blood bodies from the ground up. The eyeball monster had disintegrated at least a dozen people. Yet those same people were restored to life.

She wondered if they were the same people or if the

universe had simply built flawless duplicates that would carry on their lives exactly like the originals with no one the wiser. Not even the clones themselves. Invisible imposters manufactured by a reality fighting a never-ending battle against a relentless barrage of weirdness.

Was she one of them herself? She had no way of knowing if she'd been killed in some previous incarnation. Maybe she was Diana mark two. Or three. Or fifteen. Maybe a strange dream she no longer remembered hadn't been a dream at all, but the forgotten last moments of a former Diana.

Vom the Hungering waved a hand in front of her face. "Hey, everything okay in there?" He tried snapping his fingers, but the fur made that difficult.

"Maybe you should try slapping her," suggested the eyeball.

Diana glared at him. "That's not necessary."

"Are you hurt?" asked Sharon, now in human form.

"I'm fine. Just fine."

She moved a few steps away from Sharon. Diana couldn't transform into a monster like Sharon could. But she wasn't so sure she was human anymore either.

"Give her some space, guys," said Sharon.

"No, I'm fine." Diana cleared the haze out of her head. "Just adjusting."

It seemed that was how she spent the bulk of her time now. Adjusting. Dealing with new absurd situations, new strange perceptions. Every time she grew used to one change, another was waiting just around the corner.

She set aside her cue. "I think I need to go home."

"Yeah, sure," said Sharon. "Want me to call you a cab?"

"No, I have a car."

The eyeball hovered forward. "I call shotgun."

"I always get shotgun," said Vom. "Right, Diana?"

Another adjustment. She'd just gained a new cosmic horror. The eyeball, named Zap, sat in the backseat with Smorgaz.

"Are you sure you're okay to drive?" asked Sharon.

"I'm fine, thanks."

Diana tried to shake the image of beastly Sharon from her mind. Vom, Smorgaz, and Zap were relatively easy to accept. They were monsters, plain and simple. Maybe not in personality, but certainly in appearance and origin. But Sharon was a person. A person who could become something monstrous. That seemed more unnatural somehow.

It also blurred the lines. Diana hadn't been aware of it, but subconsciously she'd been making it by convincing herself that, deep down, she was a human being and that all the magical powers, monstrous roommates, and otherworldly perceptions couldn't change that.

Now she wasn't so certain.

"It was nice meeting you," said Diana, though it had actually been quite unpleasant. Although that wasn't Sharon's fault. "Thanks for saving my life."

"You're welcome."

Sharon pulled a card from her pocket and offered it to Diana.

"I want you to have this. I know you're going through some crazy stuff. I've been there. And your friends"— Sharon pointed at the occupants crammed in Diana's car—"I'm sure they mean well, but it'll be easier if you have access to someone who sees it from a human perspective."

Sharon made sense, but Diana wasn't sure if Sharon qualified as human. But Diana wasn't sure she was the right person to make that qualification.

Diana took the card. Mostly to be polite.

"Call anytime," said Sharon.

"Will do," said Diana reflexively as she climbed into the car.

"Can you turn up the air?" asked Zap. "It's a little stuffy back here."

She repressed a frown and gave the creature a bit of advice that had become her lifeline.

"Deal with it."

CHAPTER TWELVE

Back home (though she hesitated to call it that) she entered the building at the same time as the guy from Apartment Number Two. She was surprised to see his dog had allowed him outside. He carefully trod the steps while carrying two overflowing grocery bags.

"Hi," she said. "Need some help?"

"If you're offering." He handed her one. It was full of canned goods and heavier than it looked.

"Want me to carry that for you?" asked Vom.

She decided letting a ravenous monster carry groceries was a bad idea and just soldiered on.

As they walked toward his apartment, she tried to think of something clever to say. Something witty. Something, at the very least, memorable.

"Getting kind of cold outside, huh?"

Chuck, his back to her, kept walking. "Beg your pardon?"

"Outside," she said. "Cold."

"Didn't notice," he replied.

They climbed the short flight of stairs to the second floor. She screwed up her courage and tried again.

"A bit late for grocery shopping, isn't it?"

"I don't pick my schedule," he replied. "Have to take my opportunities when I get them."

At the top of the stairs, she noticed his monster hound was missing from its post at his apartment door.

"Where did it go?" She regretted asking it. She didn't want to step into a sensitive area.

Chuck's response was deadpan.

"Away. It does that sometimes."

The door opened by itself as they approached. He went inside.

She paused on the threshold, waited a few moments for Chuck to reappear. He didn't. She set the groceries down.

Vom inspected the contents of the bag. "Oh, is that salami?"

She glared with disapproval.

"All right, all right." Vom and Smorgaz walked to her apartment just a few feet down the hall.

She glanced down the length of the hall. The dog was still not there.

Diana called into Chuck's apartment. "Hello?"

He didn't answer.

She grabbed the groceries but hesitated. Casually entering one apartment had gotten her into trouble recently.

Perhaps she would be wise to think about it this time.

She scanned the room. Everything looked normal. The décor of the place was difficult to pin down. It was like a designer had cut it into zones, and each tiny zone had its own theme. The couch was from the sixties, bright orange and covered with fringe. The television was a wood-paneled monstrosity from the fifties. The coffee table was a thin, irregular piece of metal that must've been from the future because it floated without any means of support. The flooring was equal parts carpet and wood, broken into a checkerboard pattern.

It didn't look dangerous. But her life was already weird now, and peril was something she was getting used to. She stepped into the apartment. A light, sticky sensation hit her face as she did so, as if she had walked into a spiderweb. Her first instinct was to brush it away, but there was nothing there.

The door started to swing shut behind her. Quietly. If it was hoping she wouldn't notice, it was mistaken. She stopped it with her foot. She found a wedge of cheese in the bag and shoved it under the door. Then she followed the sounds of activity to join Chuck in his kitchen. It was bigger than the living room area. Much bigger. A window cast bright light into the room, but she couldn't see anything outside but the brightness. His back was to her, and he must not have heard her.

"Where do you want this?" she asked.

He jumped, knocking the bag over. Several cans rolled across the counter and clattered on the floor. A can of peas rolled to her feet, and she ducked to pick it up.

"Sorry," she said.

"What are you doing?" he asked.

"I just wanted to know where you wanted me to put this down."

"No, not that. What are you doing in here?"

"Your door was open," she said.

"It was?" He walked past her and checked for himself.

"I propped it open with your cheese," she said. "I hope that's okay."

He glanced at her, then the door.

"It's fine. I guess so, anyway."

He smiled slightly and returned to putting away the groceries. She thought about helping but didn't know where anything went. He was a good-looking guy. Better-looking than she'd assumed from her first impression. Tall, slim but athletic, closely cropped dark hair, and a lantern jaw that was almost cartoonish, but kept just on the right side of that line. He reminded her of Superman. Or his mild-mannered alter ego in a rather poor disguise. Although his eyes were brown. And his nose was a little big. And he had a bit of stubble on his chin. Still, a handsome guy, just her type. Although it was strange to think she had a type at all, since she'd never been romantically linked with a guy like this.

"I just moved in," she said.

"My condolences."

"Oh, it's not so bad. The apartment is nice at least. Not sure how I feel about the monsters, but I've had worse roommates. How long have you been living here?"

Chuck, his back to her, crumpled his grocery bag.

"You should probably go."

"Oh. Okay. Sorry."

She exited the apartment. Chuck followed.

"Sorry to bother you," she said.

He unwedged the cheese from the door. "You aren't bothering me. It's just probably better if you aren't here when he gets back."

"He? Your dog, you mean."

He nodded.

"You aren't allowed visitors?"

He rubbed his chin. "I don't know. Don't get many. Although Stacey and Peter drop by and bring me a baked good every so often."

"Does everyone bake in this building?"

"Stacey turned me on to it. Helps to pass the time."

Chuck smirked. It was a lopsided grin, charming in its imperfection.

"I'm thinking of picking up knitting," she said. "Or maybe juggling."

"Whatever works."

They shared a chuckle that he cut short abruptly.

"He's coming. You should go."

"Okay. It was nice—"

He shut the door.

"—Meeting you."

It was a stroke of cruel irony that she'd finally moved into an apartment across from a good-looking guy who liked to cook, and he was being held prisoner by an inter-dimensional beast hound. It wasn't a problem. Not exactly. But it was irritating as hell.

She walked the few steps to her door. A glance over her shoulder confirmed that the dog was back at its post in front of Apartment Two.

"See you 'round, Chuck," she muttered to herself before going inside to her own monsters.

CHAPTER THIRTEEN

For the first time Diana didn't push her dresser in front of her door when she went to sleep. She had never expected it to be a deterrent to the monsters that shared her apartment, but it had been a psychological bulwark against the tide of madness that threatened to engulf her. It could no longer serve that purpose. She was fairly certain she was crazy already, or at least well on her way.

She awoke staring into a giant tentacled eyeball.

"Hey, you're awake," said Zap.

"I'm awake."

She climbed out of bed. Zap handed her a robe.

"Thank you," she said.

"My pleasure."

Diana wondered how long he had been staring at her

but decided not to ask because there wasn't really a good answer to that question. She'd have to set some boundaries for the new monster, but that could wait until she had some breakfast.

She took a quick shower. When she pulled back the shower curtain Zap was hovering over the toilet. He handed her a towel.

"Get out," she said quietly.

"Yes, ma'am. Right away, ma'am." He darted out of the bathroom.

She got dressed, brushed her teeth, combed her hair.

The monsters were all waiting in the living room. Vom and Smorgaz sat on the couch. Zap floated in a corner.

Staring at her.

That was going to get old real fast, but before she could confront him the doorbell rang. She didn't remember having a doorbell before, but maybe it was new.

It was West. "Do you have a minute, Number Five?"

"Yes."

"Do you have six minutes?"

"Sure."

He counted on his fingers. "Might take up to seven minutes, now that I think about it."

"I have the time," she replied.

"Good. Follow me."

She followed. Any excuse to get out of the apartment. She couldn't shake the sensation that Zap was still watching her.

West read her mind.

"He can't. The building occupies a null point in space-time. A being like your friend cannot see through its walls."

"That's good to know."

West took her downstairs, turning right at a split in the hallway that she was certain hadn't been there before. A layer of gray filth coated the walls. As they went farther and farther down the seemingly endless corridor, the grime grew blacker and thicker until the sludge under her shoes made a sticky squish with every step. She looked over her shoulder, but an inky darkness crawled along behind them. This was not a metaphor. She could see tentacles and gnarled limbs reaching out, dragging the shadows at a slow, steady rate. She wondered what would happen if they caught up.

West must have read her mind again. "They're nothing to worry about. All talk."

She heard them then. Distant, disquieting whispers speaking in insensible languages.

"I wouldn't listen too closely if I were you," said West. "You have a strong constitution for this sort of thing, but they can still screw with you."

Being told *not* to listen only made it harder not to. Most of the whispers didn't register, but several voices tried to spoil the endings of movies for her. They failed, probably because the darkness seemed a little behind on the latest cinema.

Darth Vader is Luke's father. Norman Bates is the killer. Rosebud is a sled.

They reached the end of the corridor before the voices could get to anything more shocking. The door was covered in the same grime. West wiped it from the lock, drew an old-fashioned key from his pocket, and unlocked the door. It opened slowly, and a chill swept from the darkened room on the other side. Hissing fearfully, the shadows retreated from the hall.

He passed over the threshold. Diana paused. She was placing an inordinate amount of trust in a guy who had tricked her into a cursed apartment. She was fairly certain he wasn't human. He might have been at some point, but now he was something else. Something inscrutable, indefinable. Vom and Smorgaz were monsters, but at least they were up-front about it. For all their dark impulses and inhuman qualities, they were more accessible than West.

He spoke from the interior. "This way, Number Five."

The hall behind her stretched off into infinity. She got the distinct impression that if she tried to walk down it without West as her guide, it would swallow her, trapping her in an endless walk. She didn't know where that information came from, but she didn't doubt it. Her only choices were to tarry here outside the door or go inside. She'd come this far. It was a little late to chicken out.

She pushed open the door, expecting a chamber of horrors beyond mortal ken, but it was only another apartment. It was dusty and cluttered with boxes and junk pushed against the walls. The furniture was old and battered. Stains spotted the carpet. The whole place smelled musty and stank of stale pizza rolls.

Music came from somewhere. It filtered through the walls. The distant, atonal tune could've easily been mistaken for random noise but buried underneath its discordant melody lay a hidden harmony that beings from beyond time and space would find comforting. A purely human mind would've found its sanity knocked a smidge ajar in ways that wouldn't have been immediately obvious until it discovered its crippling fear of red shoes and obsession with banana pudding. But Diana only found the music strange and disquieting. And just a touch beautiful.

This should've shocked her, but she had already suspected that she was a little bit crazy at this point. She'd seen too much not to be. Sanity and insanity were just words anyway, and only lunatics obsessed over silly little things like words, she'd decided.

A tall, twisted lamp flickered. Diana wasn't even aware she was reaching for it until West grabbed her by the arm.

"Don't touch anything, Number Five."

For only a moment she saw the lamp as something else. Something indefinable but baleful. A foreign thing that lived to devour whatever souls fell into its flickering trap.

"Mind the rug," said West.

Just a few inches from her right foot a yellowed oval of carpet slowly, almost imperceptibly, crawled toward her. If she stood perfectly still it might reach her in an hour or two. The scratched old coffee table stalked her with the same lack of speed. The paintings stared at her with hungry eyes. The piles of boxes against the walls teetered ever so slightly, trying to work up enough momentum to bury her alive.

Everything here wanted to kill her. Or worse.

"Just stand there," said West. "You should be fine."

He walked to an old recliner. He waved his hand in front of the chair and a phantom materialized. It was a withered, malformed creature with skin indistinguishable from the chair's cracked vinyl.

"Say hello, Number Zero."

The figure opened its mouth. The lips moved. Eight

seconds later, the sound crawled across the room to reach her ears. The word was faint, scratchy.

"Hello."

Zero turned its head toward Diana. Its eyes were two tiny white dots. There was no malice in its expression. Only vacancy.

"I trust I've made my point, Number Five," said West.

She didn't know what that point was, but she nodded. Anything to get out of this dark corner of discarded insensibility.

West wasn't fooled.

"Number Zero wanted power," he said. "I tried to warn him of the consequences of it, but he wouldn't listen. And now here he dwells until the end of this universe. And quite possibly until the end of the next one after that."

She nodded again.

West's hairy eyebrows furrowed, and he snarled. For the first time, she saw his teeth. They were pointy. Like a shark's teeth.

"Don't just nod, Number Five. Listen."

"I am listening," she replied. "I just don't get what you're trying to tell me."

"They never listen. Why do I bother?" He shook his head. "They never listen."

"I'm sick of this," she said. "Everybody is so goddamn mysterious all the time. Nobody just comes out and tells me anything. They always just hint and warn and say cryptic nonsense. Why can't anyone just tell me straight out what they mean?"

"It's not that simple."

"Maybe it is. Maybe you're just trying to make it more complicated."

This time West nodded.

"It's not easy, Number Five. Not easy for me to remember. Remember the way it used to be. Remember the way you see the world. It's been a long time. A long, long time…"

His gaze drifted across the room, fixed on some far-off place.

"Number Zero was like you," he said. "He thought he could accumulate all the power in the universe without anyone noticing. He thought there would be no consequences."

West frowned. His beard writhed ever so slightly.

"There are always consequences, Number Five."

"Uh-huh." Diana nodded politely. "With all due respect, what the hell are you going on about? I'm not accumulating power. I'm just trying to avoid getting eaten by the unholy menagerie you've stuck me with. I took an apartment and had my life turned upside down. I didn't ask for any of this."

"Didn't you?"

"No, I didn't. And don't try to feed me any of that karma or subconscious-desire bull. If life worked like that I'd have gotten a winged unicorn when I was six, and I'd be an astronaut who hunts vampires in her spare time."

West said, "You are not an ordinary person anymore."

"Maybe not, but I'm going to stay as ordinary as I can despite all the strange monsters and supernatural bizarreness your universe is throwing my way. Now can we go? This place is giving me the creeps."

The thing in the chair (she couldn't think of it as a person or as ever having been a person) gurgled at her.

"No offense," she said.

West smiled. "I think there's hope for you, Number Five."

"Damn right," she said. "I can beat this thing."

He chuckled drily.

"Nobody beats it. The crushing weight of madness is a burden no human mind can carry without strain. All victories are temporary, all defeats inevitable."

"That's a cheery thought."

"Just calling it like I see it."

"Well, if I can't avoid it, why bother warning me at all?"

"Because I like you, Number Five. I see something in you that I don't see in many."

"And that something is?"

He shrugged. "Something. If I could've given it a better label, I would've."

They left Apartment Zero behind. The journey back wasn't nearly as unsettling.

"I never said you'd be trapped in the apartment. I wouldn't imagine you will suffer the same fate. There are too many possible dooms in these worlds that I doubt either of us could suspect or imagine the one that will come for you."

"Great," she replied. "Because I'd hate for it to be something predictable and avoidable."

"Be careful, Number Five," West said. "But not too careful."

"I'll keep that in mind."

"You do that." He smiled at her, and she was so taken aback by the expression that by the time she recovered her senses he'd already shuffled back into his apartment.

CHAPTER FOURTEEN

Diana hesitated before knocking on the door. This was a weird building, and everyone who called it home was chained to that weirdness. She'd met only a handful of the residents. They'd all seemed nice, but having all of them crowded into one apartment was perhaps more abnormality than her mind could take. She knew she was going to go mad someday. West had practically guaranteed that, but if she was going to lose her mind, she'd rather put it off for as long as possible. At least one more night.

She pondered what horrors awaited her on the other side of that threshold. Alien beasts? Time warps? Smooth jazz? She couldn't begin to guess. Except for the jazz. She could hear the muffled tones of easy-listening sax.

That alone was almost enough to convince her to turn around and forget the whole thing.

Her monsters changed her mind. They were all so eager to party. She couldn't pull the plug on the evening. Even eternal other-dimensional entities could get bored. Hanging around the apartment, playing cards and watching TV all day had to get old. And a gaggle of monsters in desperate need of a good time would probably be trouble in the long run.

She knocked. Stacey answered the door. She was hosting the horrid bat creature at the moment, and Diana was surprised at how readily she accepted this and annoyed at how unthreatening she found the misshapen hulking woman. Stacey-thing smiled as widely and friendlily as a mouthful of four-inch fangs would allow.

"Diana come to mixer," she said in a guttural growl. "Diana bring friends."

"Yes, I hope that's okay."

A hacking, wheezing racket shook Stacey-thing from deep within her spasming torso. It sounded painful and looked agonizing, and Diana assumed it was a convulsion before she figured out Stacey-thing was chortling with delight.

"More fun, more merry."

"See? I told you they'd be cool with it." Vom sniffed the air, even though he had no visible nostrils that Diana could see. But he didn't have eyes either, and that never seemed to bother him. "Do I smell snickerdoodles?"

"Baked fresh," said Stacey.

Murmuring approval and excitement, the monsters went inside.

Diana held up a loaf of misshapen banana bread. "I

don't have much baking experience," she said by way of explanation and apology.

Stacey seized the offering and gobbled it down. "Banana bread good," she said, spewing crumbs. "You come in now."

Diana had expected the apartment to be a remnant from the fifties to fit with the Ozzie-and-Harriet style of harmless congeniality that Stacey and Peter so effortlessly embodied, but it was remarkably functional and modern. Everything was straight out of the upper end of a Pottery Barn catalogue. Except for the bizarre masquerade masks hanging all over the walls. They were all different shapes and colors, many with twisted and odd designs. Some of them had eyes in them that stared at her, following the action around the room. She pretended that was normal, and maybe it was at this point.

The party was dead. The only guests were Diana's monsters, and they were crowded in the kitchen, devouring cookies and probably baking tins, silverware, and whatever else they could stuff in their mouths. Although Zap didn't have a mouth, so how he was eating anything was a mystery she left unsolved.

"Guys, be careful," she said.

"Oh, let them enjoy themselves," said Peter, rising from the couch. He wore a festive Christmas sweater vest, and he was smoking a pipe.

"So glad you could make it."

"Glad," repeated Stacey-thing.

"Did I get the time wrong?" Diana asked. "I'm not early, am I?"

"No, as a matter of fact, you're fashionably late."

"Fashionably," said Stacey-thing.

"And I see you brought a treat. You really shouldn't have."

Diana shrugged. "It's not very good."

"It smells absolutely delicious. Perhaps I'll try a piece next time."

Stacey-thing stuck out her long, blue tongue and let some of the slimy banana bread fall into her hand. She offered the soggy lump to Peter.

"Good," she cooed.

"Thank you, dear, but I'm saving room for dinner."

She licked her hand and fingers.

"Are people usually late to these things?" asked Diana.

"No, not usually," said Peter. "Usually no one shows up. Except for Keith in Apartment Seven. Have you not met him yet? He's a terrific fellow. Why, if he existed, I'd be tempted to set you two up. A single young lady could do a lot worse."

Diana just nodded. Honestly, being set up on an imaginary blind date didn't sound too bad. If it worked out, she could see herself with two imaginary kids and a fictional dog named Dusty. They'd summer in a floating condo and winter in Shangri-la, take vacations in a hybrid realm where Paris, Disneyland, and Atlantis all merged into one wondrous place. Sometimes she and Dusty the Wonder Dog would solve murders and uncover sinister Martian conspiracies.

The fantasy was running away with itself, but she indulged for a few more seconds.

"Is Keith not in the bathroom, dear?" asked Peter.

"Him not sitting on couch last time I not see him," said Stacey-thing, squinting as she turned her head in an awkward direction.

"Oh yes. There he isn't." Peter pointed to a spot, then pointed to another spot. "Or maybe he's not right there. Well, I know he's not here somewhere. Why don't you have a seat while I make you a drink? I should warn you. My martinis are legendary."

Diana, locked in a rigid posture, sat on the sofa. She placed her hands on her knees. She tried to relax, but this idea hadn't panned out. She hadn't expected much, but this was promising to be the third or fourth most boring party she'd ever been to.

"Nice weather we're having," said someone nearby.

She glanced around but saw nobody. She looked to the nearest mask, and the bloodshot eyes looked back at her. "Did you say something?"

The eyes blinked, then rolled around in what she interpreted as a negative response. She was just guessing, but she assumed that if the eyes could talk, they would have just answered.

"How is the outside world?" asked the voice again. "Did they ever get around to impeaching Nixon?"

Peter was mixing a drink at the minibar while Stacey-thing was entertaining the other monsters in the kitchen. Diana couldn't find the source of the voice, but she decided that she didn't care either. It was just one more inexplicable event. She'd experienced plenty of those recently. Too many to even bother cataloguing at this point.

Stacey passed off hosting of the thing to Peter, who lumbered over with a martini glass delicately clutched in his giant claws. "You drink."

"Thank you." She took the glass and sipped it. It wasn't bad, though she wasn't much of a drinker and had never had a martini in her life, so she couldn't tell if this one qualified as the stuff of legend.

Someone knocked on the door.

"Guests!" growled Peter-thing as he lurched to answer the knock.

"Never really a fan of martinis," said Diana's unseen conversationalist.

Zap floated over and had a seat in a recliner. The eyeball monster laid his tentacles on the armrests and leaned back. "Feels good to take a load off."

"You're doing it again," she said.

"I beg your pardon?"

"You're staring at me."

"I see the multiverse in ways your pathetic senses cannot fathom. If I'm looking in your direction, rest assured that I am not staring *at* you. I'm simply staring *around* you at something much more interesting, at levels of reality that you would find both awe-inspiring and psychosis-inducing."

"If you're staring at the universe, why does it tend to be the universe behind me?"

He blinked. She'd never seen him blink before. Given that his body was more or less one basketball-sized eye, it took longer than a standard blink. At least three times as long. This was still very fast, but noticeably long for a blink.

"The hubris," he said. "The unapologetic egotism. Do you really think that with everything I can see, the worlds upon worlds that fall within my merest glance, that you, a speck of dust floating in a roiling sea of infinite possibilities, would be able to hold my interest for even the briefest, most fleeting of moments?"

Diana folded her arms across her chest and stared down Zap.

"I'm just suggesting that you behold the wonder of that roiling sea of infinity in some other direction. If you don't mind."

"Oh, indeed," said Zap with a sarcastic squint. "Yes, sir! Right away, sir!" He offered a crisp salute with one tentacle. "As you command, so shall it be done."

"Knock it off," she said.

He sputtered, rotated thirty degrees to the right, and focused on one of the masks staring back at him.

Peter-thing approached. When the misshapen host moved to one side, Chuck was revealed.

"New guest. Chuck, this Diana. Apartment Five. Diana, this Chuck—"

"Apartment Two," she interrupted. "We've met."

Peter-thing clicked his fangs together. "Chuck brings pie."

"Just a little something I whipped up," said Chuck.

"Pie good."

Peter-thing was scant moments away from devouring the gift when Stacey snatched it from his hands. "Now, dear. Leave something for our guests."

The creature glared, baring his terrible teeth, flexing his long, claw-tipped fingers.

She rapped him on the knuckles with a wooden spoon. "We still have leftover carrot cake in the refrigerator. Have some of that."

"Did someone mention carrot cake?" asked Vom from the kitchen, already opening the refrigerator. Peter-thing dashed off to scrap with the other monsters for his piece.

"I'm sorry about those guys," said Diana.

"Oh, they're no bother," said Stacey with her unflappable June Cleaver smile. "It's just nice to have company."

She went over to try to keep order among the monsters. If anyone could, Diana figured, it would be Stacey. Chuck sat on one end of the couch.

"Hello," said Zap, waving a tentacle.

Chuck nodded. "Hi."

"So, some mixer," said Diana, without any thought behind the statement. Just something to say.

"Yeah," he replied in his own vague manner.

She opened her mouth, but then shut it. She was about to comment about his evil puppy dog and how it had let him out again, but she assumed he was probably tired of talking about that.

Small talk proved difficult. Every subject seemed either inane or absurd. The problem with being trapped in an abnormal situation, even with company, was that there was no normality to seize hold of to balance things out. A harmless topic was hard to find.

"Seen any good movies lately?" she asked.

"No. Dog won't usually allow me out of the apartment that long, and my TV only picks up Hanna-Barbera cartoons."

"Oh. Well, *Scooby-Doo* can be fun."

"Don't get *Scooby-Doo*," he said with a sour frown.

"*Flintstones*?"

He shook his head.

"*Yogi Bear*?" she tried. "*Hong Kong Phooey*? *Captain Caveman*? *Squiddly Diddly*?"

"No. None of those either." He half-smiled at her. "I don't think I've met anyone who was such a Hanna-Barbera fan."

"I have this tendency to remember unnecessary trivia," she replied. "And yes, I do realize that unnecessary trivia is a redundant phrase. But some bits of trivia are more unnecessary than others, and I assume that knowing nearly every Hanna-Barbera character ever created is probably in the more unnecessary category."

He laughed.

"Well, what do you get?" she asked.

"It varies. Mostly *Galaxy Trio* reruns and the occasional *Speed Buggy* episode. Sometimes, if the planets are in just the right alignment, *Fangface* comes in."

"*Fangface* was a Ruby-Spears production," said Diana. "Not Hanna-Barbera."

"Boy, you weren't kidding about the unnecessary trivia, were you?"

"Everybody's got a talent."

"Just do me a favor," he said. "Don't tell my TV that. *Fangface* may not be great, but I'd hate to lose it."

She put a finger to her lips. "Mum's the word."

"I was always partial to *Grape Ape*," said Zap.

The invisible voice spoke up behind her. "I think it's criminal that *Wait Till Your Father Gets Home* is all but forgotten."

She jumped. It wasn't a big reaction, but Chuck noticed.

"That's just Keith," said Chuck. "He doesn't exist."

"So I've been told."

He tapped his temple with his finger. "It helps not to think about it too much."

She imitated the gesture. "Can do."

They shared a smile. Diana wasn't given to romantic fantasies, but she felt a connection, a spark. She noticed it because she'd so rarely come across it before. They had something going on here. Something undefined, but promising.

Vom came over and plopped onto the sofa between Diana and Chuck, ruining the moment.

"So what are you two crazy kids up to over here?" he asked.

"Flirting, I think," said Zap. "Fascinating ritual, really. I'm not familiar with how the custom proceeds, but I believe they were about to engage in intercourse."

"By all means," said Vom, "carry on. Didn't mean to interrupt."

"Actually," said Smorgaz, "mating usually only proceeds when the female has been properly inebriated to levels that impair her judgment without imminent threat of inducing vomiting."

Chuck excused himself to go to the bathroom.

"Thanks a lot, guys," said Diana.

"Did we do something wrong?" asked Vom.

"Forget it. It's no big deal."

She caught Zap staring at her again. He folded his tentacles and turned his giant eye toward the ceiling.

Stacey and Peter-thing came over with a plate of cucumber sandwiches.

"Everyone behaving over here?" asked Stacey with her warm smile.

"Snack snack," said Peter-thing.

"Don't mind if I do." Vom grabbed two handfuls and devoured them in one gulp. There was one left, and he gently plucked it from the tray and, with one furry green pinky out, moved it toward his mouth. "Uh...anyone want this last one?" he asked.

Nobody did.

"Delicious," he said. "Absolutely delightful. You must give me the recipe."

"It's an old family secret," said Stacey. "My lips are sealed."

"Cucumbers and mayonnaise," said Peter-thing.

She wagged her finger at him, and he recoiled.

"Now, Peter, why would you do such a terrible thing. I don't think I'll ever forgive you."

Peter-thing pouted. His large, red eyes welled up with tears.

"Sorrrrryyyyyy."

"Oh, you know I can never stay mad at you, you silly boy."

Grinning, he leaned forward, and Diana assumed he was about to bite her head off. Instead, they kissed, and the bat-thing switched hosts as their lips touched.

Despite all efforts not to think about it, Diana wondered how the couple managed sex. She could imagine it, but managed, through sheer willpower, not to dwell on the images that went through her head.

"You'll excuse us," said Peter.

When Stacey-thing turned around, he slapped her rump. The thing jumped hosts again, and Stacey giggled.

"Oh, Peter, you naughty boy."

Diana smiled. The couple weirded her out, but they were also kind of sweet at the same time. Take away the bat-creature one of them always had to be, and they probably had the best relationship she'd seen in a long while. They seemed to enjoy each other's company and were making the best of a tough situation. There was something special about that. Weird, but special.

She got up and caught Chuck as he came out of the bathroom.

"Hey, sorry about the monsters," she said.

"Don't worry about it. You get used to that sort of thing around here. And you can't really blame them for getting confused about how our reality works. Hell, I was born here, and I'm still figuring it out."

He ran his hand through his hair, and a few strands fell across his forehead, cementing forever his resemblance to Superman for her. She'd always loved Superman. Never been a fan of the bad boy. The rock-solid, dependable good guy was underrated.

She caught herself staring into his brown eyes. They twinkled.

"You want to grab a drink?" she asked. "I hear Peter is a superb mixologist."

"Don't mind if I do."

Bowing, he indicated he'd follow her, and when they walked he put his hand on her back. Not too high. Not too low. Just the right spot to indicate friendliness without familiarity.

You could keep Batman, she decided. She'd take the Boy Scout any day.

CHAPTER FIFTEEN

Greg stood before the small banquet. He didn't like standing behind a podium, saying it distanced him from his audience, triggering sense memories of long, dull lectures that a lifetime had taught most people to tune out. But Greg had a message to spread, the good word, and for all his faults, for all his smarminess, all his one-dimensional eagerness, he was a believer. That was what bothered Calvin the most about Greg.

He believed.

Over the millennia Calvin had been associated with many people like Greg. The words might change, the setting might differ, but it was all the same. Where once mortals whispered the secret names of unfathomable things in shadowy temples or sacred grottos, they now did so at invitation-only brunches or casual pool parties. Most people who wanted to touch the unknown were drawn to it like moths to a bug zapper. They didn't know why, and they weren't usually smart enough to wonder about it until it was too late.

But Greg believed. He was that rare breed of human capable of understanding a vast universe in which he was just a mote of dust, and not being driven into a deep depression or raving lunacy by that knowledge. It helped that he had a direct pipeline to something bigger than his tiny universe, but even in this Greg wasn't fooling himself. He didn't believe that Fenris cared about him or that, when the time came, the monster-god chasing the moon would even notice him. He only wanted to get what he could from Fenris while he could get it, and it wasn't greed or fear that compelled him. It was the belief that this was the best a mortal could hope for, and that it was his duty to share that information with his fellow specks of dust and help as many as he could, because he was a humanitarian. And Calvin wasn't so certain he disagreed.

Greg's intentions were noble, and he was merely using the tools of his time to spread the word. Calvin still didn't like him, and he was looking forward to the cataclysm. Even if whatever waited for Calvin beyond wasn't worth going to, at least he could avoid these brunches.

He sat at the big table in front of the audience, meaning he had to at least pretend to be listening. It was fortunate Sharon was there to prod him every time he appeared bored.

"Hey," said Greg to his listeners, "do you want to be the best you you can be? Of course you do! We all do!"

He smiled. His teeth were so perfect and white that

they made him look like an artificial being designed specifically for the purpose of smiling, like a toothpaste-pushing robot residing on the precipice of the uncanny valley.

"My friends, a change is coming. A change to this world, a primal revelation, is about to unfold, and believe me, in the new world, how much money you have won't matter. Civilization is an illusion, a delicate gossamer fantasy that will not stand."

Calvin slouched in his chair. He'd heard the speech dozens of times, had every nuance committed to memory. He even had a habit of mouthing silently along without realizing it.

Sharon nudged him with her elbow under the table. They conversed in a series of quick glances. It wasn't telepathic. They'd just had the exchange so many times that saying it aloud was unnecessary.

Stop that, she said with a raised eyebrow.

Nobody cares, he replied with a furrowed brow.

She pursed her lips, nodded toward the audience. *We're sitting in front of people. Sit up straight and try not to look as if you're bored out of your skull.*

But I am bored out of my skull.

Sharon's face went blank. He hated that. He also hated that she was right. Greg didn't ask for much, and in return he gave Calvin a nice place to live, money, and Sharon to take care of all of life's little annoyances. Calvin didn't need these things, but while he was trapped in this world they certainly made his life easier. He'd spent the Dark Ages hiding in a cave. Time had just dragged on and on and on. Video games, movies, books, and other distractions helped to pass the time at least.

He straightened. Smiling, she adjusted his collar.

"The end is coming," said Greg. "Sooner than anyone thinks. But it isn't an end. It's really a beginning, and each of you here has the chance to be a part of it."

He sprang thirty feet across the room, landing on a table with a silent catlike grace. The audience gasped, and a smattering of applause filled the banquet hall.

"No, please, please." He waved away the clapping. "What I just did, there's nothing special about it. I've merely unlocked the potential within myself, the potential within all of us. In the new world, power, real physical power, is what will decide where you stand and who you stand with."

He backflipped into a handstand. He shifted his weight, balancing on one hand.

"You're here because we believe that you have a place with us, because when the time comes we will be the new power to shepherd in the new age. We will be ready. And you will be ready with us."

Greg dismounted from the table. He loosened his tie and strode back to the front of the room with a slow, easy grace. The walk had just a hint of confident swagger. He stopped in a feigned spontaneous moment and touched an old man on the shoulder.

"Come with me, Mr. Francis. I have something wonderful to share with you."

Greg led Francis to the front of the room.

"How would you like to feel better than you have in years? Better, in fact, than you have ever felt in your life?"

He hesitated just long enough to give Francis the chance to reply, but interrupted just as he opened his mouth.

"Of course you would. We all would. There is a secret buried in these bones of yours, and it is a secret we are about to unleash."

He nodded toward Calvin.

"That's my cue," mumbled Calvin, pushing away from the table.

Sharon winked. "Knock 'em dead."

"Mr. Francis, I'd like you to meet a very special person," said Greg. "Don't let his appearance fool you. Our friend Calvin is nothing less than a god, and his merest touch will reveal the glorious future awaiting all of us in this room."

Calvin forced a smile. Not too big. He was supposed to be inscrutable, an unknowable force. He extended his hand. Francis took it. A charge passed from Calvin to the gray-haired man. Francis collapsed in a twitching heap on the stage. The crowd gasped.

That wasn't supposed to happen.

Greg didn't miss a beat. "Relax, friends. This is perfectly usual. Weakness leaves the body reluctantly, but in a moment, you'll see a wonderful change in Mr. Francis."

He glanced at Calvin, who shrugged.

Greg helped Francis to his feet. "Can we get some water for our friend here?" He chuckled. "Can you feel it? Can you sense the power within?"

Francis's wild eyes rattled around in his head, and he gnashed his teeth. He pulled away from Greg, and confusion and rage fell across his face. He was a wild animal, disoriented and baffled by the world around him. A low growl escaped his throat, and he coiled in preparation to spring on Greg.

Greg remained calm. In different circumstances he

would've just punched Francis until dominance was established. This crowd wasn't ready for that. They needed to dip their feet into the savage future, one toe at a time.

With his back to the audience, Greg furrowed his brow and bared his teeth. His eyes went a bright red and glinted with barely concealed savage fury. His teeth grew into fangs. He allowed the wicked claws to extend from one hand, hidden from the crowd. He snarled and took a single threatening step toward Francis.

It was risky. It was possible that Francis would meet the challenge for alpha status head-on. While Greg had nothing to fear if challenged, the crowd would've probably lost interest in what he had to offer. That wouldn't make much difference, but Greg would be disappointed.

Francis proved to be all bark. He cowered before Greg, and the animal within retreated. When Greg held out his hand, Francis took it and stood.

"I'm sorry," he said. "I don't know what came over me."

"It's fine. Everything is just fine." Greg chuckled, patted Francis on the back. "So tell me. How do you feel now?"

"Much better." Francis bounced on his toes. "Better than I have felt in years, actually." He stretched. "And my back...it doesn't hurt anymore."

"Wonderful, isn't it?"

One of Greg's minions sneaked up and knelt behind Francis. Greg planted both hands on Francis's chest.

"It gets better."

Greg gave Francis a shove. The older man stumbled over the minion, but rather than fall flat on his back he flipped over, landing on his feet. Eyes wide, he laughed.

"Marvelous!"

Francis performed a few tentative jumps. With each bounce he sprang a few more feet in the air until he was nearly reaching the ceiling. Then he ran forward, grabbed one of the large banquet tables, and hoisted it over his head.

"Absolutely marvelous!"

His body shook with laughter as he jogged around the room, still carrying the table.

"Yes," agreed Greg, addressing his audience. "Marvelous is exactly the right word. Not miraculous. Because this isn't a miracle. Miracles are capricious. Miracles pick and choose without rhyme or reason by forces on high, but I am offering each and all of you a chance to be part of the new age."

At this point Calvin usually thought about the conglomeration of decaying flesh and bones that was the human species, and how they'd learned to live with that, given no other choice. They might comfort themselves with magical thinking, pretending that the universe was made just for them, or at the very least convincing themselves that they were an important and vital part of a vast cosmos. But most of them didn't honestly believe this, even with the benefit of miserably short lives and wholly ineffective perceptions of a universe more complicated and fantastic than they could ever comprehend.

He'd usually follow this by contemplating his lot. From a cosmological perspective he was a far greater being than anything born in this humble nook of reality. He was immortal and privy to truths the human race would probably never be ready for. But he was still just as much a prisoner as anyone in this room, on this world, in this universe. And after all of them were dead and gone, he'd still be here, tangled in a reality that held him in its unbreakable embrace. That this universe was no happier with the situation than he only made it more annoying. It seemed no one, not the humans, Calvin, Fenris, not the smallest grain of sand nor the universe itself had any control over its fate.

The realization, one that Calvin had had countless times before, never ceased to annoy him.

This time that chain of thought was derailed by Francis's boisterous, increasingly frenzied laughter. It walked on the edge of madness as he dashed around the room like a man possessed. Greg was too deep into his routine to notice, and it wasn't unusual for the sudden influx of power to fill the recipient with glee. This was different. Francis was losing control.

He flipped a table over, sending its contents flying in every direction. He seized a woman and pulled her roughly to him and planted a kiss on her worthy of a lusty pirate from a romance novel.

"Now see here," said the woman's husband, rising to defend his wife's honor.

Francis punched him in the face, breaking his jaw. He threw aside the woman like a forgotten prize and eyed the room like a caged animal let loose on the world. In his primitive perception everything boiled down to fight or flight, and the rage in his contorted face told everyone which option he'd chosen.

He ripped out of his skin, changing into a hulking, four-armed beast with a caricature of a head that was nothing but a set of massive jaws and flesh-ripping teeth.

Like a whirling typhoon of destruction Francis

charged through the banquet hall, smashing and clawing at anything and everything within reach. There were screams. Screams and blood. And brutal, merciless savagery that was thankfully cut short when several of the established temple members burst into their own savage forms and pounced upon the mad Francis.

Calvin just watched, transfixed by the sight. The primal order Greg had preached was here, and the humans found themselves in the unwilling role of prey. At least six or seven were dead or nearly dead, having been attacked in the few moments Francis had run amok. Others cowered in absolute terror or ran, shrieking, out of the building.

This was the future of humanity.

The cult members dragged Francis before Calvin. Though they were every bit as strong as Francis, he was the more primitive, more furious soul, and they were having a hell of a time keeping him under control. He flailed and snapped, growled and hissed. It was mesmerizing. Calvin wondered if this was all because of what he'd put into the human, or if the human had had this inside all along and Calvin had only given it permission to arise. Was civilization humanity's creation? Or humanity's lie? He had no way of knowing.

"Well don't just stand there," said Greg. "Do something."

Calvin stepped toward the snarling Francis. Calvin was invulnerable and immortal, but he found himself put off by Francis's savage frenzy. He put his hand on Francis's muzzle and felt the jump of power. Except it was going the wrong way. Francis doubled in size and cast off the beasts constraining him. He grabbed one of the cultists in a hand and bit her in half.

The other beasts jumped back. Everyone but Calvin. The giant creature that had been Francis leaned forward and snorted. It screeched at Calvin, who let its rancid breath wash over him. Bits of blood, fur, and gore splattered his face.

Calvin had nothing to fear, and without fear to feed it the creature was confused. It sniffed curiously at him. He put a hand on its nose and smiled.

"Sit."

The monster did as commanded.

"Good boy."

He gave it one more reassuring pat on the muzzle. For now the creature was dominated, but there was only one way to get it out of Francis. It had to be scared out, reminded of its place in the cosmic order.

"Sorry about this."

Calvin laid an uppercut across Francis's face. Several giant teeth were knocked loose, and the creature tumbled over with a stifled whimper. It shrank into its human form.

"What the hell was that?" asked Greg.

"I don't know," said Calvin. "Something went wrong."

Greg kept his voice calm and steady, as always, but an edge danced around his enunciations. "Brilliant. Something went wrong. That's your explanation, is it? Something went wrong. Do you know how hard this will be to clean up? And this isn't going away on its own."

Calvin's destructive influence on reality was rarely permanent. Sometimes a few small things slipped through, but for the most part, as a foreign element, his corrosive power was quickly countered by the universe's innate dislike of his unnatural presence. But occasionally the universe was fooled into accepting the damage. Usually by a secondary agent slipping under the radar. Francis must have qualified as that agent.

And now people were dead.

Calvin didn't know how to handle that. He'd been walking on this planet for a long, long time, but he'd rarely been responsible for the death of anyone. And in most of those cases the death and destruction had been impermanent, shadows edited out of existence.

But these people were staying dead, and in the very near future they'd be the lucky ones.

CHAPTER SIXTEEN

"I don't see what kind of future you can have with this guy," said Vom.

Diana paused in the application of her eyeliner. She couldn't talk and put on makeup at the same time. She didn't wear makeup enough to have gotten to that level of skill.

"Who said anything about a future together? I'll be lucky if one of you doesn't eat me by the end of the month."

"I resent that."

"I didn't mention you specifically. I could've been talking about Zap."

"But you weren't talking about Zap," said Vom. "You were talking about me."

"You're right. I was. And I'll apologize right now if you look me in the eye and say that you weren't thinking about eating me then or right now."

"I don't have eyes," he said.

"Isn't that convenient?"

"Okay. You got me. I was thinking about eating you then. I was thinking about eating you when I first met you, and I've been thinking about eating you every day since. But I think about eating all the time. An hour ago I almost ate Zap when his back was turned."

Zap piped up from the other room. "Not cool, dude!"

"Yeah, yeah." Vom shrugged. "The point is that just because I'm thinking about eating you doesn't mean I'm going to."

"Maybe you won't," she replied. "But if you don't devour me then Smorgaz will probably smother me beneath an avalanche of clones. Or Zap will disintegrate me. I'm not saying it'll happen on purpose, though I expect it will because, as you just pointed out, you—all of you—have innately destructive natures that you are struggling against every day. And all it takes is one slip, and it's over."

Vom said, "You're exaggerating."

"No. I'm not. And even if one of my roommates doesn't kill me then some other confused beast from beyond will. And if by some miracle that doesn't happen then I'm practically guaranteed to either go stark raving mad or be deemed too dangerous to exist and be shoved into exile in Apartment Zero. And I'd most definitely prefer to be eaten or zapped or smothered over that anyway."

Vom stepped toward her. She thrust her mascara wand at his reflection.

"Don't get any ideas now."

Vom smiled innocently.

Diana continued, "And let's not forget that Chuck—who does appear to be a nice, funny, and handsome guy—has a vicious little creature of his own that keeps him locked in his apartment for days on end. And that he'll probably either die a violent death at the hands of that monster, or go insane, or end up in Apartment Zero."

"So you're just looking for a good time then?" asked Vom.

"I don't know what I'm looking for. I'm just taking it one day at a time. So could you let me enjoy this?"

Vom said, "Fair enough."

She finished putting on her makeup, checked herself in the mirror one last time. It'd been a while since she'd put on her little blue dress. It looked good, but a touch on the formal side of casual. If they had been going out, even if only to a movie or a restaurant, then it would've been a good choice, but she wondered if it was too much for a dinner in his apartment. Maybe jeans would've been a better choice.

She was halfway to her closet when she decided she was overanalyzing. Jeans and a nice top might've been more appropriate, but this was a date. She hadn't been on a date in a while, and if she wanted to wear her little blue dress, she'd wear it.

She gave her inhuman roommates instructions not to wait up and walked down the hall to Chuck's apartment. The dog was at the door. It made a peculiar gurgle, and its long, barbed tail whipped in dangerous circles as she approached. The creature moved to one side as she approached.

"Thank you," she said. For a hideous demon from beyond, it was almost cute.

She knocked on the door, and Chuck answered.

He wore a T-shirt and slacks. For a moment she considered excusing herself and changing, but from the way his gaze lingered on her she knew he liked what he saw. This dress did do amazing things for her. She had a good figure, but the dress pushed things in the right directions and gave her narrow hips a little extra oomph. She was also wearing a push-up bra, which she knew was cheating. But she'd yet to meet a guy who cared once the illusion was unclasped. If it even came to that. She was getting ahead of herself.

"You're early."

"Traffic was light."

Chuck smiled. He ran his fingers through his hair, and a forelock fell across his brow.

He stepped aside and let her in.

"Something smells good," she said.

"Lasagna," he replied.

"Great. I love Italian."

"That's good, because it's really the only thing I can cook."

While he checked on the meal she relaxed on the sofa and took stock of the mishmash of styles in his apartment. The floating coffee table interested her the most. She tested its stability by pressing one hand against it, then two. Lightly at first, then harder. It didn't budge. She tested the underside, but it remained steady.

"Yeah, I can't figure out how to move it," he said. "Can't move any of the furniture actually. Although sometimes when I'm not looking it changes. That sofa is only a few weeks old. Before that it was a rocking chair."

"Do you think it makes any sense?" she asked.

"They're both designed for sitting."

"Not that. Not just that anyway." Diana made a sweeping gesture. "Any of this."

"I don't know. Maybe." He offered her a glass of wine. "Maybe it all fits together on a cosmic scale that we'll never be able to understand. Could be that there's a master plan going on, and we're just bumbling our way through it. Or it could all be chaos, entropy, and any sense we try to make of it will only be the elaborate fantasies of small, inadequate perceptions. Either way, I don't see how we'd be able to perceive the difference."

"You've thought about this a lot," she said.

"You haven't?"

They clinked their glasses together in a toast.

"How could you not?" she said.

"You'll want it to make sense," he said. "You'll never stop wanting that. But after a while you realize that it doesn't matter. You just take things day by day and don't expect order. You just hope for some semblance of stability."

"Yeah. That's what I miss most. Stability. Predictability. I don't know if the real world is any more sensible than this, but it was at least steady. Now everything's up in the air. If I went back to my apartment and found everything had turned purple, I probably wouldn't even bat an eye at this stage. But it's still hard to get comfortable when everything can be topsyturvy in a moment."

She gulped down the wine and licked her lips.

"Wow. Don't normally like wine, but this is yummy."

He poured her another glass. She swallowed this with

another swig. A drop ran down the corner of her mouth and she dabbed at it with her finger, then sucked the moistened fingertip with a satisfied sigh.

Chuck looked away like he'd caught her in the middle of an intimate moment.

"Sorry," she said. "I guess this is really good wine."

"I guess so."

She chuckled. He joined her, and the awkwardness dissolved.

"Want some more?" he asked.

"No, I'm good. Two glasses is my limit." Diana eyed the bottle. "Well, one more glass wouldn't hurt anything."

A timer buzzed in the kitchen, signaling the lasagna's readiness. She watched him pull it out of the oven.

"It'll probably be too hot to eat," he said. "We'll have to let it cool down."

"It smells too good," she said, presenting her plate. "I can't wait."

"Okay, but don't get mad at me if you burn your mouth."

"Can I even do that anymore? I'm told I'm immune to conventional harm now."

He dropped a slice on her plate.

She frowned. "Oh, come on. Don't be stingy. I'm starving."

He served her more, and when her frown remained he gave her another slice. Her mouth watering, she pulled away the heaping plate, grabbed a dirty fork out of the sink, and started eating.

"Did you skip lunch?"

It took Diana a few moments to chew all the food

jammed in her mouth. "No, I'm just hungry for some reason. This is really good by the way."

"Thanks. It's an old recipe my dad—"

She threw open his refrigerator. "Got anything to drink?"

"Uh, sure. There should be—"

"V8? Can't stand the stuff." She grabbed a bottle, opened it, and chugged a healthy portion. Some of it dribbled down her chin. Red drops stained her little blue dress.

"Oh great." Diana yanked at the dress, pulling it to her lips.

She was making an unpleasant sucking noise when she looked up and noticed Chuck was watching her with a slight, yet noticeable, revulsion.

"Oh, jeez. I'm sorry. I don't know what's gotten into me. Just really hungry all of a sudden, that's all."

"I noticed."

They took a seat at the table. Diana pushed her appetite to manageable levels and forced herself to eat at a leisurely pace. It was surprisingly hard to do.

"This is really good."

"You said that already," he remarked flatly. "Several times."

"Did I?" She speared a small bite, stuck it in her mouth, and chewed. "Sorry, but I'm just really hungry."

"You said that too."

Her stomach growled, and they both pretended not to hear it.

The conversation went flat after that. Neither said much of anything for several minutes. She kept trying to think of something to get everything back on track, but the only subjects that came to mind were lasagna-related. Whenever he spoke, she was usually too busy chewing to offer more than a nod and a murmur.

She had three servings. Three heaping servings. She emptied the lasagna pan in the time it took him to finish off his one plate. The more she ate, the hungrier she seemed to get. She tried to ignore the problem, hoping it would go away on its own. When she accidentally ate her own fork, she decided the problem wasn't one that could be ignored.

Diana studied the stub of silverware in her fingers. She'd sheared it off at the handle, and was chewing the prong end. The metal had a peculiar tang, not altogether unpleasant. And since half a fork wasn't much good to anyone, she went ahead and finished it off.

By now Chuck had stopped registering the weirdness of it.

"Maybe I should leave," she said.

"Maybe."

"I'm sorry."

"There's nothing to be sorry for. You said it. There's always something new to deal with."

He smiled at her, gave her a slight hug that was friendly without being presumptuous. He really was a great guy, and she almost convinced herself that she could just ignore her hunger pangs and push on with the date. Then her stomach rumbled.

"Excuse me."

She rushed over to her apartment, threw open the door. The monsters were sitting in the living room, watching television. Except Vom.

"Where is he?" she asked.

They pointed toward the kitchen.

"Of course he is."

She found Vom the Hungering hunched over the counter, spreading tuna salad on bread.

"What are you doing?"

"Making a sandwich," he said. "Want one?"

"No, I don't want a sandwich, and don't play dumb. You're doing something to me."

The furry green creature swallowed the sandwich in one bite and started making another. "Sure you don't want one?"

"Don't try to distract me."

"If I were trying to distract you, I wouldn't be offering to feed you." He held out a plate of a dozen sandwiches and offered it to her. "Eat. Trust me. You'll feel better."

She grabbed one and bit into it. It tasted so good. It was the best sandwich she'd ever eaten. The best sandwich anyone had ever eaten, she decided.

"The secret ingredient is whipped cream," said Vom. "Also, I find that sawdust adds a delightful texture."

She rolled her tongue around her mouth and nodded. He was right.

"You know what would be good with this," she said. "Copper. I think I have some pennies on my dresser."

"Intriguing."

Diana went to retrieve the coins, but she made it only a few steps before stopping herself.

"Am I seriously thinking about eating pennies?"

"Is there anything you're considering not eating?" asked Vom.

She performed a thorough mental scan and found that anything she thought of, no matter how bizarre or unappetizing, seemed reasonable to consume. She tried not to dwell on anything too disgusting, even as her mouth watered.

"I wouldn't eat shag carpeting." The insight both pleased and revolted her.

"Good. Although shag carpeting is pretty tasty if I do say so myself."

She joined him at the table and forced herself to eat a sandwich with slow, deliberate bites. Just the act of eating seemed to relax her. The functional grace of the chewing motion as her jaws worked. The wonderful transformative process where something was destroyed only to become part of something else. She'd taken it for granted her entire life, but she felt the particles dancing between her teeth, skipping lightly on her tongue, sliding down her throat. It was erotic and holy, pure and primal. It was beautiful, a sacrament.

"Oh God." She closed her eyes, tasting every element of her meal. She was closer to an orgasm than she wanted to admit.

"It's transference," said Vom.

"Stop it."

"I can't. It's not something I'm doing. It's just something that happens sometimes. When the conditions are right."

"What conditions?"

"I don't really know. It's not like I have a manual on this."

"It's like I'm hungry, and I know that I can never satisfy that hunger but I have to try anyway." She grabbed another sandwich and gobbled it down without concern over table manners. "How do you live like this?"

"I was made hungry, and I'll always be hungry. It's just something I deal with."

"That must suck."

"It's not always easy," he said, "but it is my natural state of being. I've always thought it must suck to be a decaying bag of flesh that is constantly struggling against entropic forces that will eventually cause all your systems to break down into their component matter and then be redistributed, reprocessed, and repeated in an endless struggle against the chaos you deny is waiting to consume you."

"Hadn't thought of it like that," she admitted.

"Why should you? It's like being a frog enjoying the taste of flies. It's not something the frog has to think about. It's just something it accepts."

Vom beat her to the last sandwich. He opened wide to swallow it, then stopped, tore the sandwich in two, and handed one half to her.

"Thanks. I know how hard that was for you to do."

"Not as hard as you think," he said. "Sure, where I came from, when I was just a single-minded eating machine, it would've been impossible. But the transference process works both ways. You might have my appetite, but I have your self-control, your empathy."

She chuckled. "Never thought of myself as having much self-control before."

"Most humans have infinitely more self-control than we horrors do. It's how your species functions, bred into you. You need it to have a civilization. Where I come from, civilization isn't even a word."

"What's it like?" Diana didn't expect to understand his answer, but she was just trying to distract herself from the gnawing hunger. Eating kept it in check, but it didn't seem to satisfy the endless appetite within her, which seemed stronger than before.

"Sometimes it's hard to remember," said Vom. "Probably because memory itself is something else I've borrowed from you. The laws of physics as you know them don't exist. It's a much smaller place. Only a single planet and a handful of stars. Everything springs into existence from molten pools of primordial goop, where it immediately begins the process of devouring and avoiding being devoured. And there, I am a god. Of sorts. In a reality where everything lives to eat everything else, I am at the top of the heap. I sit on the great mountain and things kill each other just for the right to crawl into my gullet."

"Sounds nice."

"Believe it or not, it was. Especially if you're lucky enough to be the devourer and not the devoured. It was what I was made for, and I was good at it. Then I fell into the void between worlds and ended up here, with all the accompanying baggage that goes with it. Existence here is a lot more complicated, and I still don't know if that's a good thing or not."

She could relate. Right now sitting on top of a mountain, having people throw an infinite supply of cheeseburgers down her throat, sounded pretty damn appealing. Knowing that this wasn't her, but coming from Vom, only made her realize how alien life in this reality was for him.

"I'm sorry," she said.

"Apology accepted." He took the plate and swallowed it. "Sorry about what?"

"I'm sorry that I didn't understand how hard this must be for you."

He nodded. "Yeah, I guess I should apologize to you for the same thing."

"There has to be a way to get you back there."

"I'm sure there is. And I'm sure one day I'll go back. I am infinite. I have all the time in this universe and the next. But I sometimes worry that when I do go back I really won't be the same. Eating everything sounds great. It does. But I'll miss being able to talk to people and think about things. People don't like talking to primal devouring gods. They mostly chant placating dirges and scream."

Vom held out his furry palm. "Give me your hand."

"Why?"

He offered a close-mouthed smile, and she knew he did so to hide his many rows of sharp teeth. "Trust me. Just this once."

Against her better judgment, she put her hand in his. A spark stung her fingers, leaving her hand numb. And just like that, she wasn't hungry anymore.

"You took it back."

"I don't know how long it'll last, but it might be long enough to finish your date. Hope you don't mind, but I borrowed some of your self-discipline too. Just to make things more bearable."

"If it means never being hungry like that again, you can take it all."

Diana stood, collected her thoughts. She wasn't hungry anymore, but she felt stuffed and bloated. Now that Vom had taken back his hunger, she wondered if he'd taken his omnivorous nature with it. She hadn't been worried about the fork or the sawdust or the whipped cream when eating them, but now they sat in her gut like a lump.

Vom assured her that everything would be fine. "Go on. Have a good time. We'll be here when you're done."

She wasn't about to let a queasy stomach end her date at this stage. She pushed away from the table and stood, and when she didn't throw up or fall to the floor in crippling pain she counted herself lucky.

"Thanks, Vom."

The fuzzy green monster shrugged as he rummaged through the refrigerator. "It's no big thing."

Having held even the smallest sliver of his ravenous appetite, she understood how overwhelming it could be, and how being free of even a tiny bit of it was a relief. If the positions had been reversed and she could've given away the burden, she wouldn't have been able to take it back.

"Yes, you would have," he said.

She almost reprimanded him for reading her mind again, but that wasn't his fault.

"Go on," he said between gulping down whatever he could get his hands on. "Have fun."

She left him to his appetite and returned to Chuck's. He opened the door.

"Oh," he said with a note of surprise. "Everything okay?"

"Everything's great," she said with a shade too much enthusiasm.

"Glad to hear it."

He looked so damn handsome and huggable that she did just that. She didn't plan it, and she didn't plan the kissing either. She eventually pulled away, feeling a bit embarrassed. Or thinking she should've been embarrassed. Only she wasn't.

Embarrassment came from being afraid of embarrassment. Like a snake eating its own tail, if you had no embarrassment to feed it, it just slunk away into the nether whence it was spawned. It also came from fear of putting others in an awkward position, and it was clear that Chuck had liked the kiss as much as she.

He grinned. His face was a little flushed.

She waited for him to respond. To seize her passionately and sweep her off her feet. At the very least to say, "Thank you." Instead he bit his lip. He moved his hands in small motions that didn't go anywhere.

Diana didn't feel bad about it. She wasn't herself. Although that wasn't true. She was exactly the same except for a few slivers of self-control that Vom had borrowed from her. While self-discipline was a good thing when it came to stopping yourself from eating the universe, it could sometimes hold you back from doing what you really wanted to do, and she'd been wanting to do that for a while now.

"Sorry."

She turned. He grabbed her by the arm.

"Wait. I—"

Diana fell into his arms and kissed him again.

Neither was surprised by it this time.

CHAPTER SEVENTEEN

Fenris's anguished howl awoke Diana.

She was getting used to it. It happened at least once a night. She was careful not to wake up too fast, to avoid ending up in the nightmare world of the dream eaters. The trick was to keep your eyes closed, to let unconsciousness fall away like a layer of whispery veils.

She opened one eye and glimpsed a shadow slinking away into the darkness. By the time she dared look around, it was gone to the otherworld or imagination that spawned it. She sat up, looked at Chuck.

She didn't regret sleeping with him. He was a good guy. Maybe it was a bad idea getting involved with a guy like this, saddled with his own weird problems, but she'd worry about that tomorrow.

Diana was hungry now. She'd been hungry for a while. It was the hunger as much as Fenris's pain that had woken her. She got up and went to the kitchen to find something, anything, to eat.

Somewhere along the way she got lost. She must've taken a wrong turn because she found herself standing on the shores of paradise. The transition was subtle enough that she didn't notice until her feet were wet. The cold liquid between her toes caused her to jump back. Her first instinct was to expect something horrible. Slime or blood or the pools of drool of a horrible creature.

It was only water. An endless blue ocean stretched out to the horizon. A golden beach rested under her feet. And a lush forest grew only a few yards away. The sun warmed her face. It was like a dream.

But it was real.

It was beautiful. Not just because of the pristine waters and the forest. It was all so ordinary. The water and sky were blue. The sun was neither too big nor too small. The trees were recognizable, with green leaves. Seagulls passed overhead, and the air was fresh and pure.

She didn't question it. She was positive that soon enough a giant squid would rise up out of the ocean or the sand would come alive and attempt to eat her. But for now she was content to pick some berries off the bushes and eat them while enjoying the view.

"You don't belong here, Number Five," said West from behind her.

"I was wondering when you'd show up to ruin everything." She held out her hand. "Berry? They taste like chocolate."

He passed.

"What's wrong with this place?" she asked.

"Nothing. It's an unspoiled realm, where everything lives in harmony. There's death here. And chaos. Enough to make it viable. But for the most part it's a world at peace."

"No people, huh?"

"Oh, there's people. Not humans. But close enough. And they're really quite pleasant. They follow a philosophy of cooperation, respect among individuals, and moderation in all things. You'd hate them."

"I get it. This isn't a world I can live in." She smiled slightly. "Not really made for me."

"Technically, you're not made for it. But that's close enough."

"Nice place to visit, though."

He nodded. "Yes, it is."

"How can a place like this exist at all? From what I've seen so far the universe is a big, ugly place. There has to be something I'm missing. Something bad about it. Doesn't there?"

"You still don't understand," said West. "Just because the forces of the universe are indifferent to you that doesn't make them malignant. They're not out to destroy you or drive you mad. They just don't care. Paradise exists, as your human mind defines it. In a thousand different worlds, in a thousand different forms. As do ten thousand hellish realities and everything in between."

"Well, that's just keen."

She scooped up a handful of sand. It ran through her fingers. Trying to hold on to the grains was impossible, just like trying to hold on to this beach.

A swarm of bugs blew past her face. She brushed them

aside, only to have more appear. She felt more of the things crawling up her legs. They were in the sand. Thousands of them.

So much for paradise.

Diana jumped to her feet. The bugs seemed harmless. They hadn't stung her yet, but she shooed them away, swatting at her arms and legs. She ran a few steps, and they stopped pursuing her.

She wiped the dead bugs from her hands and pajamas. Some had gotten in her mouth. She spat those out, rolled her tongue around to look for more.

A single gnat landed on her nose. She was about to crush it when she noticed that it wasn't a bug at all.

It was a tiny, tiny person. No bigger than a gnat. Too small to make out in great detail, but if she squinted she could see its humanoid shape.

"Oh my God."

The corpses of a few dozen of the tiny winged people stuck to the backs of her hands.

"Oh my God."

The sand churned with life. Hundreds of thousands, millions of the creatures, had been brought to the surface. Clouds of the winged ones circled her.

"I'm sorry. I didn't mean to. I didn't think..."

They couldn't understand her. Even if they could, an apology wouldn't do any good. West had told her she didn't belong here, and now she knew why.

His legs were covered in the tiny people. He stood perfectly still, and she followed his example. If she didn't move, she couldn't do much damage.

"I warned you that you wouldn't like the people of this world," he said.

They were just bugs, she told herself. Weird bugs with human bodies, but bugs nonetheless. And it was just an accident. It wasn't her fault. It wasn't as if she'd asked to be here. It was all a cosmic mistake.

The people—damn it, that was the only way she could think of them now—crept up her feet and ankles while flocks of the flying ones hovered around her head.

"Go away," she said. "I don't want to hurt you."

But she had. Her slightest step, her most careless gesture could destroy thousands. Intent was irrelevant. The damage was done. She was become Diana Malone, destroyer of worlds.

The sickening realization punched her in the gut.

The people continued to swarm around her. She didn't know if they were trying to defend themselves or merely confused. She couldn't know. Just like they couldn't fathom why she would attack them without provocation.

"What do I do?" she asked. "West?"

She turned her head slowly in his direction, but he was gone.

It took every ounce of willpower to stay still as the teeming millions crawled over her. She closed her eyes. That only made it worse. It allowed her to concentrate on the unpleasant sensation across her skin.

Diana broke. It was too much. She couldn't take it. She had to get away. Some place where she wouldn't do any damage, where she could escape the hordes. She ran across the beach, every step crushing hundreds, swinging her arms in wild deadly arcs, slicing through the swarms with deadly grace.

She tripped, falling flat on her face.

She spat out sand and wiped the genocide from her face.

There was a palpable snap throughout the universe. She heard the pop as she was ejected from the beach and onto Chuck's kitchen floor.

She pushed to her knees. Most of the tiny people had been left behind. Only a few corpses remained on her pajamas and the tile. Not all had been killed, though. Some of the people skittered across the floor while others hovered in confusion. She'd dragged them from their paradise to a hostile place.

They flew off to explore their strange new universe. She hoped they had a better time of it than she had.

She carefully swept up the dead, collecting them all in a plastic bag she found. There had been billions of the creatures. Trillions of them. This handful of a few dozen souls, smashed by her carelessness, didn't amount to much. But they hadn't asked for this, didn't deserve it.

In the morning she buried them in the park.

CHAPTER EIGHTEEN

For her second date with Chuck, Diana had her self-control back. She still ended up sleeping with him. Once the genie was out of the bottle, she couldn't think of a reason to go backward.

They lay in his bed. The previous night it'd been a water bed. Or something like a water bed. The liquid within hadn't moved like water. There was a rhythm that reminded her more of something breathing. She decided not to overthink it, though, and just to pretend it was a water bed.

Tonight the bed had changed, as he had mentioned his furniture had a tendency to do, into an asymmetrical oval covered in yellow fuzz.

She'd been picking up a weird vibe from Chuck all

night. She assumed at first that she'd been imagining it, but it remained. He was awkward, on edge. Something was bothering him. At first she didn't assume it had anything to do with her. They'd only been on one date at this point, and he must have had other things going on in his life. So she played it cool, and just enjoyed being in his arms. Cuddling was one of the few things that reminded her of what it was like to be human.

"I've had a great time," he said.

She laughed. "I should hope so."

"Oh, I didn't mean it like that." Chuck hugged her tighter. "You're great. You really are."

Diana let the statement sit there for a minute.

"Are you breaking up with me?"

"What? No." He repeated himself, more emphatically. "What? No! No!"

She moved away from him.

"Are you sure? Because I've done this before. Seems awfully familiar. You get one last screw in and then you drop the hammer."

Chuck put his hand on her cheek and looked into her eyes. "I'm not breaking up with you."

"It's no big deal," she said. "We've only been on a couple of dates. Not like it's serious yet. I'm not sure an official breakup is even necessary."

He pulled her closer, gave her a kiss. She moved closer to his naked warmth.

"I'm just saying it's okay if you've decided you're sick of me."

"Stop it."

"We're both adults."

"Just stop."

They made out, accompanied by some heavy petting. He rested his hands on her butt, and she debated whether to wait for him to signal the start of something more serious or if she should just go for it herself.

"Drop the hammer?" He chuckled.

"Don't laugh." She playfully tousled his hair. "It's happened to me. Twice."

"Twice, huh?"

Diana mumbled. "Okay, once. The second time I did it."

"You dropped the hammer?"

"Yes, I dropped it." She said, "I was a bad girl, and took advantage of someone for one last sexual escapade even though I knew I was going to dump him at the end of the night."

"I had no idea you were such a bad person."

"Oh, I have a dark past." She got up, threw on a robe, took a detour into the kitchen. She found a slice of carrot cake in the fridge, which she started eating.

Chuck, in sweatpants, stood in the archway.

"Sorry." She sheared off a small portion with her fork and took a bite, being very careful not to eat the silverware. "Mind if I eat this?"

"All yours. Still having appetite problems?"

"Comes and goes, but it's mostly under control." She held out her fork to him. "Want some?"

"No thanks. I'm good."

He sat across the table and watched her eat. She wasn't uncomfortable with that, but it did keep her from really enjoying herself. When she was finished she picked off a few stray crumbs but resisted the urge to lick the plate for any cake residue invisible to the naked eye.

"I don't know how you do it," he said.

"Do what?"

"Live with it. With them. Those things that share your apartment."

"It's not so bad. At least they let me out whenever I want. Not like your little monster." She regretted saying it almost immediately. "I'm sorry. That sounded kind of mean, didn't it?"

"No. It's true. I can't control the damn thing. You manage three, and I can't even figure out how to live with one."

"Maybe yours is harder to control than mine are."

"No, it's not that. You come and go whenever you like to my place. It doesn't bother you at all."

"Maybe it's because I don't let him bother me," she replied. "You have to be firm. You have to remember that he's probably not any happier with the situation than you are. Empathy goes a long way."

"You want me to empathize with that beast?"

"Couldn't hurt." She took his hand from across the table. "Having met a few of these..."

She hesitated to use the word *monster* to describe them. They were monstrous in appearance. They didn't view the world as humans did. Yet *monster* seemed too harsh, too black-and-white.

"They're just trying to get by. In a perfect universe they'd be in their reality, and we'd be in ours, and everyone would be happy. But that's not the way it works."

"Well, why doesn't it?"

She laughed. He didn't.

"Don't ask me," she said. "But you just deal with it. Isn't that what you told me on our first date?"

Chuck pulled his hand away from hers.

"How can you be so calm about it? Doesn't it drive you nuts?" The edge was back in his voice. "Every day it's out there, on the other side of that door. Just waiting. I used to wonder why it didn't just kill me. After a while I wished it would. Anything to get out of here."

She rose, put her arms around him. "Take it easy. It'll be okay."

"You really don't get it, do you? We're trapped here." He laughed. A soft, bitter sound that unsettled her. "You should go."

"What's wrong?"

"Nothing. Just get dressed and go. Please."

He went into the bathroom and she heard the lock click. There was no arguing with that.

Diana put on her clothes and went back to her place.

"You're home early," said Vom. "Trouble in paradise?"

"Give it a rest, Vom."

She slammed her bedroom door shut.

CHAPTER NINETEEN

Every apartment came with a price. West lived in Number One and was the keeper of the building's many secrets. He was responsible not just for keeping the building happy but for safeguarding reality from all manner of bizarre, unknowable threats. Very few of these threats were in the destroy-the-world category. That would've been far too simple.

Reality was a flexible thing, easily bent, but not easily broken. It had its own ways of protecting itself from such ordinary threats as apocalypse. But that every day the human race woke up to discover the dinosaurs were still extinct, the speed of light hadn't slowed to fifteen miles per hour, and the continents were indeed where they had left them when they went to sleep was due, in some small way, to an obscure, hairy landlord who never actually set foot in the universe he kept running properly.

If Vom was destruction incarnate, and Smorgaz was creation personified, then West was order in its ultimate obsessive-compulsive form. It wasn't an easy job. He wasn't perfect. He still hadn't found the time to nail down the confusing jumble that humans foolishly labeled quantum physics. And once, when he'd eaten a bad hot dog and been sick in bed for a week, the result had been the ludicrousness of superstring theory. A few extra dimensions leaked through here and there at the wrong times, and the human race just couldn't let it go.

He'd never found the time to fix the error. And it'd probably work out fine in the end. Like when he'd accidentally let space-time become curved. At first it'd bugged him, but now he hardly noticed. And the humans seemed to get a kick out of it.

Someone knocked on West's door. He was surprised. There was no rent, beyond the obligations the apartments gave their occupants, and nothing ever broke. The tenants rarely had anything to do with one another. Except for the pair from Number Three. They baked pies and distributed them on a schedule. He was due for a boysenberry sometime in the next week, if he remembered properly.

It was Number Five.

"Hi." Diana held up a bag. "I got this for you. It's a hamburger." She hesitated. "You do eat hamburgers, right?"

Vom piped up from behind her. "If he doesn't want it, I'll take it."

"I eat hamburgers," said West. "Don't suppose you brought a shake too, Number Five?"

"Had one, but someone got to it."

"If it's any consolation," said Vom, "it was a bit watery."

West took the burger. "Thanks, Number Five."

He started to close the door, but Diana asked, "Can I talk to you for a second?"

"I can't get you out of the apartment," he said.

"I wasn't going to ask that. I kind of assumed it. No, I wanted to know about Chuck."

"Who?"

"The guy in Apartment Two. The one with the… dog."

"Number Two? What about him?"

"What's his deal?"

"He lives in Apartment Two."

He unwrapped the burger, took a bite. She waited for him to finish chewing, but he was a painfully slow chewer. And an even slower swallower. He scratched his beard. His furry eyebrows arched.

"S'good."

"You don't find there's too much mayo?" asked Vom. "I thought they overdid the mayo."

"Is that why you only ate five on the ride here?" asked Smorgaz.

"Guys, could you do me a favor and go back to the apartment?"

Grumbling, the monsters walked away.

"Chuck…Number Two, how dangerous is that dog?" she asked.

West took another bite, chewed, and swallowed in the time it would take a normal person to eat the whole burger.

She sighed.

"I'm just worried about Chuck."

His eyes narrowed.

"Chuck. Number Two."

"Uh-hum," said West neutrally.

"Is there some way to make friends with it?" she asked. "The dog outside of Apartment Two? If I gave it a burger, would it let Chuck out more often?"

"Hmm?"

"Number Two, would the dog let him out more often if he fed it something?"

West's already sallow flesh paled. "Don't feed it. Whatever you do, Number Five, don't do that."

"Because...?"

"Because it would be a bad, bad thing to do."

"Bad how?"

West's brow wrinkled. "You ask a lot of questions, Number Five."

"How am I supposed to understand any of this if I don't?"

"There are things the human mind was never meant to comprehend. And things the inhuman mind can never comprehend. Incomprehensible things."

She nodded. "Uh-huh. Yes, that's very clear. Thank you."

The building trembled violently, nearly knocking both of them off their feet.

"What was that?"

"Bugs," said West. "One tremor is nothing to worry about."

A second quake rattled the building.

"Two is acceptable. Only pressing if it's—"

A third shudder, less powerful but three times as long, shook the walls.

"Ah, damn. It's always something."

He walked past Diana and opened the front door. The city was gone. A glowing green wasteland stood in its place. A mosquito the size of a fighter jet soared overhead, kicking up radioactive dust.

West shut the door and trundled into his apartment. He found his old green toolbox. Diana stood in the doorway, blocking his progress.

"What happened?" she asked.

"World changed," he replied. "It happens. Now if you'll excuse me, I have to fix the boiler."

She stepped aside, but she followed him down the hall.

"That's how it ends?"

"It didn't end," he said. "It changed. *End* implies it's over, but it's just different than it was. But it's always different than it was. Just usually not so obvious about it. Or you're not in a position to notice. The only reason you noticed this time was because you were in here when it happened. Otherwise, you'd have changed along with it.

"Last count, there are fourteen viable radical transitions poised to take place at the moment. It varies, of course. This is not an exact science." He stopped at a dusty door beside the stairway and fumbled with a giant key ring.

"But just like that?" said Diana. "One second it's there, the next it's all changed?"

He took note of her voice, tinged with concern, but not overwhelmed with confusion. He smiled to himself. As a general rule, he didn't get to know many of the tenants. The apartments consumed most souls within a few days. Some lasted longer. But only a rare few had the right combination of curiosity, common sense, and temperament to last a year.

He jammed a key in the lock and wrestled with it for several seconds. He gave the door a few kicks and rammed his shoulder into it.

"Are you sure you unlocked it?" she asked.

"Oh, it's unlocked." He took a moment to catch his breath. "The Hive must've blocked it."

"What's the Hive?"

He gestured toward the door, letting her know she should help him. Together they put all their weight against the door and pushed.

"Tomorrow a mutagenic radiation will cause all insects on the planet to grow to enormous size. Within a year they'll devour all noninsect life on Earth. Within ninety years they'll establish an interplanetary colony that will cover half the Milky Way galaxy. I call it the Hive. Although it probably calls itself something different. Or maybe they don't even bother with words. They might not even have language. Never tried to have a conversation with the damned things."

The door opened a few inches. A sticky substance oozed through the cracks.

"Don't let the mucus get in your eyes unless you want to see how you die," he warned.

With a bit more work they managed to open the door halfway, which was enough for West to squeeze through. He descended a few steps, stopped, and spoke without looking back.

"Are you coming, Number Five?"

She poked her head into the dim stairway. "Is it dangerous?"

"Worst that can happen to you is you die."

"Oh, is that all?"

From most people this would've been sarcastic, but Diana understood, just as West did, that there were far worse things than death in this universe.

Diana followed him into the dark. He dug a claw hammer out of his toolbox and handed it to her. "You'll want this. Your powers won't work down here."

"If you know it's going to happen, can't you stop it before it happens?"

"Doesn't work that way."

"Why not?"

"Because the radiation always hits tomorrow. If we succeed in fixing the problem, then it will just hit the day after tomorrow. And if we stop that—"

"Got it."

"Near as I can figure it, the Hive functions on a reversed temporal axis. Not quite a hundred and eighty degrees from what all other life on Earth uses. Maybe about one hundred and seventy-three degrees. Maybe one hundred and seventy-four."

They plumbed deeper into the depths. At the bottom of the stairs a faint yellow glow emanated from the goo-coated walls.

"The Hive's future pushes against our past. If the Hive succeeds in pushing itself forward, or backward if that's easier to comprehend, it'll eventually rewrite all of history, erasing all of human civilization in the process."

"That sucks."

"Not really. Already happened three times before. Four, if you count the fall of the Neanderthals. And really, you should, because they were a fine primate civi-

lization in many ways superior to humanity. The Neanderthals invented the telegraph a full week before *Homo
sapiens*. And they made a hell of a chicken sandwich."

"So if it's the future and we can't stop it, then what are
we doing down here?"

"Just because it's the future that doesn't mean it happens tomorrow. The Hive pushes against our past. And
our past pushes against the future that is the Hive's past.
It's entirely possible for the future of the Hive to always
be tomorrow, to always be out there." He waved his pipe
wrench in a vague manner, as if pointing toward a distant
horizon. "Somewhere else, but never quite here."

"Ah," she said. "Makes sense."

"Does it?"

"It's like the future, but not necessarily the future that
ever comes."

"No, it's nothing like that, but never mind. If it's an explanation that works for you, we'll leave it at that. Mostly
I make this shit up as I go along, so it's not like I understand any of it either. Theories and explanations are just
tools to be used and discarded as needed in this job, Number Five."

A sac of eggs burst open, and puppy-sized maggots
squirmed down the wall.

"Don't mind those," said West. "They're grown for
food, harmless."

A trio of four-foot-tall ants appeared and started collecting the maggots, placing them in baskets.

"Drones," said West. "Harmless too."

"So how do we keep the insect apocalypse at bay for
another day?" she asked.

"We fix the boiler."

As they went deeper the basement became hardened slime catacombs and worker drones. After a few minutes every trace of the man-made world vanished.

He stopped at an intersection of eight tunnels.

"Been a while since I've seen it this bad." He opened his toolbox and pulled out a map. "Mmm-hmm. According to this, the boiler is either that way or that way."

"It doesn't know?"

"At the point where two histories meet, certainty is replaced by probability." He folded the map. "I'll go this way. You go that way. One of us is bound to find it."

Before she could argue he was already halfway down his chosen corridor, vanishing in the sickly glow of the nest.

"Wait! If I find the boiler, how do I fix it?" she called out.

"Use your hammer!" he shouted back. His voice echoed, ringing against the walls for several long seconds. Then there was only silence, and she was alone in the murky luminescence.

She wondered why she wasn't terrified, but all of this was becoming too ordinary. She couldn't remember which tunnel West had told her to take. Rather than think too much about it, she just picked one at random.

She walked leisurely through the nest. She ignored the larvae and drones, and they paid her the same courtesy. Once flies the size of small birds buzzed her. One landed on her shoulder and stayed there like a hairy, clicking parrot. She tried shooing it away. It kept returning, and after a while she gave up and let it perch. Whenever she came to a junction she'd turn in a random direction.

She was lost. She imagined herself forever wandering

through a future that never happened. It more irritated than frightened her. She had far too many dooms, many worse than this, hanging over her head to be bothered by it.

Diana entered an alcove. Aside from the bioluminescent walls, a single lightbulb dangled from a cord in the ceiling. Several crates sat stacked to one side. A rusty boiler stood in the center of the room.

It couldn't be this easy, she thought.

A fat red beetle the size of a compact car lumbered into the chamber. Diana pressed against the wall into one of the gray pools of twilight. The beetle wheezed with each breath. It scanned the room, its hundred of glowing green eyes sweeping from side to side. She thought for sure it would see her, but she resisted the urge to run for it. Even if she escaped, she doubted she'd find the boiler again. And if she was going to get eaten by something lurking in this nest, then she figured the beetle would finish her off quickly. Only a bite or two at most.

The creature retched, spitting up an arm, a pipe wrench, and a toolbox.

"Damn," she muttered.

The beetle snorted. It tilted its head to one side. She held her breath, remained very still, and mulled over her choices.

West was dead. That left her as the only one capable of fixing this problem, and she had to fix it. Otherwise the bugs from the future would destroy the past, and even if that didn't end up erasing her because she lived in an apartment building that didn't play fair with the space-time continuum, she didn't think she wanted to live in a world of giant mutant bugs. Her world was strange enough already.

Fixing the boiler would fix the future. She didn't know how to fix a boiler, but she might be able to figure it out if she didn't have to contend with the beetle in the room too. Her only weapon was an old claw hammer. Unless it was magical, it wasn't going to do much against the creature.

She tightened her grip. It didn't feel magical.

The fly on her shoulder made a loud buzz. The beetle swiveled in her direction.

Diana stepped out of the shadows. She didn't know why. The best justification she could arrive at was that if she was going to die anyway, she might as well go down swinging. If there was a Valhalla, she'd be dining with the Vikings tonight with one hell of a story to tell.

She remained calm. Where once a giant bug would've shocked her, now it was just another oddity that wanted to eat her. Her heart beat faster. Her muscles tensed. She tapped into a part of herself that could view this from a distance, as if she were playing a survival horror video game in which she had only one shot at this level.

The creature didn't advance. It just stood there, studying her. She wondered if it was impressed by her bravado or confused by her stupidity. She didn't look it in the eyes. It had so many that that would've been impossible. She watched its legs, its body language, trying to be ready for when it tried something.

Diana took one step to her left. The beetle pivoted. Its raspy wheeze quickened.

Speaking softly, she held the hammer in both hands and leveled it at her opponent. "Make your move, big guy."

But the monster just stood there.

"What are you waiting for?" she growled through clenched teeth. "Come on, you stupid bug. Come on!"

The beetle took a step back, and its wheezing ceased. She'd scared it.

It was ludicrous, but just for a moment she'd managed to intimidate the damn thing.

Maybe it was only surprised. When you were as big as a car you probably weren't used to being yelled at by little women with littler hammers.

The beetle moved toward her. She shouted. It backed away with a startled shriek.

Diana drew in a deep breath, then unleashed the loudest roar she could muster. It echoed through the chamber, and even she was surprised by it. The beetle turned and dashed away, slamming into a wall with enough force to stagger itself. She stamped her feet, jumping up and down, shrieking. The creature regained its senses and bolted down a tunnel.

She smiled at the fly still perched on her shoulder. "What a wimp."

She checked the boiler.

"Now how the hell do we fix this thing?"

The fly hopped off her shoulder and walked in small circles on the rusted boiler.

She raised her hammer. "When in doubt..."

She struck the boiler, sounding a peculiar gong that literally rattled the nest. The quake shook dust off the walls. She wasn't sure if it was a good thing or a bad thing, but it was something.

She hit it again with the same results. This time the noisy buzzing warbles of alien crickets also sounded. Several drones entered the chamber. They didn't do anything other than watch her and make clicking noises to each other. She took this as a positive sign.

"Sorry, fellas. It's nothing personal."

Diana struck the boiler several more times. Each blow sent shock waves through the nest and drew the attention of more and more of the Hive. Three of the giant beetles arrived too, but none made a move to stop her. She kept her guard up, expecting a rush any moment. It never came. And after a few minutes of smacking the boiler, everything went back to normal.

It was a bit anticlimactic, actually. She wasn't even sure when the change happened. She just looked up and noticed that the nest and all the bugs were gone, that she was back in the ordinary basement.

The part of her that had seen too many horror movies knew that this was the fake-out, the false moment of triumph. When the monster jumped from the shadows, she'd deal with it. Diana climbed the stairs out of the basement. There was no bug behind the door. And when she checked the world beyond the front door, everything was normal. As normal as she could expect.

"Good job, Number Five."

She turned. West stood in the doorway of his apartment, eating a hamburger. She was unsurprised to see him alive.

"Thought you'd gotten eaten," she said. "I saw your arm, your toolbox."

"Lot of arms out there. Lot of toolboxes," he replied. "But if you didn't see me get eaten, you didn't really see anything, didja?"

"No, I guess I didn't."

West offered a crisp salute before retreating to his

apartment, and Diana, accustomed to such things, didn't give the incident another thought. Except to be glad that the world outside her building wasn't a hellish landscape of mutant insects. Just the one she knew, with a healthy dose of cosmic monsters and indescribable horrors sprinkled here and there.

It wasn't much, but she'd take what she could get.

CHAPTER TWENTY

Diana met Sharon at a sushi restaurant. The thought of sushi used to make Diana queasy, but that was before the transference with Vom. Now she could eat anything. She limited herself to conventional edibles, though this wasn't always easy. Every so often she'd spot a succulent pigeon or smell a halfeaten burger in the trash. But years of living as a human had given her enough self-control to avoid surrendering to her less discriminating urges.

She glanced through the menu. Everything looked delicious.

"So I have to say I'm surprised you called," said Sharon. "I thought you were a bit freaked by how our last encounter ended."

"The four-armed monster werewolf thing?" said

Diana. "Yeah, I'll admit that threw me for a loop at first."

"So why did you call?"

"I don't know. Guess I just needed someone to talk to who could understand it from my perspective. I have friends, but…"

"But they're from the old life," said Sharon. "Even if they were willing to listen, they'd just think you were crazy."

"Why shouldn't they? I'm still not sure I'm not."

"I've been there. Except I was lucky enough to choose my fate, not just fall into it. I can't imagine what that must be like. I'm just glad you felt comfortable enough to call me."

"I hope it's not an imposition," Diana said.

"Don't even worry about it. It's nice to have a friend outside the church."

"You go to church?"

Sharon smiled. "Nondenominational. Primal force worship."

"Like Wicca?"

"Not at all."

Sharon offered nothing more, and Diana didn't feel comfortable enough to pry.

"So you actually chose to live like this," she said. "That just seems…" She trailed off, unwilling to finish the thought.

"Crazy?" asked Sharon in a flat tone.

"Oh God. I'm sorry. I wasn't trying to offend you. Not after you were nice enough to—"

Sharon cracked a grin. "I was just messing with you."

Diana chuckled uncomfortably.

"Sorry. Couldn't resist," Sharon said. "I don't know.

I guess it is kind of crazy to want to touch something beyond yourself, something greater than you can ever truly comprehend. But isn't that human nature? This universe is far stranger and more beautiful than most of us will ever know, than most of us will be given the chance to know. When the opportunity came, how could I not take it?"

Her gaze focused on some distant point and an expression of hushed wonder crossed her face. It was almost an intimate moment.

"I suppose I hadn't really thought about it," said Diana softly.

Sharon didn't reply. She stared off into space for a few more seconds before shaking off her silent delirium. She glanced around the restaurant as if seeing this world for the first time.

"Sorry. That's happening more often lately."

"No problem."

While waiting for their food, they chatted. It was all small talk. Nothing about monsters from beyond or other-dimensional weirdness. It wasn't that they were avoiding the subject. It just seemed irrelevant. It was nice to talk to someone like a normal human being. Strangely, Diana found it hard to engage in harmless conversation with normal people. She just kept wanting to explain how little they knew. But Sharon knew just as much as Diana, and this freed them to talk about nothing important.

"So are you seeing anyone?" asked Sharon.

"There's this guy," replied Diana. "But I'm not really sure about it."

"Is he cute?"

Diana nodded. "Yes, he's cool. But he's like us."

"And that's a problem?"

"I don't know. I just get a weird vibe off of him sometimes."

"Bad vibe can be a dealbreaker," agreed Sharon.

"But I'm not sure I can trust my vibe-sensing powers anymore. He seems like a good guy and it's not like I have a lot of options. Don't see how I could date a normal person the way my life is now."

"I hear you."

"What about you? Anyone special?"

"Sort of. It's complicated."

Diana waited for Sharon to elaborate. She didn't.

"Sorry," said Diana. "Didn't mean to pry."

"No, it's all right. I asked you, didn't I? Seems only fair. I'm in a relationship now. I guess that's what you could call it. It's more of a professional capacity, but it takes up most of my time. Makes it hard to meet anyone else. Although I'm not sure I'm interested in anyone else."

"Crush on the boss? That can be trouble."

"You have no idea. Especially since he doesn't see me that way."

"How do you know?" asked Diana.

"Because he can't. I know he cares for me, but he doesn't have the capacity for anything more than we have. Anyway, he's leaving. I knew he would be one day. I just didn't expect it so soon. But it's probably for the best. I know it's the best for him at least."

Sharon stirred the ice in her drink and studied the cubes as if they held the answer to unasked questions.

Diana chuckled to try to lighten the mood. "As if dating wasn't complicated enough before this."

Sharon smiled. "I won't miss it."

"You shouldn't give up so easily. I'm sure there's a guy out there."

"When things change, it won't much matter."

"What's going to change?"

"Oh, nothing important. Nothing worth worrying about."

Diana considered pressing, but their food arrived. Her appetite demanded her full attention. She forced herself to eat one piece of sushi at a time, to chew each piece twenty times, and to wait at least fifteen seconds between bites. It took most of her concentration, and the conversation returned to inane small talk, which was just fine with her.

Sharon spotted someone entering the restaurant and lowered her head. Diana glanced toward the entrance.

"Who is that?"

The tanned and immaculately groomed man saw Sharon. Waving, he called her name and made a beeline toward the table.

"Well, hello." He smiled, and the whiteness of his teeth nearly blinded Diana. "Didn't know you came here, Sharon."

"First time," she replied.

"Mind if I sit with you for a moment? My party has yet to arrive." He sat without waiting for permission. "Promising new disciples. We haven't much time left. We have to save as many as we can."

"Mmmm," replied Sharon while chewing on a spicy tuna roll.

"I don't believe we've been introduced." He held out a hand to Diana. "My name's Greg."

His grip was surprisingly strong, even a bit aggressive. She squeezed back. They stared into each other's eyes. She sensed the challenge inherent in his gaze. He dared her to look away. She didn't.

Greg smiled through clenched teeth and a tight jaw. "And who might you be?"

"Diana."

She was aware of a challenge of her own buried in the reply. She didn't like this guy. She couldn't say why, but she trusted her instinct.

At some point the handshake become awkward and the aggression between them noticeable to the nearby patrons. They released at the same time and dropped their stares simultaneously. It was the only way to end the battle of wills in a civilized manner, since resorting to a fistfight would have been frowned upon by the establishment and Diana still had half a plate of spider rolls to finish off.

"Where did you find her?" asked Greg of Sharon. "She's got fire. I like that."

"She's taken, Greg," replied Sharon. "I don't think she'd be interested in what you have to offer."

He laughed. On the surface it was polite, jovial. Underneath it was rehearsed and flat. "Don't be absurd. Everyone wants what we have to offer. When the glorious transition comes, even those attached to lesser gods will wish they had chosen more wisely.

"Tell me, Diana," said Greg. "Have you ever considered your future? The future of this whole world?"

"Can't say that I have," she replied. This was a half-truth. She hadn't contemplated the future for most of her life, but the last few weeks had changed that. But she wasn't going to feed him anything to keep him talking. His slightly leathery skin, doll teeth, and perfectly shaped eyebrows just put her off. Everything about him was wrong, and every instinct told her she wanted nothing to do with this guy.

"You really should," he said. "When the great upheaval is upon us, only the strong will stand with us. And I can sense you have that strength in you. But it's undirected, unfocused."

"Do we have to do this now?" asked Sharon. "We were just trying to have dinner."

"If not now, when?"

"How about never?" said Diana.

He was taken aback. So was she. She wasn't usually this rude, but she could tell Greg wasn't the kind of guy to take a subtle hint. He was one of those people most everyone found likable, even charming. But for a small group he was only irritating. Diana belonged in the latter category.

His smile dropped. Just for a moment.

"You really should reconsider. This is a rare gift I'm offering."

"Pass."

"Suit yourself." He handed her a business card. "I'll just leave this with you. In case you change your mind."

She didn't want the card, but she feigned enough civility to stuff it in her pocket.

His party arrived just then, and he excused himself.

"Sorry about that," said Sharon.

"He's not the guy, is he?" asked Diana. "The one you work with that—"

"Oh, God no." Sharon laughed. "I can barely stand him. But, believe it or not, he means well. He might be an egotistical jackass, but most people don't seem to notice. And his heart is in the right place."

"What was all that stuff about the great upheaval?"

"Shop talk. I'd rather not get into it."

"Fair enough."

They finished their meal without talking about anything weird again.

CHAPTER TWENTY-ONE

The door to Chuck's apartment opened a crack.

"Are you alone?" he asked.

"Yes."

The door closed quietly. There was rattling behind it, but it didn't open. When she tried the handle, it was still locked.

She knocked again.

His door parted, allowing half his face to be seen. "What do you want?"

"Weren't we supposed to have dinner tonight?" she asked.

"Dinner? Dinner?" His eye darted to and fro. "I can't right now."

"Is something wrong?"

"Something?" Chuck laughed mirthlessly. "Is something wrong? Everything is wrong. What isn't wrong? It's all wrong."

He shut the door again.

Diana stood in the hall a minute, waiting for Chuck to reappear. He didn't. She placed her ear against the door. She heard talking, maybe two or three voices in a rapid exchange, followed by a thump and a crash.

She considered knocking again, but he was going through something. She didn't know what that something was, but she withheld judgment. She knew Chuck came with baggage. Everyone did.

She was halfway down the hall when Chuck's door was flung open.

"I need you!" His eyes flashed with manic energy as he dashed out, grabbed her by the arm, and pulled her back to his apartment. "I know how to stop it! I know how to make it all go away!"

She didn't resist, allowing him to tug her along.

"See? It's all about corners! Corners! Corners?"

Diana didn't recognize him. The tall, good-looking man was there, but everything had changed. He was stooped, twitchy. His eyes were squinty, darkened slits of suspicion.

He grabbed her by the shoulders. "Don't you get it? Don't you see?"

"The corners," she replied. "Sure, I get it."

He stared deep into her eyes, then scanned the room, taking a few seconds longer to scrutinize the ceiling.

"I knew you'd know. I knew you'd understand." He grabbed a roll of duct tape and started slapping it along the bend where two walls met. "They need corners. They need them to come through, to stay here. But if I get rid of the corners, all of them, then it'll be over. Finished!"

He cackled.

The air of madness around him was distracting, but now she noticed that the apartment was covered in silver tape. Every corner. Every joint. Every place with an angle. He'd done half of the living area.

"Chuck, maybe you should take a break."

"Not now. If I stop now, then they'll get me."

"Who will get you?"

"Them. All of them."

She watched him work, debating how to handle this. He was an entirely different person now. She wouldn't say madness had consumed him, but lunacy had taken a small bite out of him.

But was he really crazy? How did she know that he wasn't right? How did she know that all that was needed to keep away the bogeymen wasn't enough time and duct tape?

"Don't just stand there," Chuck grumbled. "Help me. You can do the couch."

"Yeah, okay."

She started taping the furniture. Not seized with Chuck's madness, she wasn't certain how best to apply the duct tape. She followed the lines as best she could, paying special attention to the edges where two or three angles met. After a while it stopped being weird, and when she finished with the sofa she stood back and appraised her work.

"That's right," he grumbled. "I knew you'd get it. I knew it."

She put her hand on his back. "Maybe we can take a break. Have a seat."

"It's not safe."

"No, I taped the sofa," she replied. "It's perfectly safe."

He frowned at her with a touch of suspicion, then his gaze fell on the sofa.

"You need a break," she said. "You can't finish this all at once. If you get too tired, you'll make mistakes."

Every bit of his manic energy subsided. He deflated, but she suspected it was only a brief respite. He was like an engine that had slipped into neutral. It didn't look like it was doing anything, but the gears were still spinning.

They sat in silence. Rather, she sat in silence while he mumbled to himself. She wanted to know the thing to say to make it all right, but what was there to say? She wasn't even sure he was crazy.

She stood. He clutched her hand a bit too tightly.

"It's okay," she said. "I'll be right back."

He clung to her. But it was more than that. He was clinging to something vital inside himself. Something intangible slipping through his fingers.

Maybe he wasn't crazy, but he was in bad shape. She understood more than she wanted to admit. She'd only been living here a few weeks, and already she could feel it. The pressure building within, trying to get out. The human mind wasn't made to know what the building revealed. Secrets and truths that could loosen the steadiest soul. Like a dripping faucet filling a bucket. It might take a long time, but eventually that bucket would have to be emptied, one way or another.

She put a hand on his cheek. He pulled away, buried

his face in the sofa, and shook as he either laughed or sobbed. She wanted to take him in her arms, tell him that everything was going to be okay. The words would've been meaningless. He wouldn't have believed her. There was no reason he should when she didn't believe it either.

Rather than waste her time with empty platitudes, she slipped out of the apartment. She tried knocking on Apartment One, but West didn't answer.

"Damn it."

Apartment Three's door opened. Stacey and Peter-thing came out.

"Is there a problem, neighbor?" asked Stacey.

"It's Chuck. I think he's losing it."

"Oh, that's a shame," said Stacey with an exaggerated frown that would've seemed ridiculous on someone else. "He was such a nice young man."

"Chuck. Good," agreed Peter-thing.

"We have to help him."

"Oh, he'll snap out of it eventually. He always does."

"This has happened before?" asked Diana.

"The dear boy just isn't cut out for this sort of business."

"But he'll be okay, right?"

"Probably."

"What do you mean, probably?"

Neither Stacey nor Peter-thing could look her in the eye.

"What do you mean by that?"

"Would you care for a piece of pie?" Stacey smiled in that wide-eyed manner of hers. It was meant to be reassuring, but Diana found it condescending.

"Cut the crap, Stacey."

Stacey sighed. Her smile faded to merely cheerful, which was as close to somber as she ever got. "I know you like him, Diana, but I wouldn't get too attached. Peter and I have seen many a soul pass through these halls, and after a while one gets a feel for these things."

"Poor Chuck." Peter-thing lowered his head and gnashed his teeth. "Poor poor Chuck."

"It takes a certain talent to live with this for any amount of time," said Stacey. "A certain way of looking at the world, of accepting the unacceptable and rolling with the punches. Chuck is strong-willed, intelligent, decent, but he doesn't have what it takes. Not for the long haul. To be honest, I'm surprised he's lasted as long as he has."

"Well, this is bullshit." Diana kicked the wall. "Absolute bullshit."

"It's not fair," said Stacey, "but not everyone has the proper temperament to live like we do."

"Wait a second? We?" Diana pointed to herself. "Like you and me." She jabbed her finger at Peter-thing. "And him."

His lips pulled away from his fangs, and he smiled.

She shook her head slowly. She couldn't verbalize her denial.

Peter-thing reached out and put a clawed hand on her shoulder.

"Diana good."

"Yes, why don't you come in and have some pie?" asked Stacey.

"No, thank you. I really should check on Chuck."

Diana pulled away and hurried back to his apartment. She didn't look over her shoulder at Stacey and Peter-thing. She wasn't one of them. She didn't belong in this place. She'd rather be driven mad.

Chuck was pulling the silver duct tape off the walls.

She approached delicately and spoke softly so as not to disturb him.

"Hi."

He turned, smiled at her.

"Oh, hi."

"Feeling better?"

"Yeah, I don't know what got into me." He tried to toss a wad of tape into a bucket of the stuff, but it wouldn't come off his hand. "Hope I didn't scare you."

She forced a smile. "No, I was just worried. That's all."

They shared an uncomfortable chuckle.

"You know how it is," he said. "How it gets to you sometimes."

"I know."

She stepped closer for a good look at his eyes. They were calm, but now that she knew it was there, she could see the hint of madness lurking behind them.

Embarrassed, he turned away.

They spent the next ten minutes quietly stripping and disposing of the tape. Afterward they sat on the sofa and watched cartoons. He put his arm around her, but neither said a word for the duration of a *Frankenstein Jr. and the Impossibles* episode.

"I have an idea," she said. "Why don't we go out?"

"We can't go out. Not tonight."

"It'll be fun."

"But he's out there." Chuck pointed to the door. "And he's not going to let me leave."

"Your dog? He's not there. He hasn't been there all night."

"That's just what it wants you to think."

She opened the door to reveal the empty hallway.

"See? Gone."

"It's there. It's just waiting."

"Waiting for what?"

"I don't know."

She took him by the hand and playfully pulled him toward the door. "We'll just go for a walk or something. Something short. Be back in half an hour. Less."

He yanked his hand away. "I said no!"

She couldn't see it, but the monster pup yipped from the other side of the threshold.

"I told you it was out there!" shouted Chuck. "Why did you try and make me leave? Now you've made it angry."

The pup wagged its spiky tail.

"It was her fault. She wanted me to do it."

The dog squealed.

"Yes, I'll get her to leave. Right away." He pushed her toward the door. "You have to go now."

"But—"

He shoved her into the hall almost hard enough to slam her into the opposite wall.

"So I'll see you tomorrow then?" she asked.

"I don't know. Maybe. We'll see."

He slammed the door shut. The demon pup paced in three small circles before sitting at its designated post. The creature lowered its head, covered its eyes with its paws, and whined.

"Who asked your opinion?"

It belched, spewing out a foul reddish cloud.

She went back to her apartment. The monsters asked her about her date, but she just mumbled something about a change of plans and shut herself in the bathroom.

Diana studied her face in the mirror. Particularly her eyes. She searched for the same troubled psyche that she'd seen in Chuck's, but she couldn't find it.

Having encroaching dementia and being unable to diagnose it didn't bother her nearly as much as the notion that maybe there wasn't anything to see. Maybe she wasn't going mad and, despite the weirdness of her situation, she was bearing up well.

That scared her more than mere insanity.

CHAPTER TWENTY-TWO

West knocked on the door.

Diana knew it was West before she even answered, because his knock was peculiar. Two quick raps, a pause, and then a third harder rap. She thought about not answering, but the thought took too long to mature. She was already turning the doorknob when it hatched, and there was no going back by then.

West held a cardboard bucket of fried chicken against his hip. While he was always a disheveled soul, now his drab clothes were covered in brown and gray dirt. It coated his wild beard.

"You like gravity, don't you, Number Five?" he asked.

Zap, sitting on the sofa, chimed in. "Gravity is highly overrated, if you ask me."

She ignored the comment, but she did take a moment to mull it over.

"I'm for it," she said.

"Good. I could use your help then." He offered her the chicken bucket.

"Thanks, but I'm not hungry."

A lie. She was always hungry now. It was only the smallest portion of the ravenous compulsion that raged throughout Vom's being. While it was rarely over-whelming, her appetite was never satisfied. But she was getting used to the hunger. A hunger she very deliber-ately did not indulge for fear of where it might lead if fed too well.

"I'll take it if she doesn't want it," said Vom.

West's mustache twitched, releasing dust particles into the air. "It's not for either of you. I just need you to carry it for me, Number Five."

He turned and walked down the hall, leaving a trail of sand in his wake. She followed.

She asked, "This isn't going to end with me facing down an army of giant cockroaches with only a bucket of chicken to defend myself, is it?"

He shrugged. "Can't make any promises, Number Five."

They took a turn down an unfamiliar hallway. She was used to that. Maybe West was the only one who knew the building's secrets, although she doubted even he knew them all, but she was getting the hang of it. The trick was not to expect anything and to be ready for anything.

They ascended several flights of stairs that led to a door.

Despite her resolve not to be confounded, she was getting a little nervous. At the same time she was excited by the prospect of what lay behind that door, excited to peel back another layer of an increasingly strange universe. She didn't quite believe there was no going back to a normal life, but while she was here she might as well find something positive about it.

West opened the door, revealing just another hallway.

She was disappointed, and that told her what she needed to know. She might have started out a reluctant prisoner of this weirdness, but something had changed. She didn't know if she was getting used to it or if she was being corrupted by the madness always around her. Either way, the peculiar didn't seem quite as peculiar as it once had, and the ordinary was...

She wasn't quite sure what it was anymore.

Predictable? Reliable? Safe?

Boring.

And boring was supposed to be good. But Diana cringed, if only just a little, at the thought of going back to it.

West walked down the hall, and she followed. The air smelled sweet, but not in a good way. It was the sweetness of decay, of milk turning and meat two days past its expiration date. She'd always had a weak stomach, but it didn't bother her.

A door opened and a pale thing stepped into view. It looked like the Pillsbury Doughboy, but with a featureless face. It wore a gray housecoat and had a gray scarf wrapped around its lump of a head.

The thing withdrew into its doorway as they passed. It shrieked, and nearly all the other doors opened. More dough people poked out their heads.

"They're not dangerous, are they?" she asked.

"They're wondering the same thing about you."

She saw his point. Weirdness was relative. Diana and West were the strange invaders from another dimension, as bizarre and inconceivable as Vom and Smorgaz.

West knocked on a door, and another pale thing answered. It was as featureless as the other residents except for a single eye in its head. It was dressed in a similar, if not quite identical, manner to West. But its disheveled appearance was close enough that, even with their physical differences, it was obvious they were kindred souls.

The creature squealed and barked.

"Yes, yes, this is the one," replied West.

The creature yipped. Once.

"Well, there wasn't much time to find another," said West. "You make do with what you can, right?"

The creature sized up Diana. It circled her once, tried to take the bucket of chicken from her, but she pulled away. It glared and growled.

"I doubt she's a virgin," said West, "but does that really matter?"

"It's tradition," said the creature.

Although it hadn't said that. It had clicked, growled, and hissed as before. Diana had just understood it this time. Its inhuman language was suddenly laid bare. It shouldn't have been possible. The syntax and grammar were so strange that a master linguist could've spent a lifetime deciphering a handful of sentences, only to realize that to truly understand the language would require having heard the first word uttered by the first gray sludge that slithered upon the shores of this world.

But she understood.

"It is written that the Great Thing prefers virgins," said the creature.

"The Great Thing will take what it can get," said West.

The creature snorted. It stomped away into its apartment.

"What's going on here?" she asked.

"Just hold on to that chicken," West said and went inside.

She hesitated. Maybe boring, predictable reality wasn't such a bad thing. A glance behind her showed that the denizens of the building were watching her from the safety of their doorways. She doubted the frightened creatures would get in her way if she retreated to her own universe.

But she'd come this far, and her own building in her own sphere of existence wasn't much of a shelter when it came to weirdness.

She followed West.

The apartment was normal. A bit cluttered but otherwise unremarkable. West and the creature stood across from each other. They were busy moving the furniture from the center of the room, including a rather large and heavy coffee table.

"Need some help?" she asked.

"Just hold on to the chicken." West strained to drag the table to one side. "Your part is almost here."

"And mind the throw rug," said his pale, one-eyed equivalent.

The table must've been even heavier than it looked. It took them several minutes to drag it out of the way. When they finally pushed it up against some bookshelves, a hot gust of wind blasted from under the huge square throw rug that occupied most of the floor. It stank of that same sweet decay.

West and the creature stood on either side of the rug and rolled it away. Underneath was an inky hole that took up most of the floor. It didn't bother her that the heavy coffee table should've sunk right into the hole while sitting on the unsupportive rug. Those sorts of physics didn't mean much to her anymore. She certainly didn't take them for granted.

But there was something down there. She couldn't see it, and the air was dreadfully still. Yet in the darkness…there was…something.

The Great Thing.

She gazed into the abyss. It didn't gaze back, being indifferent to her presence. Its apathy was hypnotic, consuming. This hole was the universe. Deep, unfathomable, and disinterested. It threatened to swallow her up. It wouldn't have to do anything. It wouldn't stalk or tempt her. It would just wait with endless patience until she cast herself into its hungry jaws.

"What are you waiting for?" asked the creature. "What is she waiting for?"

"The human mind grapples with the incomprehensible," said West. "Give her a moment."

Diana stepped away from the hole, and the world quaked.

"The chicken, Number Five," said West.

Her feet slipped out from under her. She fell slowly toward the ground. When she finally hit the floor, she bounced and floated. The furniture hovered a few inches off the floor. Everything did. Except West and the creature, who managed to remain earthbound.

She threw the chicken into the hole. Tried to. It was difficult to do when things had stopped falling. Diana kicked off the wall, grabbed the bucket, and threw it into the pit. It drifted into the abyss. She floated aimlessly while the bucket disappeared into the dark.

"Is it working?" she asked.

"I told you we needed a virgin," said the creature.

"Just give it a minute," said West.

She stared at the void beneath her. If gravity came back right now, she'd be in for a long fall.

"Give me your hand, Number Five."

West reached out for her. She took his hand. His skin was scaly, cold. Her first instinct was to pull away, but she ignored that.

A cold wind blasted out of the hole, and she was falling. She clung to West with a desperate grip, but there was no way he could keep her and himself from falling into oblivion. But he didn't budge and, with a single tug, he pulled her to safety.

"Would've worked faster if she'd been unspoiled," said the creature.

"It worked," he replied. "Does it really matter?"

West and the creature unrolled the carpet, covered the Great Thing, and dragged the coffee table back into place. It all seemed perfectly ordinary, business as usual. Visit another dimension, feed a bucket of chicken to a big hole, fix gravity, go home. West exchanged a few words with the creature in private while Diana waited in the hall. West assured her she could go back without him now, but she had a few questions.

She started with "What the hell was that?" knowing that the question was too general, and that West wouldn't answer it. Either because he didn't want to or possibly because he couldn't.

"What's in the hole?" she asked.

"I don't know."

"That guy back there called it the Great Thing."

"There are some who believe that a cosmic something dwells at the center of all realities. It does something important there. There are those who worship it as a god, although why anyone would worship a god they all agree couldn't give a damn about them always escapes me. But that's the Great Thing. While I don't know what's down in that hole, nobody else does either. I'm skeptical, though, because there are a lot of holes in this universe and while one of them might lead to the heart of everything, I have to figure most don't."

"Well, something has to be down there, right?"

He shrugged again. "Don't know about that."

"Something ate the chicken."

"That's an assumption. All I know is that there's a hole and every so often, it's necessary to throw a bucket of chicken into it to keep everything from floating away. What happens to the chicken, where it goes, if something eats it or if it just sits at the bottom of the hole with a thousand other buckets of fried chicken, these are things I don't know, most probably never will, and don't really concern me."

"But why chicken?" she asked.

"You'll drive yourself mad if you don't stop asking unanswerable questions."

"Bull."

West stopped. He turned slowly with a genuinely perplexed expression.

"I'm not like you," she said. "I can't just go with this. I think about this. I know I can't understand it, but it doesn't stop me from wondering about it. Curiosity isn't a sin, and asking unanswerable questions is something human beings do from time to time."

His beard writhed. He nodded to himself.

"Okay. That's fair. Ask all the questions you want. Just don't expect any satisfying answers."

"I guess I can live with that. If I have to."

He smoothed his beard, and the faint trace of a smile was visible under it. "Then you should do just fine, Number Five."

They were back in their apartment building, and West prepared to part ways with her. She stopped him.

"One last question. Why did you need me at all for that?"

"Tradition demands that a maiden make the offer. It's nonsense, of course, but easier to have you do it than argue about it with him."

"That's it? It's just because of some dumb tradition?"

"Does there need to be a better reason?"

"But I could've died," she said. "I almost jumped into that hole. I don't know why, but I almost did."

"Some people do."

Reading West's face was always difficult, but this time she could see exactly what he was thinking.

"You son of a bitch. You knew that I might jump."

He lowered his head and mumbled.

"What was that?" she asked.

"I didn't think you would, but I've been wrong before."

"Is that what I am? Just another disposable resource?

Something to be used and discarded just to make your life a little more convenient?"

"I didn't want you to jump, and I could have taken the chicken myself. But I like you, Number Five."

She stepped back instinctively.

"The things I do, somebody has to do them." His shoulders slumped. "Or not. It's not like any of it really matters in the long run. But I do them anyway because...because that's what I do. And when I look out into that world of yours, I sometimes wonder why I do it."

West straightened. As straight as he ever stood.

"Someone like you reminds me why. Someone with the strength of will not to jump into madness when most others would, who can ask unanswerable questions with unsatisfying answers. Someone who doesn't give up."

It was her turn to slump. "You're wrong. I give up all the time. Giving up is what got me here in the first place."

"No, Number Five. You're wrong. If you weren't, you'd be at the bottom of that pit, solving the mystery of the Great Thing. But you're here, and that says something about you."

"But what does it say?" she asked.

He ran his fingers through his thick hair and shrugged. "Don't know. Maybe that's up to you to decide in the end. If you'll excuse me, Number Five. I can't sit around talking all day. Some of us have things to do."

He closed his door.

She didn't know what she thought about any of this, but if the decision was hers, she decided right then not to worry about it.

CHAPTER TWENTY-THREE

It'd been a week since Diana had seen or heard from Chuck. After the duct tape incident she wasn't sure if she should be relieved by that or not. The few times she tried knocking on his door he didn't answer. She decided to give him some space and hope he could deal with his problems.

He finally showed up at her place. She answered his manic beating on her door. He pushed open the door and slammed it shut.

"Hey, Chuck," she asked. "What's up?"

"Quiet. It's out there."

"What's out there?"

"Hi, Chuckie-boy," said Vom.

Chuck paled.

She asked Vom, Smorgaz, and Zap to leave the room so she could talk to Chuck alone.

"Why do we have to leave?" asked Zap.

"Yeah," said Vom. "It's movie night, and I just microwaved a fresh batch of popcorn."

She glared at them.

"Oh, fine." Vom picked up the bowl of popcorn and shoveled handfuls down his throat.

"Save some for me," said Smorgaz.

"Get your own," replied Vom, shoveling faster.

The monsters went into the kitchen. When they were gone Chuck relaxed a bit. He was still on edge, but he was nowhere near the wild energy she'd seen last week.

Her first instinct was to ask what was wrong, but she already knew the answer.

"Maybe we should go for a walk," she said.

"Out there? I can't go. It won't let me."

"How do you know?"

"Because I know."

"Chuck, if I could maybe offer you some advice, I think you have to stop being afraid of it."

"What are you talking about? It's a monster, a creature that lives to torment me. I'd be stupid not to be afraid of it."

She said, "But that's just it. I don't think it actually wants to torment you. I think it's just responding to the emotional vibe you keep putting out. If you keep acting fearful, then it will think it should be feared. These things, these monsters, they don't really mean any harm. They just can't help it."

His brow furrowed. "Why are you talking about them

like they're people? They're horrible things that don't belong here."

"I know, but that just means they're confused and disoriented. They need something or someone to ground
them in our reality."

"Maybe you're right," he said, "but I don't see how
anyone can choose to not be afraid."

She wanted to tell him it wasn't that hard, but it was a
lot harder than she'd realized. She remembered her first
reaction to meeting Vom. It had shattered everything she
understood about the universe, and while she'd gotten
over that, she couldn't explain how.

Maybe it was a question of temperament. Maybe some
human minds were more ready for the unknowable than
others, and there was nothing anyone could do to alter that.

"Come on. Let's go for a walk."

She took him by the hand and led him toward the door.
He moved stiffly but didn't fight.

"It'll be easy." She used a soft, relaxing tone. "We'll
just walk out the front door, and the creature won't care
because we will stay calm."

She opened the door. His demon pup was on the other
side of the threshold. It raised its hideous head and
yipped. Chuck squeezed her hand tight.

"It's okay," she said. "Everything is just fine."

The dog bared its pointed teeth and growled.

"Oh, God," he whispered. "It doesn't like this." He
pulled free and stepped back.

"You can't let this thing rule your life," she said.

"That's easy for you to say. You don't have to deal
with it every day."

She frowned. "Just a second there. I have three unholy

beasts in my kitchen right now. So I think I know what I'm talking about."

He scowled. "Yours are easy. Not like that little creature. It's just waiting for me to drop my guard so it can kill me."

The dog howled.

"Close the door!" he said.

"Chuck, you can't—"

"Close the goddamn door!"

The dog snapped its lipless mouth open and shut several times.

Diana shut the door.

"It's still out there," he said. "Oh, God, I can feel it watching me through the walls."

She wanted to reassure him that he was probably just feeling the unrelenting stare of Zap, but reconsidered. He probably wouldn't find that very reassuring at all.

She excused herself to grab a drink from the kitchen.

"Sounds like that boy is near his expiration date," said Vom.

"He's going to be fine," she replied, though she noted she didn't sound convinced.

"Believe me," said Zap. "I've seen his future. It isn't pretty."

"So now you can see through time?"

"The very use of the phrase highlights the fallacies of your limited perceptions. One does not see *through* time. Rather, one sees *along* time."

"What does that even mean?"

Zap waved his tentacles in a condescending manner. "It means that trying to explain it to you would only be a waste of time for both of us."

"You are such a pretentious prick," said Smorgaz.

Vom snickered.

Zap glared.

"He's right," said Vom. "You are."

"Well, if being privy to the mysteries of the universe makes me a pretentious prick, then I guess I'm guilty as charged."

Vom and Smorgaz laughed.

"That is such a prick thing to say," replied Vom with a snort.

"Philistines," said Zap.

She left the monsters to their debate.

Chuck paced back and forth. He was losing it again. She wondered how often this happened to him. Was he just having a bad month or were the sane moments the anomaly? She didn't need to deal with this. It was selfish on her part, but keeping him sensible wasn't a responsibility she wanted or needed right now.

"Chuck..." She wasn't certain how to put this.

He jumped at her, clamped a hand over her mouth.

This was definitely not a healthy relationship, she decided right then.

"Listen," he whispered as he stared at the door. "Can't you hear it?"

She did catch the faint scratch of claws on wood.

Diana pushed Chuck away.

"Okay, this is not cool," she said. "Not cool at all. I'm going to have to ask you to leave right now."

He wasn't listening to her. He curled up in a corner of the couch and covered his ears.

"Oh, no. Don't try that with me. I have my own monsters to deal with, so—"

Something pounded hard against the door. The creature struck three more times, and the hinges showed signs of buckling.

"Ah, guys," she called. "I think I could use a little help here."

Her roommates entered the room as the assault intensified.

Chuck cackled like a madman.

"Damn it." She put her hands on his cheeks and tried to get his attention. "Chuck, it's responding to your confusion and fear. If you stay calm and in control, then you have nothing to be afraid of. It doesn't want to hurt you. It just doesn't understand."

For a moment she glimpsed reason surfacing in the storm of madness in his eyes. It didn't last.

The door burst open as the demon pup sprang into the room. It was the size of a Bengal tiger, and its twisted body oozed and popped as it boiled. Vom, Smorgaz, and Zap pounced on the beast. Howling, it thrashed to free itself.

"I got it! I got it!" Smorgaz was kicked across the room. He bounced off the wall, shook his head clear, and jumped back into the battle.

The demon dog's serrated tail sliced off one of Vom's arms. "You little son of a—"

"Stand back!" said Zap. "I'll blast it!"

"No!" said Diana, Vom, and Smorgaz in unison.

"Just a little blast," said Zap.

"No blasting," repeated Diana.

"Oh, fine."

She had to do something fast. It was only a matter of time before the demon dog slipped free and pounced on Chuck.

She slapped him. A shock to the system was all she could think of. It worked just long enough for him to punch her in the throat and scramble away. No serious harm was done, but by the time she caught her breath he had managed to lock himself in the bathroom.

He was going to hide. Facing an incomprehensible threat, his only instinct was to retreat from it. It was sensible, but it wasn't going to work. Not this time. When you couldn't run from the unfathomable, your only other choice was to confront it head-on, but Chuck didn't have the capacity.

The dog threw off Vom and Smorgaz. Zap slowed it, but in three short steps it'd tear Chuck to pieces.

Diana stepped between the dog and the bathroom. She planted her feet, folded her arms across her chest, and squinted with steely determination. She almost shouted at the monster, but it seemed unnecessarily dramatic.

The hound growled at her.

"You're confused, scared. I get it. You don't have to be. Not anymore."

The creature tilted its head left and right, trying to decipher her like a puzzle.

She moved toward the dog. Rule number three was don't pet the dog. So she held out her hand under the creature's multitoothed mouth. Its tongue darted out and wrapped around her arm. It cooed.

"Yes, you can stay with me."

The dog shrank to its less threatening puppy size.

Vom groaned. "Are we running a halfway house here?"

"I'm not cleaning up after it," added Zap.

Diana attempted to coax Chuck out of the bathroom,

but gave up after a few minutes. He'd have to come out eventually.

She sat on the sofa with the dog and watched television with her roommates. Two hours later he finally stepped out.

"Hey," he said.

"Hey," she replied.

There was nothing more to be said after that. He quietly slipped out of the apartment and was gone from the building by the next morning without even a casual good-bye. She would've liked to get mad about that, but she couldn't blame him. She probably would've done the same in his situation.

They named the dog Pogo.

CHAPTER TWENTY-FOUR

Bowling was Diana's idea. Bringing along her room-mates was Sharon's.

"I'll bring my guy," she said. "You bring yours. They'll get a kick out of it. Trust me."

The monsters seemed less interested in meeting another cosmically misplaced entity and more interested in getting out for a few hours. For beings that lived outside of time, they had a peculiar tendency toward restlessness.

"Sharon's going to be there?" asked Vom.

"Yes."

"I'm out then," said Smorgaz.

"What? You guys have been bugging me for days about getting out of the apartment."

"I don't like her. She makes my head buzz. And not in a good way."

"Well, I'm in," said Vom after a bit of thought. "I can put up with the buzz if it gives me a chance to stretch my legs."

"Me too," said Zap.

"You don't have legs."

Zap glared. Sparks of lightning danced around the edges of his single giant eye. "Har har."

"Are you sure you don't want to come?" she asked Smorgaz.

"Pass. Don't worry about it. I'll keep myself company."

He budded a full-grown spawn and plopped on the couch. "Want to get us some popcorn, buddy?"

"Why me?" asked his identical spawn.

"Because I'm Smorgaz prime."

"That doesn't give you the right to boss me around."

"Have it your way." Smorgaz prime snapped his fingers, and the clone dissolved into a puddle.

"Hey, watch the rug," said Diana.

"Sorry." Smorgaz budded off another clone. "Now are you going to get me some popcorn, or are we going to have a problem here?"

The clone lumbered into the kitchen.

"Have fun," said Diana. "And clean up your mess."

"We'll get right on it," promised Smorgaz.

"I call shotgun!" shouted Zap.

"I always get shotgun," said Vom. "Right, Diana?"

"Sorry, but he did call it."

"Ah hell."

Vom sulked in the backseat, and Zap played with the radio on the drive to the alley.

The moon was glowing tonight. Transference from Zap had given her supernatural sight. She could perceive auras around people and objects now. Not all people and not all objects. Not even every monster she passed on the street had an aura, and the auras would sometimes disappear. Vom always had one. Zap never did. And Smorgaz prime was usually encased in a soft yellow glow, while his clones tended to be wrapped in purple.

The moon always shone like a light. Threads of luminosity stretched from the silver orb to Fenris, its eternal pursuer, who himself always glittered almost as bright. The two auras were so bright that they were a pair of virtual midnight suns. Except that the light they spread across the night sky was a prism of colors, many of which humans had not invented names for yet.

Diana was getting used to this stuff, but the night sky unsettled her. It was like gazing into a kaleidoscope that showed the end of time. She could accept that the universe was finite, but she didn't like the idea that there were things on the other side. Horrible things. Unfathomable to mere mortal minds and to inhuman creatures like Vom and Zap alike.

Zap put his tentacles on the dashboard and looked up at the sky. "That Fenris is up to no good."

"I could've told you that," said Vom.

"It'll happen soon," said Zap.

"What will happen soon?" asked Diana.

He blinked. "I don't know. It's too hard to see it from this point in the space and time, but something is going to happen."

Vom laughed. "You're like a bad psychic. Could you be more vague?"

"Mock me if you must—"

"Oh, I must. *Something* is going to happen! And soon! You want to know what I think? I think you're full of it."

"Hardly surprising," mumbled Zap, "considering that you are nothing but a pair of mouths on legs with the perceptual capacity of all that requires and nothing more. I, on the other hand, am a cosmic observer birthed from the very first star to bear witness to the universe."

"Guys, can we knock off the bickering?" asked Diana. "At least for a few hours. I don't want to make a bad impression with these people."

The entities grumbled but agreed to do their best to play nice.

At the bowling alley Diana had to rent three pairs of shoes. They didn't have any in Vom's size, and Zap didn't even have feet. But the man renting the shoes insisted. She still hadn't deciphered how human minds transformed the monsters into something ignorable, but she'd stopped trying to figure that out.

"What am I supposed to do with these?" asked Zap.

"Just carry them, I guess," she replied. "You have plenty of arms."

Sharon's monster wasn't what Diana had expected. She'd come prepared for something bizarre, and instead found a man so ordinary that she wasn't sure he was a creature at all. Calvin did have a weird aura, a crackle of light like tiny sparks were created as he dragged himself across the surface of reality. If she looked hard, they seemed like rips in the universe, but they disappeared almost immediately. Even these weren't readily visible or constant. They only seemed to manifest with sudden movements.

Introductions were passed around. Diana noticed Calvin didn't offer his hand to shake. Vom and Zap went to pick their bowling balls.

"Been forever since I bowled," said Diana.

"We go all the time," replied Sharon. "I'm still pretty lousy, but Calvin is fantastic."

"She's exaggerating," said Calvin.

"Don't be modest."

He lowered his head and smiled. "I do all right."

Vom and Zap returned. Vom had selected a thirteen-pound ball, but only after he'd eaten several others. Diana had seen him do it. She elected not to say anything. Zap's ball was only six pounds, but he was having trouble levitating while carrying it. He might have been privy to secrets of the universe, but he wasn't very strong.

Vom grinned. "Need help with that?"

"I got it," Zap grunted, swaying a bit.

Calvin bowled the first frame and scored a strike.

"Whoa," said Vom. "Looks like we have a ringer."

By the third frame Calvin had a clear lead. Vom trailed in second. Sharon and Diana ended up knocking over a few pins, competing for third place. And Zap, barely able to push his ball down the alley, had a score of three. He sat in a hard plastic chair and grumbled.

Cosmic monsters were an immature lot, mused Diana, having come to this conclusion several days earlier.

Vom offered to get some snacks, but she told him to stay put. Diana and Sharon went to the vending machines. Diana didn't have any change. Then she discovered a handful of quarters had materialized in her pocket. As reality-altering slips went, she could live with it. She started dropping coins into the slots without much thought. Whatever she brought back would be fine with Vom.

"So Calvin is nice," said Diana.

"Oh, yes. He's probably the nicest guy I've ever met. Wouldn't hurt a fly."

"Hard to believe he's one of…them."

"I know, right? I've never met a guy who was so levelheaded and sweet. Maybe it's because he's been around forever, but he never loses his temper. And he's thoughtful and intelligent. And funny, too, though you have to get to know him to find that out. He has some stories about the Ice Age that'll make you laugh until your sides ache."

Diana pushed some random buttons and let the machine dispense whatever it felt like. "Wait a second. Is this the guy you like? The guy you work with?"

"Do you think I should get a Mars bar or a Twix?"

"Twix," said Diana. "Don't change the subject. Is this the guy?"

Sharon nodded very slightly, as if confessing to some terrible sin. "But you can't tell him. You have to promise me."

"I wouldn't tell him. But what makes you think he doesn't already know? Don't you two already live together?"

"Sort of." Sharon leaned against the machine, resting her forehead against the display window. "It's complicated. I told you he just doesn't see me in that way. In most ways he's very human. But not in that way. He doesn't function like that."

Sensing she was encroaching on dangerous territory, Diana didn't ask any more questions. Sharon volunteered answers without being asked.

"He's not a sexual being. I'm not just talking about the act of sex itself. I'm talking about the entire reproductive element of what makes us humans tick. He's eternal. He doesn't need to. And I'm not sure he finds us attractive. I've never even seen him check out another woman. Or man, for that matter.

"I know he likes me and appreciates what I do for him. But I'll always just be a friend. That's all I can be."

They gathered their candies, chips, and sodas.

"I guess there are worse things to be," said Diana.

"I'm lucky to have known him. Luckier to have been so close to him before he leaves."

"Where's he going?"

Sharon hesitated.

"Away. Just away." She paused, then pasted on a smile. "It's not important."

Diana wanted to ask more questions, but she didn't know Sharon well enough to press.

Vom pounced on them. "Oh, Butterfinger."

Diana held up her hand. "This is for everyone. So you have to share."

"But Zap is just going to vaporize his."

"Remember our discussion about sharing? Now you can have a soda and two candy bars."

He wasn't happy about it, but he'd take what he could get. Zap picked out a pack of Skittles. He disintegrated the snack with tiny bolts of lightning. Whether or not that qualified as eating for him, Diana couldn't guess.

"Ah, I wanted a Mars bar," said Calvin.

"Here. You can have mine." His fingers brushed her thumb as he took the candy from her.

The universe exploded.

Not literally, although it took her a few seconds to realize it hadn't self-destructed. This was all a misfire of
her senses, an overload in her perceptions. She lost sight
of the ordinary world. In its place, dancing patterns and
swirling vortexes. She could smell eternity and taste the
color blue and hear the atoms as they crashed against the
shores of uncertainty.

Everything she knew and everything she didn't know
were little more than intangible knots of colors and
shapes. Laid bare, they were too much for her to absorb,
but her sanity was saved by a singular object that drew
her attention away from the more unsavory, unfathomable secrets exposed to her.

In this ethereal wasteland Calvin was the only thing
with any weight. Tubes of color flowed up and out, and
her eyes followed them skyward, although there was no
sky anymore, so she was just guessing at that.

The moon was the second thing she could really see.
Like Calvin, it was a sparkling diamond, making everything else pale and immaterial by comparison. The third
and final object was the shrieking, writhing form of Fenris.

The moon god howled. Its pain was overwhelming.

Diana's instincts screamed, but she ignored them. She
was getting used to this, and while this experience was
beyond her ability to withstand for long, she knew pan-
icking would only make it worse. She closed her eyes and
covered her ears. Most important, she made no attempt to
understand what was happening to her. To open herself
up in any way was sure to destroy her mind. This would
pass. She only needed to wait it out.

Even with her eyes closed she could see the future un-
ravel, the world come undone. Time was just another di-

mension, a flat plane spreading out before her. And on the horizon a storm was brewing, a moment inescapable and so overwhelming that it rippled through history written and unwritten, causing her universe to fold and bend on itself.

The storm was the reason her reality was broken, the cause of all the glitches that allowed inhuman monsters and dangerous alien things to slip into realms they were never meant to touch.

But it wasn't just one storm. There were three. Three swirling vortexes of anarchy drawing closer with each day. The storm was coming to a head, and a universe that struggled daily to hold itself together against the thrashing tentacles of an unspeakable horror was in for a hell of a time. She had no idea what waited on the other side. Or even if there would be another side to see. It was possible that there was no future and that the storm would even undo the past, a tide of annihilation sweeping throughout the planes of time to swallow everything in perpetual stillness.

Her vision cleared. Or was obscured, depending on how one chose to look at it. Either way, her perceptions of her universe fell into more human ranges.

"Thanks," said Calvin.

Diana opened her eyes. What had seemed like twenty seconds of terror had been less than an instant. Nobody else had seemed to notice. Not even Calvin.

"You're looking a little pale," said Sharon. "Are you okay?"

"I'm fine." Diana sat down. Her head cleared, and the memories of what she'd seen were fading. In a few minutes she doubted she'd remember any of it.

"It's your frame," said Vom.

She gave him permission to bowl for her, and nobody minded. Diana sat beside Zap and waited for her head to clear. She almost convinced herself that it was all an illusion. The doom lurking over her portion of the universe was merely a misfire of her underdeveloped human brain trying to make sense of realities it had never been meant to contemplate, much less actually witness.

"It's doomsday," said Zap.

She looked into his giant eye. He'd seen it too.

"Damn it."

She didn't want to know this, but she didn't want to know a lot of things she now knew. She decided to ignore the vision. It was easier to do than she had imagined. She didn't see a destroyer of worlds in Calvin, who was an affable fellow. Or at least a realistic enough simulation that she couldn't tell the difference, just as long as she didn't touch him. A second touch might give her another revelation, but she had no interest. She could only gaze at the secrets of the universe so many times in a day before her sanity was forfeit.

After the game was over, Sharon suggested getting something to eat.

Diana's first thought was to cut the evening short, but the best excuse she could think of was a fictional early doctor's appointment in the morning. But it was barely eight o'clock, and she didn't need to go to doctors now.

She didn't see the point anyway. Whatever Calvin was, the future, past, or present wouldn't be shaped by whether she had a meal with him or not. And Vom was always up for a bite to eat.

They picked a buffet place, which Vom liked even more.

"Only ten trips," said Diana.

"But it says all you can eat."

"Yes, but I don't think they had someone like you in mind with that rule."

He frowned. "And how is that my fault?"

"Look at it this way. If you put all the buffets out of business, where will you go to stuff yourself?"

He had to admit she had a point.

They all got their food. Without planning it, Diana arrived back at the table with Zap. They stared at Calvin. It seemed to her that the universe revolved around him. Not just figuratively, either.

Diana wolfed down a chicken wing, bones and all. The need to know overwhelmed her. That was Zap's passion. Not just to witness and observe, but to know.

He obliterated a slice of pizza and some French fries. "Do you think Sharon knows what he is?"

Diana didn't have the answer, but there was an obvious way to find out. She caught Sharon at the buffet line. Diana didn't want to ask the question, but she needed to know. Vom gave her an appetite. Zap gave her an insatiable curiosity, an endless hunger to observe everything and to understand it all.

"Do you know?"

Sharon perked up.

"Do you know what Calvin is?" pressed Diana. "Do you know what he really is?"

Sharon's lips tightened, and she used a pair of tongs to rearrange a bed of lettuce. It was all the answer Diana needed.

"He's a monster, Sharon."

"No, he's a victim. He's trapped, lost. You don't know what it's like for him."

"I don't need to know what it's like. All I know is that he's the most dangerous thing in this universe."

A woman stuck behind Diana, waiting for a shot at the meatballs, caught enough of the conversation to wrinkle her brow.

Sharon took Diana by the arm and pulled her aside. "You're making a scene."

"I'm just trying to understand this. Why would you do it?"

Sharon heaped some banana pudding on her plate, just to keep her hands busy. "I told you already, Diana. I wanted to touch something important."

"You're damn right he is," Diana said, "but he's also going to destroy our world. You have to know that."

"Of course I do. But it's not like it's something he wants to do. It's just something he has to do. It's that thing in the sky, it's that goddamn Fenris aspect."

"But that's him, isn't it?"

"No," said Sharon. "It's a part of him, but it doesn't reason. It doesn't think. It functions. It just exists. He's only a very small part of it."

They parted ways. Diana grabbed some pizza. Sharon added a few pieces of shrimp to her own plate.

"He's an anomaly," said Sharon. "And one day, he'll return to Fenris and…well, I don't know what'll happen to him then."

"Him? What about us? What about all these people?"

"They'll be taken care of. Greg has a plan to save as many as possible, but it's complicated. I can't explain it right now. Just promise me you won't bother Calvin about this."

Diana glanced to Calvin, then to Sharon.

"Promise me, please. There's no point in talking about it now. I'm the wrong person to talk to anyway. You need to talk to Greg to understand what we're doing. He's a smarmy ass, but he has a gift. He sees the world in ways that, like it or not, are true. If you can get past his smarm, you'll see that."

Diana didn't relish the idea.

Sharon said, "I'll talk to Greg, and set something up for tomorrow evening. Give me that much time."

Diana sighed.

"Just one more day can't hurt, can it?" asked Sharon.

"I guess not."

"Fantastic. You won't regret it, Diana."

"Yeah, we'll see."

They returned to the table. While Sharon forced chitchat, Diana devoured her food. She was too distracted by her thoughts to exercise the self-control to eat at a regular pace. She did her best not to stare at Calvin, and when she caught Zap staring she kicked his chair.

Calvin didn't look like something that would rip the universe to pieces one day. Knowing what he was, Diana hated to admit it, but she understood what Sharon had meant about touching something more incomprehensible than yourself.

Something beautiful.

Something horrible.

The last few weeks had altered her perception, and Diana found nothing contradictory about the notion.

She pushed aside such thoughts. She was getting used

to that, so even something like the end of the world was easy to ignore for an hour or two. She didn't mention it, and it didn't come up in conversation.

She decided to enjoy her dinner and her friends. A storm might sweep through time and erase this moment forever. And when you couldn't count on even yesterday to be there tomorrow, it only made every moment seem all the more precious and worth having.

Vom carried a plate piled with every scrap of food he could manage to fit onto it. The mound teetered on the edge of collapse. He sat, shoveled the serving down in two bites, and got up for seconds. She decided against warning him to pace himself. She could only expect so much.

She even let Vom have an eleventh plate.

CHAPTER TWENTY-FIVE

Sharon drove on autopilot. She paid just enough attention to traffic to avoid getting into an accident, although there were several close calls. She slammed on the brakes, barely avoiding a collision with the taxi in front of her.

"C'mon, you ass." She honked the horn twice.

"Is something wrong?" asked Calvin.

"Yes." She let the horn blare for a good three seconds. "People need to learn to drive in this city. That's the problem."

"Mmm-hmm. You do realize the light is red, right?"

Sharon swore. She wrung the steering wheel in her white-knuckled grip. She continued to glare alternately at the taxi and at the light for standing in her way, though if she'd reflected on it, she was in no rush.

"Are you sure there's nothing wrong?" he asked.

"Everything's fine," she said. "Why would anything be wrong?"

"Okay."

"Everything is perfect." Her voice was flat. "Everything's wonderful. Everything is just the way it's supposed to be."

"Okay."

The car behind her honked its horn. She stuck her arm out the window and flipped him off.

"Light's red, genius."

"Actually..."

Calvin didn't need to finish the sentence. The light had changed several seconds ago. The welcoming intersection beckoned. She pressed the gas pedal too roughly and their car lurched through with a screech.

"So nothing's wrong?" asked Calvin.

"No. Nothing's wrong. Why do you ask?"

"I don't know. Maybe because you almost ran over that guy in the last intersection."

"I had the light."

"He was blind."

Her jaw tightened. "So, he had a dog, didn't he? If he got hit, don't blame me. Blame the dog."

"Uh-huh. You should probably pull over before you kill somebody."

"Why bother?"

She took a turn too sharply and bounced off the curb, nearly clipping a small gathering of pedestrians.

"Pull over." He spoke with quiet authority. He didn't

give orders often, and it got her attention. She pulled into a parking lot. He reached over, turned off the car, and took the keys.

"Maybe I should drive."

"You don't know how."

"You could teach me."

He smiled. She didn't.

"Maybe I have better things to do than take care of you," she said.

"Whoa. Where did that come from?"

Sharon drummed her fingers on the steering wheel. She kept her eyes straight ahead. If she looked at him, she couldn't stay mad. She cared for him too much. Hell, she might've even loved him, and the ridiculousness of the idea made her smile humorlessly.

"Did I do something wrong?"

"You. No. You never do anything wrong."

And he didn't. He couldn't do anything wrong because he wasn't human. He was so far beyond human that you might as well call a hurricane wrong. Or label an asteroid malicious just for wiping out the dinosaurs. If he was to destroy the world, wasn't that within his rights?

Except he didn't do that. He never hurt anyone. He was the gentlest soul she'd ever come across, and while some might think it easy to be kind when you had no needs or wants, when you were immortal, invulnerable, and so above the petty squabbles of this world, Sharon suspected the opposite was true. She'd imagined herself in his position before, and it always ended with her going mad at all the insignificant specks buzzing around her, crushing them and their cities in her rage.

She closed her eyes. "I'm sorry."

He made the ill-defined noise he reserved for those moments when human behavior escaped him.

"It's my problem," she said. "I just didn't expect for it to come so soon. I thought we'd have more time."

If she'd admitted it, she hadn't expected this moment to come at all. She'd known that Calvin would leave one day. But considering the miserably short life span of humans, she'd always assumed that the day would be long after she'd died. Greg had always said it would be soon, but she'd just attributed that to the necessity of running a cult. You couldn't tell people the end of time was a thousand years away. It wasn't what they wanted to hear. People wanted front-row seats to the big show.

She apologized again. "I'm just being stupid. I know you need to go, and I should just be glad to have known you. It's more than I deserved."

"Hey, I won't hear any of that," he said. "This means something to me too. You're more than just the lady who takes care of my laundry."

"You're just saying that."

Calvin put a hand to her cheek and turned her face toward his.

"You're special."

"There are a million people out there just like me," she said.

"Maybe. But when the time comes, I won't remember any of them."

"I bet you say that to all your laundry ladies."

She didn't know if she believed him, but just that he'd said it made her feel better.

* * *

When they got home Sharon shut herself in the bathroom and called Greg. He answered the phone. He always answered, day or night, always him and not some underling. Greg, for all his faults, took the business of the Chosen as sacred and not to be shirked. He answered with his usual aplomb.

"Yello."

Sharon sat on the toilet and explained the Diana situation.

"I see. And how did she find out?"

"I don't know. She just did. She had this eyeball entity with her, and it couldn't stop staring at Calvin. I think it can see things and gives her the power to see things."

"Interesting."

"I told her you'd talk to her. Tomorrow."

"Well, I don't know if you recall, but I'll be rather busy tomorrow."

"I know, but I did promise her."

"Promises won't mean much in the future."

"Yes, but they mean something now."

"I have a lot on my plate."

Sharon said, "But what if she interferes? She is a warden. She has entities of her own."

"Now you're just being absurd. Fenris has nothing to fear from whatever influence she's amassed. Nothing can stop the future."

"I know, but you can at least consider it. One last convert, one last soul to save."

"If she has her own link to the greater universe, she's already saved."

Sharon swore. She despised that he was right.

"I'd like her to understand better, once it's all over."

"Her understanding won't matter to you, once it's all over."

"But it matters to me now."

"Sharon, I just don't see the point."

"I'm asking, Greg. That's the point. I've been contributing to this venture for years now, and I've never asked for any favors. This is my favor. You don't want to go into the future with a debt hanging over you, do you?"

"Debts won't matter in the—"

"Goddamn it, Greg."

He was silent for a few moments.

"Okay. We'll arrange a meeting."

"Thank you."

She hung up and stared at the bronze cast of a crescent moon with a human face and a great big smile hanging beside the bathroom mirror. For the first time in a long time, she saw the smile as the grim grin of a dangerous universe.

CHAPTER TWENTY-SIX

Diana found West on a ladder, changing smoke detector batteries in the hall.

"Hi," she said.

He grunted.

"You're not busy, are you?" she asked.

"Just taking care of a few things, Number Five."

He descended, and she helpfully held the ladder.

"I'm not distracting you? Because if this is important..."

He grabbed the ladder, moved it a few feet down the hall, and climbed it again. There were a surprising number of detectors. So many that West had a paper bag full of batteries in his right hand to replace them all.

"These aren't like cosmic smoke detectors or anything?" she asked. "It's not like if the batteries die in them the universe blows up, right?"

"Nope. Just being safe. Can never be too safe."

"Oh, good." She laughed to herself. It was silly to think everything West did had grand importance. It was ridiculous to assume that everything in the apartment building was connected by invisible strings to something vital to the universe outside.

He climbed down and repeated the short journey down the hall to another detector. She tried to be helpful and pointed out he'd missed one.

West stopped and wheeled upon her with unexpected energy. "We leave that one alone, Number Five. We don't ever change the batteries in that one. No matter how often it chirps for them."

The detector beeped.

He glared at it. "Shut up."

It chirped louder.

"Just ignore it," said West.

Diana pondered the small white disk affixed over her head. What great and terrible effect would it have if she slipped in while West wasn't looking and popped in fresh batteries?

She wanted to know. She blamed Zap's transferred curiosity, but it was deeper than that. The mind detested mysteries. It liked things to make sense or at least be predictable. It was human nature. It was why some people became scientists, theologians, philosophers, dedicating themselves to exploring those mysteries, and why most others took the easy way out and resolutely pretended those mysteries didn't exist. But her species hadn't crawled its way to civilization by *not* thinking about things, analyzing them, tearing them apart, putting them back together in fanciful, experimental combinations just to see what happened. Zap's influence had only amplified her natural inquisitiveness.

It wasn't all her and Zap, though. The smoke detector itself whispered temptations to her. She'd gotten used to those types of whispers and pushed them aside, along with her questions.

She made herself useful by holding West's ladder as he crept down the hall.

"I need your help. I don't know who else to talk to about this, and I thought you might have a useful perspective."

He grunted.

"You help people, right? You keep the universe running and all that, right?"

"Not exactly."

"But I've seen you do it. I've helped you."

He nodded. "I keep a few things in check. Nothing terribly important, though."

"Not important? If not for you the world would be crawling with giant bugs from the future or we'd all be floating around in space."

"Those things would take care of themselves regardless. Or not. It's not as if it matters much in the long run."

The conversation paused as they moved to the next detector.

"Doesn't matter? How can you say that? People would be dead without you. Heck, they might not have ever existed if not for you."

He leaned against the ladder. "And if they never had, who would notice?"

"You can't be that indifferent. Otherwise why would you do this job?"

"That's a strange question. Why does anyone do anything? Why does anyone take a bath when they know they're just going to get dirty again? Why does anyone eat when they know they're just going to be hungry again? Over and over again until eventually they die. And they will die. So why go to the doctor when you're sick? It's only postponing the inevitable. But at least it's something to do while waiting for the inevitable to happen."

"But that just makes it all sound so meaningless."

West replied, "And who says it isn't? Humans. You're always so obsessed with finding meaning in things. But not really. Because when you say *meaning* you really mean *specialness*. You want a nice warm hug from a cold, indifferent universe. You want everything you do to be important and everything you think to be catalogued and recorded."

"It's not like that," she said, "but it would be nice if it meant something."

"Yes, I agree. It would be nice."

He climbed down the ladder and knocked on the door of Apartment Three. Peter-thing answered.

"Here to replace the batteries," said West.

Peter-thing absorbed the information, smiled. "Safety first." He checked on a batch of baking cookies while West did his task.

"Why are there so many smoke detectors in this building?" asked Diana. "I don't remember seeing so many before."

"Do you really want to know?"

West sighed, and while he was normally a flat, unreadable soul, she sensed some annoyance on his part.

"I'm sorry, Number Five. I'm trying to see your point. I am. But I'm not exactly sure what it is."

She sat on Peter-thing's couch and blew a raspberry.

"Neither am I."

It was no wonder people went crazy. She was adrift. She couldn't think of a good reason why she should be concerned about any of this. It was like politics. Getting involved seemed like a good idea sometimes, but ultimately it only served to disillusion and disappoint. West was right about the search for meaning. Nobody really wanted meaning. They just didn't want meaninglessness. Except for maybe anarchists, but even most of them tried to shoehorn some kind of sense into it.

West's annoyance changed to something stranger. Sympathy.

"Okay, let's go then. I have something to show you."

"No."

"What?"

"No, I don't want to go on another of your bizarre, otherworldly sightseeing tours where I fight dinosaurs or destroy planets with my sneezes. Those don't make anything clearer. They only leave me more confused than when I started. I just want to figure out what I'm supposed to do. Can we just skip the weirdness this time?"

"I suppose. If that's what you really want."

"It is."

"Are you certain? Because the Isthmus of Skrunb is beautiful this time of year. As long as you ignore the shrieking butterflies."

"Oh, I'm certain."

Peter-thing lumbered over with a plateful of ginger-snaps and snickerdoodles. He offered one to each, which they graciously accepted, even though Diana didn't care for either type of cookie.

"Meaning of life is cookies."

She nodded politely, took a nibble of her gingersnap.

"Cookies are good. Cookies make people happy. Cookies don't question what they are here for because cookies know."

"You do know cookies aren't alive, right?" she asked.

"Maybe not," said Peter-thing, "but does cookie know that?"

"Okay, this is getting a little existential for me. Thanks for trying, guys, but this isn't working."

She nibbled her treat but didn't have the heart to finish it off.

She started the trudge back to her apartment. Somehow West beat her to the top of the stairs.

"It's not the end of the world," he said. "Fenris will tear his way from this reality, but the damage will only be temporary."

"Aha! I knew that you knew." Grinning, she stabbed her finger at him, though it made very little sense since she hadn't caught him lying. He hadn't slipped up. But she'd take all the victories, real or imagined, she could.

"The universe will survive. It will stitch its broken shards into something workable. It always does. It's not any different than when World War Three was postponed to next week. Or that time brown became yellow and yellow became the number seven. This change will be bigger than that, but if you're speaking of the literal end, then it's not that."

"Stop that."

"Stop what?"

"Stop trying to get me not to care."

"Are you sure about that?" he asked. "It's a lot easier when you don't."

"This is my world we're talking about. Maybe stuff like this happens all the time. And maybe I never noticed before. But I've noticed this time, and I don't like it."

"So it's about you then?" asked West.

Her first response was to deny that, but it came to her that he was right. If the world ended tomorrow, who would be left to mourn it? Just her. She didn't want it to end or change or whatever because she didn't want to be left alone, to be deprived of her lifeline to the sane and normal, although even that was an increasingly frayed thread.

"Yes. Damn it, yes. That's what it's about."

"Fenris is inevitable."

She knew she had him here. Having fortuitously, if accidentally, lured him into a verbal trap, she wasn't about to let him go.

"According to you, it's all inevitable. It's inevitable that I'll go mad, and it's inevitable that the sun will blow up someday. It's inevitable that bugs from the future will one day travel back in time and rewrite history. It doesn't mean I have to sit back and take it."

"No, you don't have to. But it'll be better for everyone if you do. Because interfering in this one will only make it worse."

"Says who?"

"Says me. When you've been doing this job as long as I have, you get a sense of these things. And I can tell you that some futures can be averted. Some changes should be avoided. And some are unavoidable. Some cannot be stopped, and to try will only cause more harm than you can imagine."

"And I'm just supposed to take your word on that."

"That's up to you. But you came to me for my perspective, Number Five. Seems strange to ignore it just because it wasn't what you wanted to hear."

His bag of batteries clacked like a maraca as he descended the stairs.

Diana almost swore, but her frustration left her drained. She wanted to save her world, but it wasn't about her world. It was about her. If she could do something positive in the midst of all this confusion and madness, then she just might be able to convince herself that she wasn't so trivial and unimportant after all. Just because she wasn't certain there was any grand plan to this didn't mean she couldn't come up with one.

She walked back to her apartment, where her monsters waited for her. Vom and Smorgaz sat on the couch, watching a version of the old *Land of the Lost* TV show that seemed to be filmed from the Sleestaks' perspective. Zap hovered in the corner, staring at the wall or maybe the greater mysteries behind it. And Pogo hopped at her feet and whimpered.

It was comforting. Like a Norman Rockwell painting populated by infernal manifestations. The monsters were just like her, lost souls, and if there was anywhere she belonged, this was it. She wasn't an outsider. Not anymore.

All things considered, there were worse places in the universe to call home.

The phone rang. It was Sharon.

"Greg wants to meet you. Tomorrow night."

CHAPTER TWENTY-SEVEN

Diana and her monsters pulled up to the estate. There was something off about it. It wasn't only that it was a huge plot of land, bigger than most neighborhoods. The entire place shimmered like a heat mirage. Like her apartment, this place had become disconnected from the rest of reality. It was an island tethered to her world, a waypoint before greater mysteries beyond.

Vom's fur bristled as he turned a sicklier shade of green. "I think I'm going to be sick."

"Oh, God," said Diana. "Don't do it in the car."

Vom stuck his head out the passenger-side window and vomited a gazelle, twenty-two pounds of gravel, and a bar stool. The bewildered gazelle stumbled to its hooves and dashed away.

Spawns jumped off Smorgaz's back like popcorn. They even made popping noises when they did so.

Zap blasted a hole in her roof before shutting his all-seeing eye.

"Sorry."

Pogo buried his head under his paws and tucked his tail between his legs.

"What the heck is wrong with you guys?" she asked.

"It's this place," said Zap. "It's throwing everything out of whack. I don't think we can go in there with you." Cosmic lightning flashed under his eyelid.

"Are you sure?"

Vom regurgitated half a shark and some slightly chewed office furniture. Smorgaz's spawn were rapidly filling up the backseat.

"Get out then," she said. "Especially you, Vom. Before you throw up acid or something."

The creatures exited the vehicle.

"Maybe you should reconsider this," said Vom, who then vomited up a misshapen limb that flailed at the air with its claws before he managed to gulp it back down.

"Agreed," said Smorgaz. "I don't like the idea of you walking into Fenris's lair without any backup."

Diana said, "It's not a lair. It's a house. And I don't need backup. This isn't a commando mission."

"Still seems a touch reckless," said Vom.

"Safety in numbers." A few dozen spawn milled at Smorgaz's feet. The strange powers of the estate limited their life span to a few seconds before they dissolved into ash, but he was still spitting out clones fast enough that their numbers were growing.

Pogo rolled over on his back and whimpered.

"I don't like it either," she said, "but maybe it's better this way. How would it look if I show up with you guys behind me like some private army of the damned? It'd be too confrontational."

"But aren't you being confrontational?" asked Vom.

"I'm not really sure what I'm doing," she admitted, "but from what I've glimpsed Fenris is unstoppable. Even you couldn't really do anything against him other than maybe annoy him."

Zap bobbed. "It's true."

"Well, if there's nothing to be done about this, then why bother going at all?" asked Vom.

She'd asked herself the same question. Several times. The only answer she could come up with was that she had to do something. If her only two choices were hiding from the inevitable or facing it head-on, she had decided the latter was preferable, if only because it gave her the illusion of controlling her own destiny.

"I know I'm your lifeline," she said, "but you don't have to worry. Everything will be fine, and you won't get stuck in the closet again." It surprised her how certain she sounded when she couldn't be sure of anything.

"Closet? Is that what you think this is about to me?" Vom shook his head. "Do you think I really give a damn if I'm locked away for a few hundred years waiting for the next witless sap to inherit me? I'm ageless. I could wait a million years in that closet. It'd be a little boring, but I've been bored before.

"No, we like you, Diana. We don't want anything bad to happen to you."

Smorgaz and Zap echoed the sentiment. Pogo wagged his spiky, whiplike tail.

She smiled despite herself.

"I like you too. Hell, you guys just might be the best friends I've ever had. But this is my reality, my fight."

They started a new round of protests.

"No arguments," she said. "I'm in charge here, right? That means we do things my way. If it makes you feel any better, I give Zap permission to keep watch over me via that all-seeing eye of his."

"I can't see in there," said Zap. "There's interference in the space-time continuum, a fifth-dimensional collapse along the polyfractal axis that's condensing all possible futures into a single unobservable waveform."

"What does that mean? You can't see anything?" asked Diana.

"Oh, I can see." Zap rose in the air, waved his tentacles. "I can see into realms beyond imagination. I just can't see much into this one."

"Does that mean it's all done? That the future is over?"

"All it really means is that someone has shoved Schrodinger's cat into a box and nailed it shut until this thing is all over. Whether that means your world is over or not...honestly, I can't say. But considering the situation, I wouldn't lay odds on anything positive. When you get down to it, reality is a stack of potentialities, some more potential than others. But when chaos becomes certainty, then that certainty is usually oblivion."

"Right then," she said. "I'm going in. Wish me luck."

They did. Except for Vom who was busy regurgitating a bus.

She pulled away, taking one last glance at the extradimensional refugees in her rearview mirror. She wondered at the wisdom of driving willingly into a place where immortal horrors feared to tread, but she'd come this far.

The unattended manor gates opened for her. She knew they were probably on an automated system or operated by a security guard via a remote switch, but it was mysterious and otherworldly just the same. A wave of heat and cold hit her as she drove onto the property. The gates closed behind her, and there was a twinge above her right eye. The heat vanished. The cold remained.

It'd been noon on the outside, but on this side of the gate twilight was falling. The full moon spread a bright blue light across the sky. Fenris glistened like a moist emerald.

The lush forest surrounding the road was a strange mix of traditional greenery and odd plants she didn't recognize. Things lurked in the shadows. Instinct told her they were nothing to fear. Just insubstantial shades caught between realities.

Eventually she reached the big house at the center of this. Sharon sat on the front porch, waiting for Diana.

That twinge above Diana's eye spread to her entire scalp.

"Sorry I'm late," she said. "I got hung up."

They shook hands. It was an awkward gesture between them. There was something about this place, something that labeled Diana an outsider at best, an intruder at worst.

Sharon led Diana into the house. They passed through the entryway, down a hall, and into a dining room, where Greg was having something to eat.

"Ah, good to see you again, Diana." He didn't sound sincere.

He offered her something. She turned it down. Since she had entered the estate her appetite had faded for the first time in a long while. It might have been a welcome feeling, if not for the weird tingles and pricks across her skin at the moment.

"Thank you for seeing me," she said.

"Oh, no need to thank me. Sharon has been very important to our cause. She made quite a case for you."

"Diana has concerns," said Sharon. "I was hoping you'd be able to help her with those."

Greg smiled as he spread some pâté on a cracker. "Concerns are only natural. You're only human, after all, right?"

He laughed. The women echoed the chuckle awkwardly.

"So what's on your mind, Diana?"

She tried to organize her thoughts, although the way the atmosphere pressed against her made that difficult. Not to mention that she genuinely didn't know how to voice her concerns.

"It's Calvin. You do realize he's going to destroy the world, right?"

Greg offered a patronizing grin. "Ah, there's your problem. Do you really think that's what's going to happen? No wonder you're so concerned."

He took a drink of wine, but he did so with agonizing slowness. He picked up the glass, swished the liquid around, sniffed it, took a very slight sip, and set the glass back into its original place with robotic precision.

"Fenris isn't going to destroy the world. He's going to purify it. He's going to strip away all the unnecessary bits and leave us with something better, more beautiful and raw."

He narrowed his eyes. His grin became more obviously sinister.

"Primal."

"With all due respect," said Diana angrily, "what the hell does that even mean?" She was getting sick of this vaguely philosophical nonsense.

Greg was taken aback. "I've been more than accommodating to this point, but it's clear you don't get it. Perhaps you lack the ability to understand the subtleties—"

"I'm sorry," she said. "I didn't mean to snap, but it's just so frustrating."

"I can imagine." And for once, he sounded sincere. "Can we cut the bullshit?" he said. "You seem like a good person, and we're so close to the end that I don't see any reason not to level with you."

He stood, picked at something in his teeth.

"It's all crap. All of it. The cult. This house. All the talk about primordial beauty. It sounds good on paper, and it brings in the cultists, makes everyone feel better, like they're part of some grand, cosmic life cycle. But it's complete and utter bullshit. New Agey nonsense that doesn't mean a damn thing.

"I only come up with it because people can't handle the truth. Or maybe they just don't want to hear it. Regardless, I can see that you don't need me to feed you the standard line. Do you want to know the truth, then?

"The truth is that I have no more control over anything that's happening than you do. I don't control Fenris. I don't exert the slightest influence over him. And I most certainly can't change his nature or stop what will happen."

"But aren't Calvin and Fenris the same thing?" asked Diana. "Can't you just talk to Calvin about it?"

"Calvin is just a very small piece of Fenris, and he doesn't have any more control over the moon god than I do. That's the truth. Fenris is one entity divided into three aspects. The moon is the physical substance of the creature. Fenris itself is all of its metaphysical bulk. And Calvin, tiny little Calvin, is the creature's intellect. Divided, each of these aspects is largely harmless. But when joined together, they become an absolute. Unstoppable. Inescapable. A united Fenris will tear this world to pieces, and there's not a damn thing to be done about it.

"But I have seen the future, and while our universe will be almost destroyed by Fenris's escape, it will not be irreparably damaged. It will fix itself. The broken threads will wrap themselves into new shapes, new forms. Our world will survive. In some savage form. I'm merely attempting to save as many souls as I can in the aftermath by harnessing the mystical force unleashed to survive the storm of chaos and ensure that some of us come out the other side alive."

Diana's vision grew bleary. She had trouble breathing.

"Oh, I can't guarantee that what people come out the other side will be recognizable as such. In fact, I can say with certainty that to survive the cataclysm we'll have to change into something else entirely. The survivors will be monsters, but at least something of us will remain. Something deep down. It's not much." He shrugged. "But it's the best we can hope for."

"But..." Her legs were weak. "But..." She couldn't think straight.

"Sorry. I guess I should've warned you. Only those who are linked with the moon god can tolerate this place for long. Your connection to other forces is going to have adverse side effects."

Diana stood halfway before falling to the floor.

"Greg, what are you doing?" said Sharon. "This isn't right."

He sighed. "Sharon, this woman means well, but she could jeopardize everything. She clearly knows just enough to be dangerous. If she'd been smarter, she wouldn't have come in here at all. If she'd been dumber, she'd have stayed out of it."

Diana twitched. She crawled in a random direction, confused by her unreliable senses.

"You said you'd help her understand," said Sharon.

"I know, and I'm sorry that I lied. But it's a lie for the greater good. If she interferes, if she disrupts the delicate balance, then Fenris will destroy everything. You know that's true. You know that this is the right thing to do, no matter how distasteful it might be."

Diana gurgled. Sharon stopped looking at the pathetic thing.

"We can't just leave her there."

"We'll put her in one of the bedrooms. She'll be fine once it's all over."

They carried her upstairs to one of the nicer rooms and laid her down on the bed.

Diana's pale flesh was sallow and waxen. If she was trying to speak, her voice came out only as a series of unintelligible noises.

"In a few hours," he said, "none of this will matter."

"What about her monsters?" asked Sharon.

"I wouldn't worry about them. The interference that's gripped her has probably destroyed their ability to focus as well. And even if they are still alert enough, they can't come in here."

"It doesn't seem right, Greg."

"Right and wrong won't matter tomorrow."

He walked out of the room.

Sharon watched Diana convulse for a few minutes. Her body became a twisted ball of knots as muscles bulged and flexed against her will. Her eyes had rolled back, and she could only drool.

Sharon hated him for it, but Greg was correct.

"I'm sorry."

Diana gasped and for a moment there was intelligence in her eyes. She grabbed Sharon's leg, tried to say something, then fell twitching again. Sharon left Diana to struggle with her own broken form.

CHAPTER TWENTY-EIGHT

Vom was back in the closet. He didn't remember going back to it, but he never did.

He moved some coats aside and cleared away some shoes for a place to sit. He couldn't see anything while the door was shut, but he didn't need to. Vom knew the closet well. Knew every pair of shoes, every hanger in it, so he was surprised when something squishy and unexpected got in his way.

"Ow," said the unexpected thing.

"Zap, is that you?" asked Vom.

"Who else would it be? Where are we?"

"The closet."

Smorgaz spoke up in the dark. "Your closet?"

Vom pondered. This was new.

Something poked him in the back.

"Watch it!"

"Sorry," said Smorgaz.

"How did we get in here?" asked Zap.

"I don't know, but it was crowded enough without the two of you." Vom shoved Smorgaz, who shoved back. In the struggle, Vom accidentally kicked Zap.

"Hey, watch it!"

"You watch it!" grumbled Vom. "This is my closet."

"Well, if we're going to be stuck sharing the damn thing, we'll have to make the best of it." Despite Zap's supernatural vision, he couldn't see anything in the darkness. For a being capable of glimpsing the hydrogen atoms dancing at the heart of stars, it was disconcerting. He probed the floor with his tentacles. They ran across the cheap carpeting, the old shoes. "Wow. This really is a closet."

"What did you think it was?" asked Vom.

"I just assumed it was different when you were trapped in it. I didn't think it would be so . . . closety."

"Nope. That's all it is. Actually, I think it's a little bit bigger now that you two are here. Maybe some space was added to accommodate all of us."

"Not enough," said Smorgaz as someone jabbed him in the eye. "So what do we do now?"

"We wait," said Vom, "for the next person to get the apartment."

"How long is that going to take?"

"Could be in five minutes," said Vom. "Could be a thousand years."

"Does this mean Diana is dead?" asked Smorgaz.

"Probably." Vom sighed. "Too bad. I liked her."

"I don't think she is," said Zap.

"I know it stinks," said Vom, "but if she were alive I wouldn't be in here. It's only if the link between us disappears that I get shoved back in this place."

"But what about us?" asked Zap. "Why are Smorgaz and I here?"

"Because…I don't know, but there has to be some perfectly good reason for it."

"Yes, and that reason is that Diana isn't dead yet. I can sense her, feel her presence. Can't you?"

Smorgaz shifted, stepping on Vom's foot. "Sorry." He moved again, knocking hangers off the rod. "Oops."

"Stand still while we figure this out," said Zap.

"Just let me move this fur coat out of the way first."

"Hey, watch the hands," said Vom.

Smorgaz chuckled. "My mistake."

Zap shouted, "Will you two shut up and listen to me? Feel it. Can't you sense Diana's influence?"

"I am feeling a bit confused and overwhelmed," said Vom. "And kind of pissed off at the same time."

"Yeah," agreed Smorgaz. "Me too."

They quieted, each tuning his personal metaphysical radio to Diana's frequency. The signal was static-filled, muffled, but it was there. That they could think clearly at all proved it.

"Something has gone wrong," said Zap. "They must have done something to her."

"Figure that out with your all-seeing eye, did you?" asked Vom.

"Shut up."

"So what difference does it make?" asked Smorgaz. "Whether she's alive or dead, we're still trapped in here until someone lets us out, right?"

"If she's not dead, then maybe we don't have to wait for that. Maybe we can get out on our own."

"Don't be stupid," said Vom. "There's no way out of this box. I've tried."

"You've tried when you were mere cosmic flotsam in a cold storage room," said Zap. "But now, I think this is just a reaction to Diana's situation. Maybe if we put some effort into it we can open the closet together."

"Can't hurt to try," said Vom.

They pushed, grunting and groaning and straining. They were inexhaustible, but after half an hour they did get bored.

Vom frowned in the dark. "This is a waste of time."

"We can't give up," said Zap.

"Why not?"

"Because Diana wouldn't give up."

"Oh, hell." Vom threw his shoulder into the door. "Let's do this."

To his surprise, the door opened. He fell out and onto the floor. Pogo squealed, lapping at Vom's face with his jagged tongue while West stood in the room, his hand on the closet door's handle.

"What were you doing back in there?" asked West.

"It's a bit complicated." Zap floated out. "Thanks for letting us out."

West rubbed his face. "Don't thank me. Thank the dog. Came and got me."

"Why didn't Pogo go into the closet?"

"The dog doesn't belong to this apartment. He belongs to Apartment Two."

Zap disintegrated the coffee table.

"All right. Back in business. Now let's go rescue Diana!"

Yipping and hissing, Pogo hopped around.

They ran from the apartment and down the hall, pausing at the threshold to the outside universe. From inside the building the flux of the universe was visible as a strange stew of bubbles floating in the air itself. Other worlds could be glimpsed in the glittering spheres. The universe was fraying around the edges. The pressure from all the outside realities might cause the whole thing to collapse, crushing it into nothingness.

"I wouldn't recommend going out there," said West. "Without Diana to anchor you and with everything falling apart, there's no telling what reaction it could cause."

Fenris roared, and the world shuddered.

"Safest place in the world is right here," said West. "Whatever happens out there, it's best to let it run its course."

"But what about Diana?" asked Vom.

"She might survive it." West shrugged. "Might not."

The monsters said nothing.

"So what should we do?" asked Smorgaz.

"Leave it be," said West. "You'll only make it worse."

"But what about Diana?" asked Zap this time.

"She wouldn't leave us behind," said Smorgaz. "She'd try to help us."

"No, she wouldn't," said West. "She'd get rid of you the first chance she could."

The monsters didn't even argue the point.

"I still like her," said Vom.

They all agreed on this. They knew she was just another human, and there were billions more out there. Or, if the humans all disappeared tomorrow, something else would be there to fill her warden position.

But they liked her.

"Oh, heck," said Zap. "What are we even risking? There's nothing out there that can hurt us. Right?"

They looked to West, who stared back at them inscrutably.

Pogo bound past the threshold. Nothing happened to the hellhound. He turned and shrieked at the others to follow him. Reasonably assured that they were beyond the primordial madness taking place, they followed. They made it only a few steps before succumbing to the strange forces and collapsing to the ground. They burst from their skins, transforming into shapes closer to their true forms.

Vom grew a dozen extra limbs and started shoveling concrete, automobiles, and lampposts into a hundred gullets in a blind devouring hunger. Smorgaz became a great misshapen blob of purple. Dozens of pods burst open as countless clones spawned. Zap crackled with power. His gaze swept across the world, blasting holes in the street.

Pogo remained unchanged because that was his true form.

The mindless horrors turned on each other. Vom bit off one of Zap's tentacles. Zap responded by burning Vom's face off. The great immobile lump that was Smorgaz screeched, and his spawn tackled Vom and Zap, clamoring over them. It was only their focus on each other that kept the block from being reduced to ruins and ash.

Pogo raised his head and shrieked. The other beasts stopped their struggle as the minuscule creature yipped in their direction. Vom, Zap, and Smorgaz turned their attention skyward. They launched themselves into the air and toward the moon god above.

"Well, I'll be," said West. "You're just full of surprises, aren't you?"

Pogo squealed, then ran off down the street.

Sharon had wanted to speak to Calvin one last time, but things were so hectic she didn't get a chance to exchange more than a few words with him. The hell of it was that the robes, chants, and ceremony all amounted to so much busywork. Nothing the Chosen did had any influence over Fenris. The cult was a parasite clinging to the moon god's belly.

Calvin sat on his throne. For once he didn't look bored. The Chosen swayed and sang his praises in nonsense syllables that Greg had given them. She stood beside the throne, phoning it in, fully aware that the creature above didn't care in the slightest about her degree of enthusiasm.

Some of the more fervent cultists stripped naked and screamed gibberish. *Morons*, she thought.

Greg stood on the other side of the throne. He was silent, relaxed. No need for the show now.

The earth rumbled as the tentacle god-beast drew closer and closer to the moon it had spent countless millennia pursuing. The hapless ordinary people who pursued their lives, blissfully ignorant of the strangeness of a much vaster universe, remained so. The coming joining was invisible, and would be until it was too late.

Fenris brushed the moon with the tip of his tentacle.

Calvin's hand tingled. He peeled away the skin like a candy wrapper. It even made that crinkling noise.

The Chosen's chant changed, transforming from nonsense into a string of syllables not made for human mouths. They swayed in unison, whispered in a language Calvin had forgotten long ago.

He remembered now.

He glanced at Sharon. He'd regret leaving her behind. The rest of the human race and the small sliver of reality they called home he'd be glad to cast off. He'd miss some things. Movies. Books. Apple pie. Doritos. The feel of a sandy beach between his toes. Toes.

Mostly, he'd miss Sharon.

His flesh fell off. He stood naked, an ebony god of pure intellect. Not his true form. He had no physical form. Even this was just a contrivance forced on him by a universe unable to accept what was happening.

Two crackling bolts lanced from his chest into the sky, connecting with the moon and Fenris. The mind, the body, and the power. Three aspects of a single entity that had been too long divided.

The estate broke free of its boundaries and spread like a green shadow across the face of the city. From there it would devour the world like an invading organism bent on rewriting itself on the fabric of the universe. Humanity would have screamed in collective terror if not for the fact that everyone within a thousand miles was transformed into piles of moss.

The cultists cast off their cloaks. The hairy, four-armed wolves howled and danced in reckless abandon as their god began his ascent. Except for the beast that had been Sharon. She stood before Calvin, lowered her head, and whimpered.

He felt the final spasm of the universe as Fenris wrapped his tentacles around the moon. And in a moment it would all be over.

"Goodbye, Sharon."

The moment didn't come.

Vom plowed into the moon god, knocking him away from his goal. Fenris shrieked as Calvin fell to Earth. False skin wrapped around him. Stifling, rotten, smothering flesh.

He vomited yellow slime onto the stone floor. Being crammed back into mortal flesh, even if only the illusion of such, was uncomfortable. It was like tight shoes he'd gotten used to wearing, and now that they were off he didn't want them back on.

The cult reverted to halfway-human forms. Calvin used the shredded remains of a discarded robe to cover Sharon's naked body.

Greg said, "What the hell?"

In the night sky Fenris clashed with only slightly less horrific entities for the future of the moon and the universe by proxy.

Pogo jumped from the bushes and landed before Calvin's throne. The dog blackened and smoked as the alien magic of the estate sizzled against his flesh. Calvin recognized a fellow greater eldritch when he saw one.

The dog gasped painfully, turning on the cult and growling. Then he ran into the house, smashing his way through the front door, bounding up the stairs, and finding Diana on the bed.

Pogo lowered his head and cried out mournfully. The roof exploded. The unnatural fog that played havoc with Diana faded. She sat up, shook the cobwebs away. She ached and had a hell of a headache, but she could think again. She could move. As long as Pogo was close enough, casting his own strange aura over her, she was functional.

She forced herself to stand, trudged with heavy steps downstairs and to the alcove where the cult stood. They stood, shocked, at this unbeliever in their midst while their lord above clashed with the monstrous usurpers.

Diana cleared her dry throat.

"We need to talk."

CHAPTER TWENTY-NINE

Fenris, the great tentacled horror, lashed out. A whip of his tendrils batted away Vom and obliterated a dozen Smorgaz clones.

Vom pounced. His countless mouths bit Fenris's unstable flesh. Bright orange and blue bile sprayed from the wounds. Zap's bolts blew searing chunks off the moon god. The cloud of Smorgaz spawn dogpiled, covering everything in a squirming mass of purple.

"What are you doing?" asked Greg, though speaking was difficult with the fangs jutting from his jaws. "You're interfering!"

Diana ignored him and the confused, twisted half-abominations of the cultists around her.

"You can't do this," she said to Calvin. "It's not right."

"You don't understand," he replied.

"I understand. I do, but—"

"Shut up!" Greg growled. "You have no right to speak to him. Our lord only speaks to predator, not prey."

"Put a sock in it, Greg. If he's going to destroy my universe, then I think someone on the con side of the argument should get a say."

The cultists encircled Diana. The flaps circling Pogo's sucker mouth waggled as he growled. While he was a thing as unstoppable and inconceivable as Fenris, most of his power was spent keeping Diana moving. He wouldn't be of use for much else.

"You really don't want to do this," she said. "You're still civilized human beings under there somewhere. You have to be."

A vicious grin crossed Greg's face. "Kill her."

"Ah, hell."

The furious cultists leaped into action, burying Diana beneath a swarm of claws and teeth.

Greg half-laughed, half-bayed at the sight of it.

Calvin stared inscrutably at the savage pack. Its bloodthirsty shrieks rang in his ears.

Above, Fenris shrugged off his opponents. Smorgaz spawn streaked across the atmosphere like meteors of white fire. They struck the tip of South America, disintegrating Argentina. With freshly grown tentacles, Fenris tossed Vom aside into Zap.

The cultists grew hairier, more beastly. Sharon groaned as her body shifted in Calvin's arms.

He didn't do anything. Just watched as the battle played out. As Fenris closed in on the moon, the change in his physical body started again. Before it went very far, though, the cultbeasts started whimpering as Diana threw off her attackers with a flurry of punches and backhands. The claws and teeth of the cult proved unable to harm Diana, and they regenerated from even the most serious injuries to bounce back into the fray. Meanwhile, Diana's monsters weren't capable of causing much lasting injury to Fenris, but they were able to push him away from the moon.

It went like this for several minutes. Sometimes the moon god would draw closer to his goal, and the cult would change into fearsome, four-armed beasts and overwhelm Diana. Then Fenris would be pushed back, and she'd start winning.

Calvin stayed with Sharon. Each of her transformations seemed more difficult, more painful than the last. And her body was losing cohesion. Her hair fell out. The outer layer of her skin liquefied, dripping into a grayish puddle at her feet.

A beast latched on to Diana's arm with its jaws, and she yelped. She'd felt it. Her monsters, the source of her invulnerability, were losing to Fenris. She punched the cultist and threw him across the garden, even as more advanced on her.

"What the hell am I doing?"

While her powers were almost unlimited right now, she was still too mortal to use them effectively, too bound by cause and effect. But she was tapped into Unending Smorgaz, and there was no reason to fight this horde alone.

Two dozen Diana clones materialized. They were naked and purple and their hasty assembly meant that they weren't great conversationalists, but they were perfect for what she needed. Her personal army engaged the cultists, keeping them busy as she approached Calvin.

Diana turned to Calvin. "You have to stop this."

He hesitated. "I can't."

"I know it has to stink what you've been through, how you've spent the I-don't-know-how-many eons trapped here, just waiting for this. But you don't have to do it this way."

"You don't understand. I can't stop it. It's not my decision."

"Whose is it then?"

Calvin pointed to Fenris. "His."

The tentacle horror had decided to ignore Diana's monsters. They did their best to get in his way, but he inched closer to the moon.

"He won't be reasoned with," said Calvin. "He doesn't even have reason. That's sort of my job."

The monsters in the sky raged. The night cracked in two, and behind the rift strange things stirred, clawing their way into the universe.

"There are lives at stake," said Diana. "Billions of them."

"What about me?" he asked. "I didn't ask for this either. It just happened. Don't I have the right to move on, to finally be free? If you stepped in an anthill and someone told you not to move your foot for fear of stepping on any more ants, would you do it?"

"It's not the same thing."

"Isn't it? To you, Fenris is a monster, an incomprehensible behemoth to be feared. To him, you're just a tiny dot on the horizon that isn't even worth noticing. Why is your convenience worth a million ants, but mine isn't worth a billion humans?"

"But you're destroying my universe."

Calvin smiled, shaking his head. "You don't get it, do you? I'm not the destroyer. You are."

As they wrestled with her clones, the Chosen's brittle limbs snapped off. With every wheezing breath they expelled gray clouds of their own vaporizing organs. The fight went out of them. She willed her clones to disappear, no longer having any need of them. The cultists lay on the ground, dying, along with the lush grass beneath them. Even the marble steps seemed to be crumbling into dust.

"I was never meant to be here. Your reality can't tolerate my presence any longer. If you don't let me leave now then your universe won't just change. It'll disintegrate with the thrashing fury of Fenris himself. One way or another, I'll be leaving this world behind. The only question is what's left in my wake."

Diana strained her senses. She glimpsed the threads of creation frayed to the breaking point. Lesser horrors like Vom and his ilk were irritants in the ordered chaos that was everything around her. They might cause weirdness here and there, might throw things out of whack, but they were tolerable nuisances.

Fenris was different. His very existence was unbearable in the long run. The universe had kept him from destroying everything up to now, but the end of the road was here.

Her monsters managed to hold Fenris at a standstill. With every bit of their titanic power they held the moon god at bay. Fenris's tentacles whipped desperately at the silver orb just out of his reach. If he had been just a bit smarter, he might have used those tentacles against his opponents, who were barely able to hold him in place. But his obsessive pursuit of the moon drove all such strategies from his absent mind.

Diana could see only pain and confusion reflected in Fenris's hundred eyes. He was just an animal trying to escape from a trap, trying to find his way home.

She didn't know what to do. Her fragile world seemed doomed. Either it would be transformed into something unrecognizable or it would be destroyed entirely.

She sat on the crumbling marble steps. It wasn't an easy decision.

Calvin and Sharon sat beside her. Sharon's body was holding together reasonably well, though her flesh was pale, her body thin and fragile.

If Diana had been able to change along with the universe and have her own genetic code rewritten to match the new world, she could have found some comfort in that. But whatever new reality awaited, she would still be herself, an alien in a twisted, unfamiliar realm.

"Damn it," she said. "This sucks."

"Tell me about it," agreed Calvin. "I don't even know what's waiting out there for me. Can't really remember. But it's all a question of scale, isn't it? Fenris might be an indestructible force in this plane of existence, but for all I know I'm just a small fish in an infinitely larger pond. I might float free of this reality, only to be devoured by something even greater."

"It's just an endless string of mysteries and questions, isn't it?"

"Maybe that's just the way life works," he said.

"Well, crap. That's just unsatisfying."

The manor spontaneously collapsed into a heap. No one commented on it.

"I can't really tell you what to do here, Diana," he said. "It's your decision."

She closed her eyes and willed her monsters to give up their fight. They released Fenris. Her roomies materialized beside her. She found restoring their sentience easier than expected. They shrank to their mortal proportions, stripped of the bulk of their awesome might.

They didn't look well. Like they'd just woken up with a terrific hangover.

"Did we do it?" asked Vom. "Did we save the universe?"

Diana shrugged. She didn't have a good answer.

Fenris squealed delightedly as it wrapped its many tentacles around the moon.

Calvin's flesh fell away. His ebony ethereal form rose into the air. The universe stopped crumbling. The Chosen rose, trapped in their beastly shapes but whole and restored. They didn't attack, instead submissively slinking toward their master.

Sharon was at the head of the pack. She whimpered, and in all the universe it was the only thing Calvin noticed. He reached out to touch her muzzle, but his immaterial hand passed through her.

He spoke, but the voice resonated from both this shape and the great cosmic monster embracing the moon.

We both knew this day was coming. I carry on, but know this: long after your world has faded to dust, I will remember you.

"See that you do," Diana said.

The moon god turned his attention to her. His gaze was a blast of heat that nearly knocked her to the ground. She dug in her heels and forced him to confront the insignificant thing before him, to remind him that all these tiny things were still down here.

"Maybe it's our nature to not worry about stepping on ants. But we'd probably think differently if we spent a few thousand years living among them. Do us a favor," Diana said. "On your way to...whatever...try not to step on too many of us."

His face lacked features, but she sensed a smile. The pressure let up, and she could stand without feeling as if a thousand worlds rested on her shoulders.

Fenris swallowed the moon. Calvin zipped away in the blink of an eye to merge with the other two parts of his divided self. The great entity glanced down at them, and though he also had no mouth and his body was nothing but a mass of tentacles and eyes, Diana thought she saw something in those eyes.

Fenris winked (or at least blinked half of his eyes in what she took as a wink). Delicately, he tore a rift in the sky with two tentacles. He exerted a fraction of his limitless might to hold the broken strands of the universe together, keeping it from falling into chaos. With a joyous howl Fenris, now possessed of the power to free himself, rejoined with the intellect to do so in subtle ways his monstrous third would never have fathomed, slipped from the universe. On his way out he tied a few threads back together, restoring all the mounds of moss to their former human shapes and erasing all the damage left in his wake. The universe itself took care of the rest, repelling the alien ecosystem and rebuilding everything as it had been.

Except for the moon. There was only a dim star-filled sky left in its place.

The cult howled with ecstasy at the triumphant departure of their god. Except for Sharon, who released a long, miserable wail. For several seconds after the other cultists had returned to their human shapes, Sharon stayed a beast, reluctant to give up the last bits of Fenris left to her. But even she couldn't hold on to it for long.

Diana took Sharon's hand. "It's for the best."

Sharon nodded. "I know."

A tendril dipped back into reality just long enough to slide along the celestial rift in Fenris's wake and seal it shut like an undone zipper. And he was gone, off to whatever and whenever, to realms of possibility that Diana didn't bother trying to imagine.

From one bewildered hapless entity to another, she wished him the best of luck.

CHAPTER THIRTY

She sat on her lawn chair, enjoying a tall glass of iced tea in the peace and quiet. Not all possible worlds were those of giant mutant insects or mole people. The universe was not just home to cosmic monster-gods and inconceivable horrors. And this reflection of an Earth that might have been (or perhaps once was or would be) was a good place to get away from it all.

This particular world was quiet. Humanity was gone. Here and gone like the hazy details of a forgotten dream. Or perhaps it had never been. The only possible trace of its existence in the endless fields of green was the silhouette of a tower on the horizon. It could've been a skyscraper. Or a peculiar rock formation. Diana had never bothered to check.

The floating door opened, and Sharon stuck her head through.

"There you are. West said you'd be here."

Diana glanced at her watch. "Oh, damn. Sorry. Lost track of time." She jumped to her feet and exited the universe.

"Are you going to leave your iced tea there?" asked Sharon.

"It's not mine."

"Whose is it?"

"Don't know. But it's always there. Sometimes it's lemonade."

Sharon didn't ask for any further explanation. She understood as well as Diana that there were mysteries meant never to be solved.

The door closed on the universe with a peculiar pop. The door was one of five in a cramped hexagonal room. The door they had just exited had the word SAFE written across it in black marker. Two of the others were marked IFFY. One was unmarked. And the last one was stained with red handprints and deep scratches.

They climbed the tight spiral staircase up and out of the room and entered the apartment hallway. The staircase was visible only from certain angles, but that was true of many things in the building. Thanks to Zap's transference, Diana was getting better at perceiving reality beyond a standard four-dimensional model. It'd bothered her at first, making her think she was losing her humanity, but humanity was found in more than limited awareness. And being able to see into the sixth dimension meant never having to lose her car keys again.

West, holding a broom in each hand, shuffled forward.

"Not Apartment X again," said Diana.

"'Fraid so." He held a broom out to her.

"Can't you take care of this one without me?" she asked.

He stared at her.

She smiled. "I've got a dinner date."

West shrugged. "Fine, but don't come cryin' to me when Dread Ghor absorbs the stars, Number Five." He shambled away, mumbling.

West wasn't so bad. In his own way he was a friendly sort, and she didn't mind helping around the building, pitching in here and there. Keeping the universe in order helped pass the time.

"Thanks," shouted Diana at his back. "I owe you one."

He made a vague wavelike motion with his hand without turning around. He passed Vom in the hall.

"Hey, hey, Diana," asked Vom. "Is it dinnertime already? Where are we going?"

"We were hoping to keep it just the two of us," said Diana.

"Oh." His mouths frowned. "Okay. That's cool."

"Let him come along," said Sharon. "He's cute."

"You've been spending too much time around monsters," said Diana.

Vom stuck out his lower lip and tilted his fuzzy green head in her direction.

"Oh, fine. But we're not going to any buffets."

On the outside Diana took a moment to study the moon in the night sky. The glowing orb was a little fuzzy around the edges. She focused her powers and willed it into place.

Fenris had absorbed the original moon with his escape, and Diana had taken it upon herself to create a replacement for the sake of the ecosystem. Such was her power now that it hadn't been difficult, although the moon's existence did demand most of her magic and required periodic reinforcement. Imagining a moon into being kept her more arbitrary wishes from forcing themselves on the universe, and she called that a win-win.

There was another other-dimensional refugee waiting at the bottom of the steps. Waiting for her.

In the few months since the Fenris incident, Diana had begun picking up strays. Some were brought to her by people like her. Wardens who had stumbled into contact with the unnatural. Others were like this newest one, simply sitting on the doorstep, drawn to her by the mysterious aura that made her a beacon for things lost in time and space.

She'd stopped being reluctant when she realized that the creatures, for all their faults, were just lost and confused. Like Fenris, they were just waiting for their chance to escape. In the meantime, all they really wanted was a safe place to stay for a while.

The furry mushroom with stumpy legs whimpered as she approached.

"It's okay," she said. "There's nothing to be afraid of. Why don't you go inside and make yourself comfortable? I'll be back in a few hours."

The creature yipped. It rapidly trundled (as rapidly as anything could trundle) up the stairs and ran into the building.

"You must be running out of room," said Sharon.

"The apartment is a lot bigger than I realized," replied Diana.

She was discovering new doors daily. Space was a more flexible concept than most ever conceived.

"I still think we should be a little more selective," said Vom. "If you keep adopting every little horror you come across, something bad could happen."

"Bad like what?" asked Diana.

"I don't know. Bad like bad. Weren't you the one terrified about too many monsters messing up your life? Or if the universe would smack you down for gathering too much supernatural power?"

"I was," she said. "But I'm over that. I don't think the universe cares if I have power. It just cares what I do with it. And if I don't do anything too radical then I think everything will be okay."

A few gray clouds sprinkled rain on the block. Diana willed them away. Small magics burned away the little bits left to her after her preservation of the moon. She couldn't help having some unwanted influence on reality, but little wishes kept her power in check. It was all about balance, a fine touch.

"I never apologized," said Sharon. "For that thing with the cult."

"You don't need to."

"But I almost stopped you from saving the world."

"I didn't save the world. I almost destroyed it."

"Don't be modest. You reminded Calvin what it was like to be human."

"He would've remembered on his own. You're the one who spent years with him, really showing him."

"Possibly. But I think you sticking around to fight was what really struck the chord."

Diana smiled. She didn't know if she agreed, but it

was a nice thought so she elected to believe it.

At the restaurant Chuck was waiting for a table too. He was with a date. Diana didn't actively avoid him, but she didn't go out of her way to talk to him either. At one point he looked over at her, and she smiled. He didn't smile back. His brow furrowed, and he turned his back to her. She couldn't blame him. She doubted he even remembered her in any detail, and the furry green world-eater with her no doubt rattled his senses. Chuck and Diana walked in different worlds, and while those worlds might brush up against each other, they would never meet for long.

"How's the cult going?" asked Diana.

"Finished," replied Sharon. "It just hasn't been the same after Calvin left. Then Greg gave it up because it conflicted with his new obsession: fantasy football league. Kind of drifted apart after that."

"Shame."

"Tell me about it. Now I have to figure out what to do with my Saturday nights."

"You still miss him, don't you?"

"Yeah." Sharon glanced up at the moon. "I know it's for the best. I know he didn't belong here. But I miss him."

"It's tough to let someone go sometimes."

"Do you think he was telling the truth?" asked Sharon. "Do you think he still thinks of me?"

"I wouldn't doubt it," said Diana.

"That's something at least." Sharon half-smiled. "I thought about trying to find a new guy, someone who needed me the way he did. But it just strikes me as pathetic, right? He was one of a kind. Even as monsters go, we won't see anything like him for a long, long time."

"If we're lucky," said Diana.

"Doesn't change the fact that I miss him."

"You need a rebound guy. One with less baggage. Preferably one who doesn't corrode reality."

Sharon laughed. "I'm not sure I would know how to handle that."

"You'll handle it, just like we all do."

"And how's that, oh wise sage?"

"Knock it off." Diana gave Sharon a playful shove.

"No, really. I want to know. How do you handle it? How do you deal with being a keeper of monsters and secrets and things this world was never meant to know?"

The universe shuddered as a hole appeared in the sky. A giant serpentine eye gazed down upon the world, and whether it glimpsed anything worth noticing or not, it disappeared.

Diana shrugged, smiled slightly.

"One day at a time."

extras

orbit

meet the author

A. Lee Martinez was born in El Paso, Texas. At the age of eighteen, for no apparent reason, he started writing novels. Thirteen short years (and a little over a dozen manuscripts) later, his first novel, *Gil's All Fright Diner*, was published. His hobbies include juggling, games of all sorts, and astral projecting. Also, he likes to sing along with the radio when he's in the car by himself. Find out more about the author at www.aleemartinez.com.

introducing

If you enjoyed CHASING THE MOON,

look out for

EMPEROR MOLLUSK VERSUS THE SINISTER BRAIN

by A. Lee Martinez

Who says supervillians can't retire?

EMPEROR MOLLUSK has done it all. Sometimes twice. He's destroyed Saturn (well fine, not all of it—but two-thirds!), created giant monsters, and until recently he was the Emperor of Earth. Yes, he still has the titles and the people are always looking to him for salvation when the aliens attack, but really, he keeps telling everyone he's re-tired. He's got better things to do...

Like feed his pet ultrapede, Woola.

Or buy groceries.

But now, he's been marked by a legendary death cult

for reasons unknown. And, honestly, feeding an ultrapede wasn't really utilizing his enormous intellect to its fullest potential. Emperor Mollusk is a supervillain, but when danger threatens, he will have to use all of his wiles, his feared intellect and superior technology to save Earth from the invasion of... THE SINISTER BRAIN!

There's no sound in space, but my saucer cannons simulated a shriek with every blast. A swoosh followed every barrel roll. And when my autogunner scored a hit, a sophisticated program supplied the appropriate level of response, ranging from a simple ping to a full-fledged explosion. I could have programmed it to provide an explosion every time, but that would've cheapened the experience.

The atmosphere burst with color as the cannons belched their staccato rhythm. My ship blasted the enemy fighters to scrap, but an impressive fleet stood between my target and me. The shields were holding, but I had only a few moments before I was disabled.

I'd gone over my exo options before mission. Neptunons might have been the smartest race in the galaxy, but outside of our exoskeletons, we couldn't do much more than flop around. We could drag ourselves across the floor, a means of mobility both embarrassing and ineffective. Our brains had grown too fast, and we just hadn't possessed the patience to wait around for nature to bestow what we could give ourselves. Over the centuries, we'd only grown smarter and squishier.

The obvious choice for an exo on this mission would've been a big, burly combative model. But I'd opted for stealth, taking a modified Ninja-3 prototype. It stood barely five feet tall and space limitations meant it didn't pack much weaponry. But I wasn't planning on fighting every soldier on the station. It sounded like a laugh, but time was a factor. Terra was a little over six minutes from total subjugation.

I slipped into my exo, loaded myself into the launch tube, and prepared to fire.

"It was a pleasure serving with you, sir," said the craft's computer.

"Likewise."

I ejected, rocketing through space in a jet-black torpedo that was practically invisible in the darkness of space. A stray plasma blast could've gotten lucky and struck the torpedo. If it didn't destroy me outright, it would knock the torpedo off course, either sending me spinning into the void of space or plummeting to Terra. But I'd done the math and decided to take my chances.

The torpedo breached the station's hull. I kicked open the torpedo's door and exited. There were no guards. Only a couple of technicians gasping for air. The artificial gravity held them in place, but the decompression had taken all the oxygen.

A security team stormed the room. I vaulted over their heads before they got off a shot. A few punches from my exo's four arms knocked them all senseless before they could even realize I was behind them. The Ninja-3 had several built-in blades, but I tried not to kill people just for annoying me.

I took a second to grab the emergency oxygen masks off the wall and toss them to the technicians.

Then I was on my way. My exo's camouflage feature allowed me to avoid guards. I slipped through the security net without much trouble, though it took a few minutes. By the time I reached the device, I was running short on time.

The immense orb hovered in a containment field. Hundreds of lights, purely ornamental, blinked across its surface. Its ultrasonic hum filled the chamber. Only a Neptunon could hear the sound without having their brain melt.

I blasted the device. It shattered into a thousand little pieces. There was nothing inside. Just a ceramic mock-up of a doomsday weapon.

A door opened, and a Neptunon in a hulking exoskeleton marched into the chamber. He banged his hands together. Their metallic clapping echoed.

"You didn't think it would be that easy, did you?" he asked.

All Neptunons look alike. We even have trouble telling each other apart. It wasn't surprising that this one looked like me, but the resemblance went deeper.

The clone had been a mistake. I don't often make mistakes, but I own up to them when they happen.

"A decoy," I said.

Emperor Mollusk, Mark Two, laughed maniacally. Had I really sounded like that? The clone carried a set of memories minus a few years of experience and the personality to match. Looking at yourself, at who you used to be, wasn't pretty.

"You should see the look on your face," he said. "How does it feel to be outwitted?"

"Someone was going to do it eventually," I replied.

"At least I can take some small comfort that I outmaneuvered myself."

"Yes, if anyone could do it…" He raised an eye ridge in a pompous, self-satisfied manner. We don't have eyebrows.

"The fleet, the personnel, the space station," I said. "This must have cost you a small fortune."

"Ah, but it was necessary, wasn't it? I knew that only one being in this system had the knowledge and ability to pose any significant risk to my plan. I couldn't hide an operation like this without something to distract you. So I devised a small game for your amusement. Little clues leading to a fun diversion then a full-blown operation that was every bit as involved and complex as the real thing. But at the heart of it…nothing."

I said, "Meanwhile, you build your weapon somewhere else, somewhere unimportant, somewhere unnoticed. It was exactly what I would've done."

"And now nothing can stop me. In three minutes, Terra shall be mine."

"You don't want it."

He chuckled, but one look at my face told him I was serious. Neptunons might not have the most expressive features, but we get by.

"Having billions of dominated souls chant your name in unison can be great for the self-esteem. Although, really, self-esteem was never our problem, was it?" I asked.

Mark Two studied me skeptically. He suspected a trap, trying to figure out my angle. There was no angle. Just a lesson learned.

"Once you're crowned Warlord of Terra, you'll see that it's a lot more responsibility than I…we…planned."

He scanned for any sign of deception. I had never been a very good liar. Strange, considering my hobby as a world conqueror, but it was a conscious choice. Being a skilled liar might have made the job easier, but telling the truth, with the occasional lie by omission, increased the difficulty level.

"Let me tell you how everything will go if you succeed," I said. "You'll become ruler of this world. You'll hold it in your hands like a beautiful blue pearl. That'll be enough at first. Just to have it.

"But then you'll start tinkering. Oh, you'll have the best of intentions. You'll fix those little pestering problems the Terrans themselves never could. Hunger. War. Poverty. Those will be easy, a long weekend.

"After that, you'll struggle against the relentless urges that drive you. You'll realize, intellectually, that there's little left to do. But you won't be able to help yourself. Terra will become your own personal science project until your inevitable nature nearly destroys the world. Several times.

"Now, providing you manage to prevent this, you'll learn some restraint. But it'll always be there. That insistent desire, that nagging need. You'll never be able to suppress it. Not completely. And you'll find yourself wondering if tomorrow is the day you destroy it, most probably by accident."

Mark Two said, "I'll learn from your mistakes."

"Or you'll just make slightly different variations of the same ones. Regardless, the Terrans have been through enough under one warlord. They don't need another."

A Klaxon blared, signaling the final countdown. I pushed a button on my exo, and the station blast shields lowered. Mark Two frowned, realizing that I'd hacked his systems.

Mark Two shook off his confusion and resumed his laughter. "I don't know what happened to you in the time since you were me, but it doesn't matter. Terra will be mine, and there's not a thing you can—"

"I already stopped it. You didn't think you could hide your operation in Minneapolis from me, did you?"

He smiled. "No, that was merely another decoy."

"Of course, it was," I replied. "As were your machinations in Lisbon, St. Petersburg, and Busan."

His smile dropped.

"I'll admit you almost had me with Melbourne," I said. "But the decoy in Geneva was sloppy work, if I may be so bold as to offer some criticism."

He wasn't angered. He was curious. He was me, after all. And I was rarely frustrated by my failures. I preferred using them as learning opportunities.

I pressed another button. I kept the gravity and lights on for convenience, but everything else in the station went dead. The countdown ended. The doomsday device, the *real* device hidden aboard this station, wound down.

Mark Two glared. "How did you—"

"I'm you, remember. Just you with a few more years' experience. Everything you've done, I've already thought of. Every contingency plan, every possibility, I already did five years ago before you were even hatched from your tank."

He hid his incredulity behind a scowl, but I sensed it. If the situation were reversed, I'd have been the same. I hadn't been one hundred percent certain that I would foil his plans. But I was a humbler guy now than I was when I had been him.

His mottled flesh darkened with rage. I could see where he was coming from. I'd failed before, but I'd never been outwitted. But I'd never had to face off against myself. Now it'd all gone freshwater for Mark Two, as the old Neptunon saying went.

His hulking exoskeleton lumbered forward. "You may have stopped me this time, but you won't be around to stop me the next."

He threw a clumsy punch that would've pulverized the Ninja-3 if I hadn't sidestepped the blow. He followed that with a haymaker that I danced under. I glided behind him and used a microfilament blade to slice open the hydraulics behind the exo's right knee. It wobbled but didn't fall.

He hadn't even bothered to change the specs. Perhaps he wasn't a perfect clone after all.

Mark Two teetered on his damaged leg as he struggled to line me up in his sights, but it was a simple thing for me to scamper up his back. I stabbed a few vital systems along the way. The last thing I hit was the stabilizer. His powerful exo tumbled over, ten tons of scrap metal.

A hatch opened, and he ejected in a smaller exo. The clear, fluid-filled dome that held his head bubbled with his frustration. I'd never lost my temper like that, but then again, I'd never been foiled so effortlessly. Or maybe the cloning process had simply been incapable of re-creating every bit of my pragmatic genius. He must've known his backup was no match for my Ninja, but in his anger, he didn't care. I dodged the blasts he sent my way and dismantled his exo with three efficient cuts. It clattered to the floor in pieces.

He flopped around, glaring daggers. Neptunons could

survive out of water for extended periods, but it wasn't comfortable.

"You can't stop me," he gurgled. "I'll be back."

"No, you won't."

I activated the station's self-destruct countdown. Just a little something I'd slipped into his blueprints when he wasn't looking.

"So that's it?" he asked. "You're just going to leave me here to die?"

"I'm afraid so. No hard feelings."

Mark Two undulated in a shrug. "No, I suppose not. I'd do the same to you if the situation were reversed."

"I guess I haven't changed so much after all," I replied. We shared a laugh.

"Just tell me something. It would've worked, right?"

"It would have worked," I said.

He grinned. "That's something at least."

"Yeah, it's something."

I made my escape without incident, boarding my automated rendezvous craft, and watched the station explode from a safe distance.

It was quite beautiful.

Then I pondered the small world below, oblivious to its own fragility.

ARTEMIS

Philip Palmer

Artemis McIvor is a stone-cold killer and a bibliophile.

Raised on the library planet of Rebus, she has a love of books in a future where reading is a lost art. Unfortunately, she's also been imprisoned for a string of brutal murders she didn't commit. Not that she hasn't killed people. She just didn't kill *these* people.

A war is coming and Artemis will find that her talents will be in high demand. But she has debts to pay and when they come due she will have a choice: fight for her freedom, or die a slave.

Praise for Philip Palmer Novels:

"Palmer's lip-smackingly over-the-top exploration of crime and retribution will delight."
> —*The Guardian* (UK) on *Version 43*

"*Red Claw* confirms Philip Palmer's position as one of the quirkiest authors working today...Palmer's playful prose, vivid characters, deft world-building and constant in-jokes keep you turning the pages...certainly brings some fun and adrenaline to the genre."
> —*SFX*

"Featuring cool-headed, sharp-witted characters who are neither heroes or villains, this strong debut belongs in most sf collections."
> —*Library Journal* on *Debatable Space*